"Ms. Warren gives readers action and danger around each turn, sizzling romance, and humor to lighten each scene. *Big Bad Wolf* is a must-read."
—*Darque Reviews*

You're So Vein

"Filled with supernatural danger, excitement, and sarcastic humor."
—*Darque Reviews*

"Five stars. This is an exciting, sexy book."
—*Affaire de Coeur*

"The sparks do fly!"   —*Romantic Times BOOKreviews*

One Bite with a Stranger

"Christine Warren has masterfully pulled together vampires, shape shifters, demons, and many 'Others' to create a tantalizing world of dark fantasies come to life. Way to go, Warren!"   —*Night Owl Romance*

"A sinful treat."   —*Romance Junkies*

"Hot fun and great sizzle."
—*Romantic Times BOOKreviews*

"A hot, hot novel."   —*A Romance Review*

Walk on the Wild Side

"A seductive tale with strong chemistry, roiling emotions, steamy romance, and supernatural action. The fast-moving plot...will keep the readers' attention riveted through every page, and have them eagerly watching for the next installment."   *—Darque Reviews*

Howl at the Moon

"*Howl at the Moon* will tug at a wide range of emotions from beginning to end...Engaging banter, a strong emotional connection, and steamy love scenes. This talented author delivers real emotion which results in delightful interactions...and the realistic dialogue is stimulating. Christine Warren knows how to write a winner!"   *—Romance Junkies*

The Demon You Know

"Explodes with sexy, devilish fun, exploring the further adventures of The Others. With a number of the gang from previous books back, there's an immediate familiarity about this world that makes it easy to dive right into. Warren's storytelling style makes these books remarkably entertaining."

—Romantic Times BOOKreviews
(4 ½ stars)

St. Martin's Paperbacks Titles By

Christine Warren

Prince Charming Doesn't Live Here

Born to Be Wild

Big Bad Wolf

You're So Vein

One Bite with a Stranger

Walk on the Wild Side

Howl at the Moon

The Demon You Know

She's No Faerie Princess

Wolf at the Door

Anthologies

The Huntress

No Rest for the Witches

Black Magic Woman

CHRISTINE WARREN

St. Martin's Paperbacks

BLACK MAGIC WOMAN

Copyright © 2011 by Christine Warren.

For information address St. Martin's Press, 175 Fifth Avenue, New York, NY 10010.

ISBN: 978-1-61129-544-3

Printed in the United States of America

St. Martin's Paperbacks are published by St. Martin's Press, 175 Fifth Avenue, New York, NY 10010.

To Beth.
Because even though it took me twenty-some-odd years
to realize I actually like having a sister, I now know
I had a good one all along.

Dear Reader,

I have a confession to make: When I set out to write my first novel (the story that started its life as the e-book *Fantasy Fix* and later became *One Bite with a Stranger*), that was all I intended to do. You see, I had this idea for a story about a group of friends who wanted to help each other fulfill their romantic fantasies, and I thought it would be a hoot if one of those friends had a fantasy that should logically be impossible to fulfill—like a fantasy about meeting a smart, sexy, dominating vampire. So that was the story I told, and I honestly meant for it to end there.

I certainly never imagined that I would end up writing *more* than five books about the original group of women in *One Bite*. I owe the continuation of the world of the Others utterly to all of you. Without your encouragement, your letters and e-mails, your words at book signings, and your willingness to read about my Others, these books would never have existed; however, after nearly eight years and thirteen books (fourteen, including this one!) even I have to admit that this world of mine has gotten a tiny bit complicated; nay, even confusing.

A lot of that comes from the fact that six of those fourteen stories were originally published as e-books, but were later edited, rewritten, and released as paperbacks, but only *after* several new stories (ones that take place later in the timeline of this world) had hit the scene. For instance, remember *One Bite with a Stranger*? That book was originally released in 2003 as the first novel featuring the Others, but it wasn't published by St. Martin's Press as a paperback until 2008, well after books like *Wolf at the Door* (2006) and *She's No Faerie Princess* (2006) had advanced the timeline of the world of the Others by several years.

I swear, I didn't do this to confuse anyone. But let me try to clear things up now by telling you what the proper order of the Novels of the Others *should* be, in terms of the chronological order of the events in the books:

One Bite with a Stranger (aka *Fantasy Fix)*
Big Bad Wolf (aka *Fur Factor)*
Prince Charming Doesn't Live Here (aka *Faer Fetched)*
Black Magic Woman (this book)
Not Your Ordinary Faerie Tale (*Fighting Faer)*
A brand-new novel (title to come)
Fur for All
Fur Play
Wolf at the Door
She's No Faerie Princess
The Demon You Know
Howl at the Moon
Walk on the Wild Side
You're So Vein
Born to Be Wild

That's it. I promise.

And yet . . .

I can hear you saying, "But, Christine, you're trying to confuse us again! I've never heard of *Not Your Ordinary Faerie Tale*, and I've looked everywhere for copies of *Fighting Faer*, *Fur for All*, and *Fur Play*, and I can't find them anywhere."

The problem here is one of compromise. In an ideal world, I'd love to release each book in the order it appears on this page, but there are two problems with that: first, I can't go back in time and fix the publication order that's already happened; and second, if I released all of the old stories as paperbacks in the order in which they first appeared as e-books, some of you out there would be cursing my name for not writing anything new for you to read (and I really hate it when you get mad at me). By staggering publication so that you get one new original book, then a reworked version of a familiar story, and then another original book, I'm trying to give everyone a little something to look forward to. If I'm failing miserably, maybe I'll at least get points for effort!

You may notice that while this book is being published in 2011, I've made a conscious effort to fit the events into my timeline so that they do, in fact, occur directly after the events of the book published immediately before it (*Prince Charming Doesn't Live Here*). This will hold true for the next several books in this series. After *Black Magic Woman* will come the new and improved version of *Fighting Faer*, now titled *Not Your Ordinary Faerie Tale*, and the events in that book will take place immediately after the ones in these pages, followed by the events in a brand-new story, then *Fur for All*, and then *Fur Play*. If I've just confused you again, look back at the list above. I promise that list is chronologically correct and will not change.

From now on, I'm a reformed author and all my books will contain events that take place in the same order in which the books are published.

Unless I delve into time travel, but that's another matter entirely . . .

With much love and sincere thanks,
—Christine
xoxo

One

So now you know. Suffice it to say, you'll never look at the world the same way again.
                    —A Human Handbook to the Others,
                                    Author's Foreword

Daphanie Carter had witnessed a lot of interesting things over the course of the last forty-eight hours, not the least of which had been her baby sister's wedding less than five hours ago. However, the sight of a small, chubby red hand reaching out from under an elegantly draped reception table and groping among the cutlery really had to take the cake. Or in this case, the diet soda, which the hand curled around and began to ease slowly through the obstacle course of discarded dinnerware.

Daphanie blinked, but the hand was still there and making remarkable progress. Considering all the cutlery, porcelain, and glassware it had to avoid, the hand and the soda were cooking. And that was when it occurred to Daphanie that maybe the hand of fate came in a variety of shapes and sizes.

And colors.

It took less than ten seconds of fascinated observation before her curiosity overcame her. Casting a furtive glance around to be sure the rest of the guests were too preoccupied with each other to notice what she was doing, Daphanie reached for the bottom of the tablecloth and lifted it so she could duck underneath. Her silk maid-of-honor dress slid easily across the antique carpet as she settled herself cross-legged in the dim light of the little cavern. Directly in front of her, the owner of the red hand started and snatched the hand and the captured prize back so fast that the diet soda inside ricocheted right out of the glass and onto his demonic little face.

"Harpy's tits!" the little creature cursed, wiping the sticky liquid from his face. Daphanie watched as he lifted the end of an incredibly long and currently dripping mustache to his lips and sucked out the moisture.

"*Baghk!* Diet cola! How do you humans drink that poison?"

"It's an acquired taste," Daphanie murmured, her fascinated gaze taking in the sight before her.

Standing less than three feet tall—probably more like two and a half, since he didn't even have to crouch to keep from hitting his head on the table above them—the creature with the dislike of diet sodas looked like nothing so much as a comic-book rendition of a devil. He had dark red skin, marked here and there with black moles, and hair the color of coal, which he wore in a short, spiky Mohawk positioned precisely between the tips of his two pointy ears. The hairstyle stopped where his forehead started, or more precisely, just shy of the two stubby black horns that sprouted there, as if he'd just walked out of a painting of a mythological faun. He also sported the Fu Manchu mustache that grew long enough to tuck into his belt, had he been wearing one. Instead, he appeared to be decked out in a pair of toddler's OshKosh denim overalls with the cuffs turned up over his tiny cloven hooves. The garment had apparently been altered further to allow for the pointed red tail Daphanie could see lashing behind him. All in all, he constituted the most amazing thing she had seen in a pretty amazing few days since her return to New York.

"I'd rather acquire a root beer," he grumbled. "Doesn't anyone drink root beer anymore?"

"Sure." Daphanie stared at his face, finally noticing the little silver ring that pierced the end of his nose. It flapped a bit while he talked, making her grin. Seriously, the last couple of days were blowing her mind. In a good way. Hadn't she been longing for something *interesting* to happen lately? Right before Danice had called to announce her engagement and add to the chorus urging her to move back to New York from her most recent home in Pennsylvania. "I mean, I don't know if anyone at this table does, but I assume that there are people who do."

"Swamp rats."

Daphanie grinned. In addition to his entertaining looks, this little guy had quite a way with expletives. His appearance had also gone a long way toward reassuring her that her sister, her family, and she had not all completely lost their minds.

When she'd arrived in Manhattan on Wednesday, just a few days before Danice's scheduled wedding, she'd expected a warm welcome from her parents and her baby sister. She'd expected to finally get to meet the man who had swept Niecie off her feet. She'd even expected to get caught up on all the family news and gossip that she'd missed since the last time they had gotten together. After all, when the stars aligned like they had to urge her to move back to the city, Daphanie liked to take the hint. What she hadn't expected had been the news that the Carters' mixed-race family was about to become mixed-species, because her baby sister's fiancé was not quite . . . well, human.

McIntyre Callahan, or Mac, as he'd informed her with a million-watt smile, turned out to be a lovely man, in more ways than one. He had the fair good looks of a Hollywood dreamboat and the body of a leanly muscled action star. Honestly, the man was more beautiful than any human being had a right to be, which was confirmed when they sat Daphanie down and explained that Mac wasn't entirely a human being.

He was half Fae, as her sister had termed it, the son of a human father and a Fae mother—what Daphanie would previously have thought of as a "fairy," and honestly still tended to. Looking at the highly masculine and utterly besotted man with his arm curled around Danice's shoulders, "fairy" had been the last description to come to Daphanie's mind, but she'd taken their word for it. She had also taken their word on a whole list of other things that threatened to blow her mind and leave her little more than a vacant-eyed, drooling, babbling mental sponge cake on the day of her sister's wedding. Having expected the mild adventure of an introduction to Mac's family and close friends, instead she'd received an introduction to the world of the Others.

Talk about being careful what you wished for.

That was what Mac and Niecie called them: The Others. It meant, as Daphanie soon learned, the collection of nonhuman beings who lived and worked in the midst of human society. They could be your neighbor or your friend, the woman who manicured your nails or the man who fixed your leaky toilet. Some were highly placed political or corporate officials, and some were sanitation workers or public servants. The Others had always been there and would always be there, she discovered, and some of them were the creatures of late-night B-rated horror movies.

Missy, Danice's quiet, kindergarten-teaching friend with the sweet face and soft manner, had married a werewolf last year, Niecie revealed. Missy had even given birth to a werewolf baby (who had not been born with fur, Daphanie had been assured). Reggie, one of Niecie's other friends, had not only married a vampire, but she'd allowed herself to be turned into a vampire as well.

And those revelations had been only the tip of the iceberg. For three days, Daphanie's head had been spinning as she tried to take in the fact that everything she'd ever thought was true about the world around her was really only a veneer of truth. Underneath the glossy, everyday surface moved an entirely new and unfamiliar world into which she'd just received a secondhand invitation. It was enough to blow a girl's mind.

Daphanie's mind, however, wasn't blown; it was intrigued.

She marveled at the possibilities. Wouldn't it explain a lot, she thought, if her college sculpture professor had actually been some sort of were-bear? It would certainly provide good reasons for his bushy beard and terrible temper during the winters. And how much sense would it make to learn that the girl she had hated from the sorority next door had been an actual as well as a metaphorical bloodsucker? Somehow, all of it just seemed to make sense. It was as if she'd subconsciously suspected this all along, and someone had only needed to point out the truth for everything to fall into place.

The most surprising part, Daphanie had quickly realized, was that most of the Others she had been introduced to had been so unexpectedly . . . normal. Except for his extraordinary good looks, Mac could have been any other man on the street, and Reggie might look a little paler than she remembered, but Daphanie hadn't detected even the slightest glimpse of fang. Really, it had all been almost disappointing. She had expected to look around her and feel like a veil had suddenly been lifted and now she could see the world for what it really was, but it turned out that the unveiled world looked pretty much exactly like the veiled one had.

At least, until now. This little guy was an entirely new experience.

Daphanie refocused on the little red creature before her and grinned. "I don't think we met before, but I'm Daphanie Carter. I'm Danice's sister. Are you a friend of Niecie's or Mac's?"

He took her hand warily and shook quickly. His skin felt warm and rough but not really any different from human skin. "I, uh, I know both of 'em," he ventured. "Name's Quigley."

"Quigley," Danice repeated, deciding it suited him

somehow. "It's very nice to meet you, but I do have to ask what you're doing lurking under the tables instead of sitting at one."

"Um, I like to keep a low profile. You know, not stir things up too much. Get everyone all excited."

Watching the way his glowing-coal eyes darted from side to side as he said that gave Daphanie the tiniest clue that his answer might not encompass his entire reason for attending the reception in hiding.

"So you crashed, huh? If you know both of the happy couple, why didn't you get an invitation like everyone else?"

"That's what I'd like to know!" Quigley's chin jutted out at a belligerent angle. "Alls I can say is, it's a fine way to thank a dude after he puts his own hide in trouble to save yer life. Some people just got no idea of gratitude, I can tell ya."

Daphanie blinked. "You saved a life? Whose life? Mac's, or Niecie's?"

"Either/or. It was a tense situation."

"What situation? Danice didn't tell me anything about her life recently being in danger. Why was my baby sister's life in danger?"

Quigley must have noticed a suspiciously militant gleam in Daphanie's eye, because he quickly shifted his feet and darted his glance to the side. Daphanie couldn't help it, though. She'd been protecting and taking care of her little sister since the day their parents had brought Niecie home from the hospital. Old habits, and all that.

"It wasn't that bad," the little creature hurried to assure her, twisting one end of his mustache around his chubby finger. "I mean, it all worked out, right? No harm, no foul. Hazard of doing business and all that." He laughed nervously.

"But why was Niecie in a dangerous situation to begi—"

"So, did ya come in from out of town or something?" Quigley cut her off with an enthusiastically jovial tone. He rocked forward on his hooves and pasted a toothy smile on his face. Somehow, the fact that his teeth were more pointed and fangy than normal human teeth didn't diminish the effect in the least. "I can't recall Danice mentioning she had a sister here in the city."

Daphanie's eyes narrowed. "She doesn't. I've been away for years now. I just came back this week. Does the situation you saved my sister from have anything to do with the reason why you're lurking under dinner tables instead of mingling with the rest of the wedding guests?"

"Ah, that explains it. Yup, I figured if Danice had a sister in New York, she'da mentioned it by now. I was just sayin' to myself, 'Quigley, if this is Danice's sister, I bet she musta been living someplace pretty far away up until now or you'da heard about her before this.' Yessir."

The creature's burning, beady eyes darted this way and that, looking everywhere but at Daphanie's face. She could almost swear she saw little drops of sweat collecting on the skin at the base of his horns. She had him backed into some kind of corner without even having seen the walls coming. She couldn't think of any other reason for his nervous twitching. The question was, what had him so tied up in knots, and should Daphanie try to squeeze him for information, or take pity on the poor thing?

"I'm going to take that as a yes." She considered him along with her options. Clearly, whatever danger Niecie had been involved in had resolved itself by now, but it bothered Daphanie that her sister hadn't told her about it. And it bothered her even more that this Quigley creature knew more about her sister's recent past than she did.

"Take what as a yes? Was there a question? I don't remember a question—"

"And that means that whatever situation you were in with Danice, it was one she didn't want to be reminded of on her wedding day. Because I'm assuming that otherwise she would have invited you."

Quigley's nervous laugh made her think of hyenas and two-year-olds, simultaneously. Which was kinda creepy.

"Heh. Come to think of it, maybe she did mention she had a sister with a bit of wanderlust to her. Haven't you been traveling for a few years now? I think I heard Danice tell Mac that her sister was some kind of gypsy, wanderin' around the world sellin' her art and lookin' for inspiration to make more. That'd be you, I take it?"

"Which means that if she or Mac knew you were here, they wouldn't like it." She saw his eyes dart nervously around, as if he expected the linens to disappear and leave him vulnerable to exposure. She was on the right track. "Given that it's their wedding day, they might not want to make a big scene and might just get someone from the staff to escort you out. That would cause the least amount of trouble, I'm guessing. But then again,

Niecie always has had a temper. If she was really upset to see you here, she might pick you up by your ears and fling you out a window herself."

"A real live artist! Fancy that!" Quigley's voice had risen to an uncomfortable and unnaturally loud squeak that made Daphanie wish for ear muffs. "Who would have thought I'd be sitting here at Vircolac's talking to Danice's famous artist sister! Now, she didn't call you a painter, so what was it you do? Sculpture? No, not that, but something similar, right? I think I remember it being something simi—"

Daphanie crossed her arms, her lips pursing. "Now, I don't know Mac very well yet, but he does seem to be awfully protective of my sister. It makes me curious. I wonder what he would do if I just let him know about his little uninvited guest under table three . . . ?"

"Hey, you know what? It's gettin' kinda stuffy under here, ain't it?" The imp cut her off with grim determination and a forced tone of good cheer. His smile looked more pained than friendly, but she guessed he was at least making an effort. "Whatta ya say we blow this pop stand, eh? You're new to the city. I could, you know, show you around. Take you to all the hot spots."

As an attempt to change the subject, the offer lacked a certain amount of subtlety, but it made up for it in obvious desperation. Daphanie quirked an eyebrow.

"I grew up in Brooklyn. I think I can find my way around Manhattan. But thanks. Maybe I should just go ask Danice about the adventure the two of you had together. I think that might be easier all around. Have a nice night, Quigley."

She placed her palm flat on the carpet and made as

if to push to her knees and crawl out from under the table. Quigley's hand slapped onto her wrist so fast, she thought he might have broken the land speed record.

"Wait!" Quigley's eyes narrowed on her face and his expression shifted from fear to calculation. "You might know what streets lead where around here, but ya don't know the city like I know the city. I'd betcha a case of root beer ya ain't never been to any of the places I could show ya."

The creature stabbed his chest with a stubby thumb. Daphanie considered him for a minute, raking her gaze over his outrageous and frankly unpleasant little form. "I'm not sure I'd want to go to any places you could show me, Quigley."

"Is that right? Huh, and here I thought you monkeys always wanted to go to the places ya ain't been invited to. The places where the real Others hang out."

" 'Monkeys'?" Daphanie repeated the insult. It took her brain a second to catch up with the rest of his statement. "Wait, what do you mean, 'the real Others'?"

The creature shrugged. "Just like I said. The real Others. The ones like me, not like this bunch of pretty, rich movie stars they got here."

"I don't recognize anyone here from the movies," Daphanie observed dryly. "I thought Niecie said this was a private club especially for the Others. She said it had been founded and run by werewolves for something like two hundred years and had werewolves and vampires and demons and all sorts of Others as members."

"Sure, Vircolac is for Others, if you happen to be an Other with a couple billion bucks in the bank or a family name that goes back to one of the first Others in

America," he snorted. "Sayin' any Other can hang out here is like sayin' anybody can live in a penthouse on Park Avenue. Theoretically, it might be true, but it ain't gonna happen for real people."

"Okay, so where do the 'real' Others hang out?"

Quigley shrugged, his gaze running over her with calculation. "We got a few places, but they ain't what I'd call suitable for most humans. Ya sure ya wanna see 'em?"

Daphanie thought about that for a moment. Did she really want to follow something that looked like a miniature devil, a creature she'd met only ten minutes before, into parts of the city she might not know all that well? Did she want to take that chance?

Part of her held back, wary, which only made sense. She wasn't stupid, after all, and she had a healthy sense of self-preservation; but another part of her whispered that this was an opportunity. An opportunity afforded her by fate, the same way all the other major opportunities in her life had presented themselves to her—the scholarship to the New School, the first chance to go to Paris, the offer to travel into China, the fellowship in San Francisco, even the little studio in New Hope where she'd settled last. The best things in her life had all come to Daphanie out of the blue, and it had been up to her to grab on and run with them.

All her life, Daphanie had had a streak of insatiable curiosity. She'd always wanted to know how everything worked, especially people. She craved answers like a drug, and now that she'd encountered the biggest question mark of her life in the form of her newfound knowledge of the Others, her curiosity was threatening to drive her crazy. She needed to know more, and who better to learn it from than an insider? She couldn't imagine anyone more inside the world of the Others than a—a—a—

She frowned at the small red monster. "What exactly are you, anyway?"

Quigley rolled his eyes. "Oh, nice. Nice manners, human. I happen to be an imp. A *greater* imp," he emphasized, glaring at her. "And you wanna watch it with questions like that. Not everyone will take kindly to that sort of thing. I mean, how rude is it to ask something like that?"

"I don't know." Daphanie shrugged. "I don't know anything about the Others, which is the reason I'm actually considering letting you distract me from talking to my sister about you. I don't know what kinds of Others there are, or what they look like or act like. I don't know how to talk to them. I don't know how not to make them want to eat me. Nothing. You might say I'm totally ignorant about them."

"You can say that again," he muttered.

"So, maybe this is the opportunity for me to learn the basics," Daphanie mused aloud. "If you show me where they gather and how to react to them, it would go a long way toward helping me understand Niecie and Mac . . ."

"Are ya asking for my opinion? Because if ya are, I gotta say that so far yer charm ain't gonna take ya real far with the kinda folks I know. Most of 'em don't take kindly to rude, ignorant humans pokin' noses into their business."

She glanced down at him. "But while I'm with you,

you can let me know if I do or say something wrong. You know, keep an eye on me."

The imp's eyes widened. "Look, Daphne—"

"Daphanie," she corrected. "Like Stephanie, only not. But you can just call me Daph."

"Daph," he echoed. "I ain't some kinda Emily Post. I offered to take ya to a club or two, not turn you into a human-Other ambassador. That ain't my shtick."

"Then what is your shtick? Hanging out under tables at wedding receptions and hoping no one will notice you siphoning off their root beer? Don't take this the wrong way but that strikes me as a touch . . . I don't know . . . pathetic."

Quigley glowered. "You callin' me pathetic?"

Daphanie shrugged.

"All right, fine." The imp threw up his hands. "Ya wanna learn all about the Others? We can do that. But ya better brace yerself, and ya better keep yer eye on me, because where we're goin', yer sister ain't gonna be able to come to yer rescue."

"Am I going to need rescuing?"

Quigley sized her up with a jaundiced eye. "Let's just say that outfit ain't gonna help ya blend in."

"Well, I was planning to change," she scoffed. "I love my sister, but this is still a bridesmaid's dress. It's not like I plan to wear it outside of this room. I've got jeans and stuff stashed upstairs. I can be ready to go in fifteen minutes."

The imp scowled and snatched up the tablecloth on the side closest to the wall. "Make it ten," he barked as he ducked out from their little sanctuary. "That way you might catch me before I change my mind."

Daphanie pushed to her knees and made to follow the grouchy red creature. "Are you saying you'd leave without me?"

Quigley laughed. "Leave without ya? And not take ya out on the Other town? Lady, I don't owe ya that kinda favor."

As Daphanie pushed through the service door at the rear of the room, slipping out of the party undetected, she wondered exactly what that was supposed to mean. A club was a club, after all, and she'd been to hundreds in her life. How different could this one really be?

Two

Most of the Others are really just like you and me—
they have jobs and friends and families. They live,
they work, and they play. They're no more danger-
ous as a group than humans are.

  Of course, you also have to remember that Ted
Bundy and Jack the Ripper were both humans.

  No, really. They were. I promise.
    —A Human Handbook to the Others, *Chapter One*

With his back to the wall of the crowded club, Asher
Grayson enjoyed the security of knowing that no one
among the throng of revelers could sneak up behind
him and attempt to take revenge for whatever plot he'd
foiled or friend/relative/acquaintance/partner-in-crime
he'd seen brought to justice recently. The thought offered
him a small amount of comfort. The position also, however, severely limited his escape routes, since in order
to leave he would have to move away from the wall and
through the crowd to reach the nearest exit.

  Life was about nothing if not compromise.

  Luckily, Asher didn't feel ready to leave. Not quite
yet. He could see the need building—crowds, after all,
did not constitute his favored environment—but he still

had half a glass of gnomish beer to finish and the night was young. By midnight, Lurk would begin to fill with its regular contingent of shifters and shifty characters, and by 2 A.M. would be bursting at the seams. If the nightclub held true to form as one of the most active and least restrictive of Manhattan's Other nightspots, before dawn it would play host to at least one magical altercation, three Lupine and/or Feline wrestling matches, and at least a handful of chairs broken by drunken imps or demons.

Asher intended to be long gone by the time any of that happened, but for now he just wanted to finish his drink in peace. He deserved it.

He also deserved a vacation after three straight assignments, all of which had taken him out of the city and kept him out for more than a year, and not one of them a stroll through the rosebushes. Unless, of course, he wanted to count the thorns they'd left in his ass. Between the man who'd unknowingly made a binding contract with a fiend known to traffic in mortal souls, and the scouting troop that had managed to plan its annual jamboree in a national park in the middle of the territory of Eastern Canada's largest Lupine pack—during the decennial wild hunt week—Asher couldn't recall taking a day off since, oh . . . birth. Five hundred and forty-three years ago. And that wasn't even counting the customers of the brothel on the Mexican border that was owned, operated, and staffed entirely by succubi. It had been a busy couple of months to be a Guardian.

Frankly, if Asher never saw another human in supernatural distress, it would be too soon. The weight of his wings was starting to give him a bad back. He could stand to put them away for a week or two. Or twelve.

In fact, after he finished his drink, he might take a little detour on his way home. Maybe if he went straight to the Watcher, he could finagle a few days of R & R before his next assignment. If he told the big man he was on the verge of losing his damned mind without a couple of vacation days, the creepy bastard might cut him some slack. After all, it would be the truth, clear and unvarnished.

Asher took another swig from his mug and swept his gaze around the room. Although the tinted windows kept out the sun during even the brightest part of the day, he could see from the level of shadows that the sun had set while he'd nursed his first beer. By the time he finished the one in front of him—his third—it would be past time to make his exit.

A quick glance at his wrist confirmed that it was now well after ten o'clock. Of course, his survey of the crowd told him pretty much the same thing. Although the club wouldn't really do the bulk of its nightly business until after midnight, many among the more mortal of the Others had already found their way inside. Asher could easily identify half a coven of witches, three half-giants, assorted varieties of changelings, and several brownies, dwarves, trolls, gnomes, and other demihumans all unwinding in the immediate vicinity. Before long, the shifters would begin to drift in, followed by the vampires and then the demons and the fiends. He wanted to be well away before that point. Too much potential for trouble to crop up, and he was decidedly off duty. Tonight it could be someone else's turn to clean up the inevitable messes.

That was precisely the thought in his head when he saw her walk in the door. It was followed closely by a resounding chorus of *Oh, shit.*

Of all the gin joints in all the world . . .

Asher knew in an instant that the woman spelled trouble. How could she help it? She was undoubtedly human, she was undoubtedly out of place, and she was undoubtedly accompanied by a greater imp who looked more than vaguely familiar to the overworked Guardian.

Damn, there went his vacation.

The woman walked into the club with the excited air and wide eyes of a first-time tourist in Times Square. Her head turned constantly as she struggled to take in her surroundings, devouring the experience in huge, ravenous gulps. And frankly, even a sip would have a more worldly soul than her good and drunk. To humans, the world of the Others could prove as intoxicating as Appalachian moonshine, and very few of them seemed to understand how to hold their liquor. It went to their heads, and inevitably something bad happened.

The kind of thing Asher's long-standing oaths left him duty-bound to deal with.

Wasn't that just a kick in the pants?

His grip tightened around his drink as he watched the incongruous pair weave their way through the crowd toward the end of the room where he sat. They made quite a picture together, the short, red imp only visible when they moved between tables—since his head barely cleared them—or when the crowd shifted to show glimpses of his denim and Mohawk between some club patron's legs. The woman's movements were a lot easier to follow, partly because she stood at least three feet taller than the imp and partly because she had the sort of look that caught the eye.

Okay, that caught a *man's* eye.

Dressed in a perfectly ordinary pair of jeans and some sort of thin-strapped top that shimmied and shimmered when she moved, the woman still managed to stand out from the other club-goers. She even managed to stand out from the *Other* club-goers, including the ones designed by nature to catch the eye.

First of all, her humanity practically glowed. It was part of what made a Guardian, to be able to identify an individual's species—especially when it came to humans—instantly, even surrounded by crowds of Others denser than this one. You had to be able to recognize a member of a species before you could expect to protect it, right? But this woman didn't just look human; she radiated humanity, like light, from her pores. He could only hope no one else noticed the aura, since to a certain breed of Others it would speak not just of innocence and ignorance, but of vulnerability. Asher didn't have trouble at all picturing a fiend eager to feast on all that vibrant energy, or a vamp unable to resist the urge to sink hard fangs into the long, elegant curve of her neck—

He caught himself on the edge of doing a little drooling of his own. Not that it wouldn't make sense. He was, after all, a man, as well as a Guardian, and the human still moving toward him was a very attractive woman. He could (at least pretend to) view that objectively. He swept a long glance over her, impassively taking in everything from the bronze-polished toenails peeping out from the ends of her strappy, sexy sandals, to the dusky skin and surprisingly toned muscles revealed by her flirty top, to the exotic tilt of her eyes and the thick fall of jet-black hair that tumbled from a high, tight ponytail. She was stunning, both sleek and curved, lush and slender, with her aura of energy and humanity simply adding to the magnetic pull he felt.

That had to be the explanation. She was just a gorgeous woman. He couldn't help but react to her, especially when he tried to remember the last time he'd managed a date, he assured himself. It was perfectly natural.

What wasn't natural, however, was seeing her here, mingling with the rowdy and inhuman crowd at Lurk on a Saturday night as the clock wound down toward the witching hour. The woman was out of her element, and if she wasn't careful, she'd find that out soon. Probably the hard way.

Asher lifted his mug, hiding a curse behind the heavy glass. He continued to watch as the imp led the woman to a small table just two removed from his and the two of them settled down to watch the crowd. Hoping the uneasy feeling sliding along his spine owed more to ingrained pessimism than his Guardian-born spidey-sense for trouble, he nonetheless turned his acute hearing in their direction. Just because she was a human in a situation no human should put herself in didn't mean she needed his help. Hopefully, he'd hear enough to reassure him of that so he could finish his drink and be on his way.

What was it the humans did for luck? Cross their fingers?

"I'm a little disappointed," he heard her say to her companion as she scanned the crowd around them. "It looks just like any other club. I thought it would be more . . . I don't know . . . exotic."

The imp shrugged, his shoulders bobbing up just over the edge of the table. "What, you expected black robes, flaming torches, and a sacrificial goat? It's just a bar. Folks don't come here to entertain the tourists; they come to unwind."

"I guess so. What is that group over there? Are those scales?"

"Shh! Don't point, for satyrs' sake! Do ya want to get our faces eaten? Who taught ya yer manners?"

"My parents," the woman shot back, lowering her hand and raising an eyebrow. "But I don't think they covered what to do in a room containing a contingent of lizard people."

"Oy, yer gonna get us killed. They're not lizards. That's a lamia and her court. And for your information, they usually only shed their own skins, but if you tick 'em off bad enough, they'd be happy to shed yours, too."

Asher followed their glances across the room to the table near the bar. The imp was right. Saskia Rughal had the sort of temper that fitted her rattlesnake cousins. Even Asher himself was inclined to give her wide berth.

"Lamia? What's a lamia?" the woman demanded, her expression fascinated. "Is that some kind of snake person? I mean, snakes are the ones who shed their skins, right?"

In that moment, a shout of raucous laughter burst from the group of patrons in the opposite corner of the bar, obscuring the imp's answer. Asher had to fill it in from his imagination. If it had been him doing the educating, he'd have pointed out that far from being simple "snake people," the lamia had once been worshipped as fierce, blood-hungry goddesses. In fact, he was aware of at least two modern cults whose members still did, hence Saskia's devoted entourage; he was also aware that people didn't decide to worship you unless you had some pretty damned impressive powers to inspire them. The human woman would do well to keep that in mind.

" 'Snake person,' " the imp mocked, burying his face in his chubby red hands. "Damnation, how you humans have survived as a species I will never understand. Yer like retarded puppies—constantly getting yerselves into trouble and then lookin' confused when something bigger than you smacks ya over the head with a roll of newspaper."

The woman fixed the imp with an impressive glare. "You try to smack me with anything, little man, and I'll show you the kind of self-defense moves that make it safe for a woman traveling the world on her own."

"Ya see, yer provin' my point. Ya think that just because yer bigger than me, ya can just stomp on me without any problem. You humans are always lookin' at the surface of things. Ya never bother to think about what's underneath. That's just stupid. Didn't anyone ever tell ya that size isn't everything?"

"Sure," the woman said with a shrug, "but I told him to put his pants back on and go home."

Asher winced and buried his involuntary chuckle in his beer. That she was stupid was not one of the impressions he'd gotten of the attractive human. She might be naïve, and she was clearly out of her element—and probably out of her depth—but she didn't strike him as stupid.

"This ain't gonna work," the imp growled, slapping his hands down on the table and shaking his head so hard that his Mohawk undulated like the crowd at a football stadium. "There ain't enough root beer in New York to make me risk takin' on the entire bar full of the Others *yer* gonna piss off tonight if ya keep this up. I'm outta here."

The woman laid a hand over the imp's and pushed back her seat. "Oh, relax. It can't be healthy to wind yourself up like that. Let me buy you a drink. Maybe that will settle your nerves. Of course, you look like that'd take half a bottle of tequila at this point, but what the hell. It's a special occasion."

The imp snorted. "Tequila? That human tap water? Fat chance. My nerves need something stronger than that if I'm gonna put up with you. I want a root beer. High-test. And tell them it's for you so they'll give ya a full glass. One shot ain't gonna cut it tonight."

Asher stifled a groan. A greater imp on a full glass of root beer? He'd rather shoot up an entire platoon of armed human soldiers with meth. It would be less messy. And less dangerous.

He heard the woman chuckle. "Root beer? You got it, you rebel. I'll tell them to make it a double."

Naïve. Yes, very definitely naïve.

The imp grabbed her by the wrist as she was about to leave the table. "Don't talk to anyone but the bartender, Daphanie. I ain't had time to tell ya who ya gotta avoid or who might get pissy at ya just for bein' human."

The woman, whose name Asher now knew was Daphanie, eased her arms away from her "guide's" grip and raised her eyebrows. "I got it, Quigley. Relax. I might be out of my element, but I'm not a complete idiot."

The imp watched her for a moment, then shrugged and released her to slump back in his seat, either satisfied or unconcerned.

Or up to something.

Asher felt the hair on the back of his neck bristle.

Daphanie stepped away from the table and began to weave a path through the growing crowd to the bar. Asher watched the imp watching the woman and saw a hint of speculation on the little creature's face. Whether it was speculation over the likelihood of the woman keeping her word or speculation over how any of her missteps might benefit him was harder to figure out. Imps tended to prioritize themselves on an entirely different level from the rest of the world, but they also tended to view every situation from the perspective of how much mischief they could cause in it.

In unison, the Guardian and the imp watched the woman's progress as she made her way to the shining, black lacquer expanse of the bar. The bartender should be safe enough. Tonight, the taps were being manned by Christopher, a young vampire who still found it amusing to play to the stereotypes. He maintained a wardrobe entirely of black, favoring black jeans and black button-down shirts that he left open significantly too far down his pale, scrawny chest. A computer geek in his previous life, he had the sort of pallor that proved how long it had been since he'd seen the sun, and he wore his dark hair slicked back like Bela Lugosi's Dracula. His own widow's peak might be slightly less dramatic, but points for effort. He also liked to affect a reddish tint to the corners of his mouth through the strategic use of lipstick. Apparently, the employment of cosmetics with the intent of titillating the masses excused any threat to one's masculinity. At least, that seemed to be Christopher's perspective. Still, it would make any impulse Daphanie had to question his identity fairly ridiculous. He might as well have stitched the word "vampire" above his breast pocket.

The vamp had no trouble identifying Daphanie as human, and therefore as potentially edible. When she reached the bar, Christopher leaned onto the counter and flashed her what was probably his most charming grin. Asher watched carefully as the woman bellied up to the glossy surface and returned the gesture with a casual smile. Located on the other side of the room, the bar was too far away for even him to overhear the conversation between the two figures, but Asher kept a close eye on Daphanie's expression. She appeared to be looking directly at the bartender, but her eyes never took on a glassy appearance and her smile remained friendly and slightly flirtatious rather than becoming fixed and plastic, or fascinated and adoring. So she wasn't entirely unfamiliar with the Others. She knew enough about vampires to avoid being charmed by one, even with Christopher making an effort at it. Good girl.

The realization did make Asher pause, though. Judging by her conversation with the imp, he had thought her to be completely ignorant of Other culture. That was certainly the way Quigley had made it sound, and her questions about the lamia had clearly shown a lack of awareness of the danger presented by certain members of nonhuman society. That all pointed to a lack of practical knowledge. But very few humans would have known to be on their guard against someone like Christopher, even if his appearance warned them of his true nature. They wouldn't have known the tricks of avoiding eye contact while still maintaining the appearance of it, or how to shield their minds against subtle probing or more direct attempts at influence. So Daphanie must know about vampires. Why, then, did she know so little about everything else?

The surge of curiosity took Asher by surprise. Since when did he care about a human not assigned to him? Hell, even the ones he was assigned rarely piqued his curiosity. They were a duty, his job, not something to affect him in his off-hours. He protected them from harm at the hands of the Others and tried to untangle them from whatever situations had put them in jeopardy in the first place. He usually couldn't have cared less about them, personally. The most common feeling he experienced for a human was exasperation, followed closely by annoyance, and occasionally pity. He never found them interesting.

And he sure as hell never found himself wondering if their skin felt as silky, warm, and smooth as it looked.

Damn it, this was ridiculous. Asher drained his beer and pushed away the empty glass. This Daphanie person was none of his concern. She wasn't his assignment; she wasn't his responsibility. It didn't matter to him one way or another if she ended up as a midnight snack for someone like Christopher, or a sacrificial offering on Saskia's minions' altar. It was none of his business.

Tearing his gaze from the tempting curve of her shoulder, he slid from his chair and plotted a course for the exit. A direct line would take him in front of the bar, which would put him way too close to the woman he'd just resolved to put out of his mind. Better to skirt around the back of the room and weave through the crowd opposite the temptation.

Carefully averting his eyes, he started forward, casting a last glance in the imp's direction. The creature still had his eyes trained on his human companion. A slight smile curved his lips.

Asher had made it less than a quarter of the way to the door when the mischief behind that smile registered and slowed his steps. The bellow stopped them.

Reflex made him look. Loud noises drew attention, which was why every eye in the club seemed to have turned in unison to the scene a few feet away from the spot where Daphanie had just stood, and fixed on the spot she currently occupied. Directly in front of her towered a huge, angry, and visibly glowering witch doctor.

Asher took his measure at a glance, with the keen and accurate eye of a Guardian. The magic the man practiced left its mark on him, making him an easy read. His character was shallow, everything about him painted on the surface like descriptive text. At least, for one of Asher's talents.

The man stood just under six feet tall with a barrel-chested build augmented by a love of rich, heavy soul food. He dressed—habitually, Asher would guess—in the bright colors and intricate patterns of African cloth and was happy to lecture for hours about his native West Africa and his hereditary connection both to there and to the New World, where his uncles had lived since the time of slavery. Never mind that his "uncles" were about six generations removed. As a man like that would point out, they existed on his mother's side, so naturally in the matrilineal society of his homeland, they still counted. And if not for that, he surely would have come up with another reason. Heritage was very important to his sort.

Since he was a man who liked to reference his long family history of shamanism and priest- and priestess-hood, the witch doctor would have every reason to cling to his relationship with such figures, however distant they might be. Having African witches and Caribbean voodoo priests in his background would bolster his claims as a man of power in Other society, despite those who would feel he was more talk than talent.

He amassed around him a following to make any cult leader envious, and an entourage of acolytes without whom he would go nowhere. He also sported a group of blank-eyed lackeys whom he would claim to have bound to him by making them into zombie slaves through the use of his dark magic.

Asher could read all this in an instant, and what wasn't written in the man's aura was easy to guess at. He wasn't the sort who could be expected to behave rationally.

"You stupid girl!" the offended and dripping witch doctor bellowed. Unless Asher was very much mistaken, that was the imp's root beer running off the man's heavy, beaded necklace. "How dare you offer such insult to my person? I am Charles Antoine D'Abo! Have you no respect for your superiors?"

As Asher watched, he saw Daphanie's expression slowly morph through a range of emotions. It had started out with embarrassed regret but shifted quickly through surprise and on to effrontery. By the time D'Abo had called himself her superior, she pretty much just looked pissed.

To her credit, though, she kept her head and betrayed her feelings through no more than narrowed eyes and pursed lips. "I apologize for spilling the drink on you, sir, but maybe if you looked ahead of you while you were walking through a crowded room, you could avoid bumping into people carrying liquids."

D'Abo snorted and gestured angrily, clearly for the benefit of his disciples. "Do not presume to instruct me on my behavior, girl. It was you who insulted me. I am the injured party."

"No, you're the *damp* party," Daphanie corrected. "I apologized, but there's no permanent harm done, so let's both just move on with our lives, shall we?"

She gestured with the glasses in her hand and turned as if to make her way back to the bar, but D'Abo shifted his bulk back into her path.

"That weak thing you call an apology will not pacify me, girl. You tried to imply that I share in the blame for your clumsiness, but I was not the one carrying drinks and spilling them on powerful men. You must admit your wrongdoing and beg my forgiveness!"

A murmur of toadying agreement rumbled among the man's followers, making Asher wince. Apparently the man lacked not only magical talent, but also common sense. Asher would hazard a guess that the Witch's Council had been denying him admittance for something like the last fifteen years. His arrogance only served to make him look like a bigger buffoon. Judging by Daphanie's expression, she thought so, too. Or she would, if she were able to see through her perfectly understandable anger.

Asher watched as she set down the empty glass on a nearby table with an audible click. In the tense atmosphere of the club, all extraneous conversations had stilled. A quick glance over his shoulder confirmed that the table at which Quigley had sat just a few seconds ago was empty. Asher swore roundly, and his senses went on high alert. Everyone concentrated on the unfolding scene between D'Abo and the unknown human, who straightened her spine, lifted her chin, and gave the blustering witch doctor a look so dirty, it wouldn't be cleared for late-night cable.

"*First* of all," she bit out, pointing a finger at D'Abo and ignoring the shocked gasps of his flunkies, "I am not anyone's girl, so I would appreciate the courtesy of not being addressed as one. *Secondly*"—she poked her finger in the direction of the man's chest—"my mama taught me my manners, which I used when I apologized for what was an honest accident. But obviously you were raised in that barn my mama always mentioned, because anyone with a sense of civility would have accepted the apology and moved the hell on with his life.

"And *third*." She stepped forward and poked again, this time barely making contact with D'Abo's kente-cloth tunic. "I. Don't. Beg. For anything. From anyone. Ever. You got that? *Boy?*"

Asher was sprinting toward the altercation before D'Abo's shocked gasp had managed to suck more than half the oxygen from the room. And here he'd thought he'd have the rest of the night off.

Leave it to a human.

Three

Among the Others, a curious balancing act is maintained between embracing one's identity as a member of a unique and powerful subgroup and desiring to be seen as more than a vampire or a shapeshifter or a demon. No Other wants to be judged by a stereotype, but very few want anyone to forget exactly how dangerous they can potentially be.
—A Human Handbook to the Others, *Chapter One*

Just where the hell did this guy get off making such a scene over a spilled drink? For God's sake, he'd been the one not watching where he was going! The bloody blowhard had been so busy pontificating to his adoring fan club that he hadn't had any idea that Daphanie was about to intersect his path, and he sure as hell didn't know how damned hard she'd had to work to stay out of his way. The jerk had almost run her over at least three times before one of his expansive and pompous gestures sent his arm slamming into the back of her shoulder, throwing her off balance, and resulting in the spilled root beer.

Sure, she felt bad about spilling the drink on his shirt. That was why she'd apologized. But it hadn't really been her fault, and she was not about to be lectured at like a

three-year-old or insulted in front of a crowd of strangers; she didn't care who they were. Let them chew off
her fingers or turn her into a toad or drain her blood
from her body. She didn't give a damn. She wasn't the
kind of girl who let people walk all over her, whether
they happened to be human or not.

Which was why she'd lost her temper.

She had tried to hold it together. Honest. But the jerk
just had to keep pushing. She'd gritted her teeth in the
face of being called stupid. There was the heat of the
moment to consider, after all. She'd even been prepared
to overlook his ungracious dismissal of her apology. But
when *any* man told her that she needed to *beg* for his
forgiveness? Oh, no. Daffy didn't play that game. Jack-
ass could go suck her left nut.

In fact, she felt pretty proud that she'd restrained
herself from telling him to do exactly that. Dude was
acting like an idiot.

Not to mention that he was putting a damper on her
entire evening. When Quigley had tried to distract her
from revealing him to her sister with the offer of a trip to
an Other nightspot, it had seemed like a real opportunity.
Since the supernatural world had been revealed to her,
Daphanie's head had been spinning with the sheer realization of all she didn't know about it. She figured an evening out with the imp would give her a chance to learn
as much as she could about the world her sister would be
living in from now on. Plus, how cool was it to be able to
meet not just vampires and werewolves and changelings,
but imps and demons and lamia and . . . whatever the
heck the ass monkey in the tribal cloth turned out to be?

Okay, so she could have lived without making his

acquaintance, but up until that moment she'd been having a blast. She'd seen things she'd never even imagined before. How was it she could have lived for half of
her life in this city and never had a clue about what was
really going on around her? How had she missed all
this before? It boggled her mind, but it also made her
vow that from now on, she wouldn't let herself miss a
thing. Fate had presented her with this opportunity,
and she intended to take these lessons from the imp
and run with them. After all, where else would she get
the opportunity to find a guide to the world of the Others? Somehow, she thought her sister might find herself
a bit preoccupied for the next little while.

Remembering Danice—and, by extension, Mac—
brought Daphanie back to the moment, annoying, insulting, arrogant prick and all. She needed to keep in mind
that this wasn't her world, but it was her sister's. Danice
might not know this jerk personally, but that didn't
mean that she wouldn't hear about it if Daphanie really
lost control and did something stupid.

Daphanie repeated that to herself as she worked to
unclench her fingers from her glass of red wine. She was
the outsider, the guest in this place. It was up to her to be
the bigger person, stop poking the jerk in the chest, and
walk away with dignity and grace.

She could do it.

"You presume to lay a hand on me! Filthy little whore!
A curse on you!"

The deep-throated fury of the words reverberated
through the room, echoing off the walls and ceiling as
if they had been designed especially for their proper-
ties of acoustical amplification. Even the floor seemed

to tremble slightly beneath Daphanie's feet. A tiny little corner of her mind wondered idly if the glass in the entry doors had shattered from the vibration, but she couldn't look to check. It would have been impossible to see through the thick, red fog clouding her vision.

What had he called her?

Whore

Whore

Whore

WHAT had he *called* her?

Daphanie watched, with curious detachment, as her left arm snaked out of its own volition. She never commanded it to move. She never intended for it to shift from its position at her waist, elbow bent and wrist relaxed. And she certainly never meant for the glass of red wine dangling from her hand to arc upward in slow motion, or for its contents to splash vividly and wetly directly into the big man's face.

Nope, that had not been part of her plan.

But neither did she have any control over the warm surge of triumphant satisfaction that flowed within her as she watched the cabernet impact its target's puffed-up cheeks, pretentious goatee, and bulbous nose. Even if she'd wanted to, she couldn't have repressed the happy glow her independently minded arm and an indifferent vintage had caused.

Not that she wanted to.

And now there was nothing left to say.

Calmly, Daphanie set her wine glass down beside the abandoned dregs of the root beer and turned to go.

If the last bellow had caused the floor to vibrate, this one should have buckled the structure's support beams.

It probably registered somewhere on the Richter scale, yet Daphanie didn't care. She set her sights on the exit across the room, intent on leaving with whatever calm she still possessed.

"*SOSA!* Get her!"

A rush of movement behind her caused Daphanie to snap her head around just in time to see one of her enemy's minions reaching for her with grasping hands and blank eyes that flared just briefly with malicious excitement. She lifted an arm to ward him off and opened her mouth to yell . . . something, but his hand snaked out beneath her guard, surprisingly swift and accurate, to grab the hem of her top.

Daphanie jerked away, hearing the sound of fabric ripping. Cursing, she looked down, expecting to see herself nude from the waist up, but luck was still with her. The flunky called Sosa had managed to tear a strip of fabric off the bottom of her shirt, but she remained decently covered.

Apparently unsatisfied, the man darted toward her again, but this time he never made contact. Instead, a large figure seemed to swoop in out of nowhere and plant itself between Daphanie and her attacker. From around the interloper, she could just make out the expression of surprise and irritation on the face of the man who had insulted her.

"What are you doing here, Guardian?" the large, sticky man demanded. "Don't try to tell me this piece of trash is one of your precious pets."

"I don't keep pets, D'Abo." The "Guardian" folded his arms over his chest so that the fabric of his coat stretched across broad shoulders and sharply defined shoulder blades. Only a pair of long top-to-bottom pleats seemed to keep it from splitting open. "And I would be careful about that sort of accusation, if I were you."

Even from her compromised viewing place, by craning her head, Daphanie was able to make out the meaningful glance her protector shot in the direction of D'Abo's entourage. It actually surprised her how *much* meaning could be packed into a face that could have been carved from stone. Or marble. By some kind of Renaissance master.

He had clean-cut, masculine features saved from outright beauty by the presence of enough crags and lines to show a wealth of experience behind the vaguely stubbled skin. Daphanie found herself itching to ask him to turn around and face her. She wanted the chance to see him full on. The glimpses she got from behind him and to the side only piqued her interest. It had been a long time since she'd been piqued by a man.

He didn't seem to share her curiosity, though. Instead, his gaze remained fixed on D'Abo and the other man's followers. Daphanie had to admit the accusation had merit. She hadn't looked closely enough at the crowd of flunkies before to distinguish that the group was made up of two distinct types of follower: one type watched their leader with eager, worshipful attention, hanging on his every word and tripping all over themselves to agree with each pronouncement as if it had just fallen from the lips of God; the second type marched in an odd sort of formation in the man's wake, eyes straight ahead, faces blank, stopping whenever their leader stopped but never appearing engaged in either the group around them or their wider surroundings. It was like watching a troop of toy soldiers, mindless automatons without any sort of independent spirit.

It kinda creeped Daphanie out.

Of course, the lack of self-determination hadn't stopped the one called Sosa from coming after her the minute D'Abo had issued the instruction. The minion might not think for himself, but he didn't hesitate to obey commands. It must feel good to be the king of your own little universe. Daphanie, however, preferred to live in the real world.

"If the girl is not under your protection, then you have no place in this," D'Abo said, waving his hand in dismissal and puffing out his chest. "Step aside. It is my right to deal with the creature that has insulted me."

"The only right you have here is the right to back off and go somewhere else before you do something I won't be able to ignore." The man standing in front of Daphanie never raised his voice above a low murmur, but the tone of command was unmistakable. Even she felt tempted to take a step back, but she'd be damned if she let D'Abo see her do it.

"I won't be ordered about by you, Guardian. You have no authority over me."

"I am called Asher Grayson, D'Abo, and I am merely one of my kind. Harm the human, and you'll have the entire Council down on your head. Not to mention the possibility that my boss wouldn't be pleased if he were to hear of it. Especially when you have no authority over a human woman who did nothing to you that a little soap and water won't fix. Do you honestly expect me to stand aside and watch you take your wounded pride out on her? You know the laws, D'Abo."

It was like sitting in her senior-year Spanish class and watching a Pedro Almodóvar movie without the benefit of subtitles—she understood about one word out of every three. It might be enough to get the gist of things, but it hardly proved illuminating.

As far as she could tell, the "Council" her protector—Asher, he had said his name was—referred to was probably the Council of Others. Danice had told her about them. They were like the senate of the Other community, although to Daphanie they sounded a lot more like the ancient Roman senate than the modern-American one. Apparently, the Council didn't so much represent the population of nonhuman New Yorkers as it ruled them. The Council of Others made the rules and it enforced the rules, and all due sympathy to anyone who decided to break the rules, because it didn't sound as if the Council as a whole possessed much of a sense of humor. Daphanie didn't want to piss them off, and she wasn't even part of their community. They had no authority over her, but she wasn't inclined to take chances.

Of course, she also wasn't generally inclined to let other people fight her battles for her.

She stepped to the side, just far enough to get a clear view of the situation, but not far enough to give the enraged D'Abo a clear shot at her. She was independent, not stupid.

Her movement caught her champion's attention. He shifted his gaze from the other man to frown down at her. It wasn't like Daphanie had never been looked down at before. At five-six she wasn't exactly short, but most men still stood at least a couple of inches taller. This guy, though, towered over her. He had to top six three, and all of it looked long, lean, and potentially lethal—the kind of man who made a woman's senses go on high alert. And in Daphanie's case, sound the alarm.

She couldn't remember the last time she'd felt the zing of an instant attraction, but there it was, shivering up and down her spine, pulling her shoulder blades together and her tummy in tight. Something about him just sparked it for her, a reaction more powerful than any she remembered from her high school chemistry classes.

He had dark, ash-blond hair cropped ruthlessly short and the sort of weathered face that she had always thought separated the men from the boys. His face looked lived in, as if he'd been through a few bumps in the road and actually bothered to learn from them. His eyes only confirmed that; they were a striking silver gray shot through with sparks of gold and backed by the kind of knowledge that said he'd faced tougher situations than this in his sleep.

Something about that both reassured and unnerved Daphanie. It was nice to know when a man could handle himself, but that ability could cost a man a lot. She couldn't help wondering about the price this one had paid.

"You should stay behind me," he rumbled.

Daphanie snapped back to attention, tearing her gaze from his and training it instead on a spot between them, just for the sake of concentration. Staring at him was turning out to be bad for her ability to focus. "Thanks, but I'm not the type to hide behind a big, strong man. In fact, I'm not really the type to hide."

The man frowned. "Stay behind me," he repeated.

Okay, he was hot, but a titch single-minded.

Daphanie ignored the order and turned back to D'Abo. She met his enraged scowl squarely and straightened her shoulders. "Look, Mr. D'Abo, we both know that the insulted party here is me. I'm the one who's been called names and condescended to; you're just the one who turned an honest mistake into a federal case.

"Now, I don't know what your childhood trauma is or why you felt the need to blow this whole thing out of proportion, but I can promise you that nothing is going to be made better by encouraging a friend of yours to 'get me.' Partly because I'm not an easy girl to get, but mostly because I will have no hesitation in reporting your stupid ass to the police, the Council of Others, the U.S. Army, and the guy in the alley out back with the knife and the .38 in his pants. So let's just let bygones be bygones, all right?"

Rage stiffened the older man's form until he trembled like the earth around an impending volcanic explosion. Daphanie almost expected to see his hair rise up off his head like a steam cloud.

Beside her, Asher shifted, bending his head to hers. "You're not helping."

"You will pay, girl! I will call Kalfou down on you and let his power deal with your impertinence!"

D'Abo grabbed the arm of his nearest servant and dragged the man forward. Yanking a knife from his belt he slashed the man across the palm, an action that made Daphanie gasp, Asher swear, and no one else so much as blink. If she'd seen a little dog anywhere nearby at that point, Daphanie would have made sure to tell it she didn't think they were in Kansas anymore.

With rough hands, D'Abo wrenched the man's hand to the side and let the blood drip to the club's concrete floor. Dozens of pairs of eyes watched the tiny trickle slide over skin and through air. Daphanie felt the hair on the back of her neck stand up and fought down the urge to take a step back.

"Kalfou, come to the crossroads! Dance in the moonlight! O great Carrefour, sh—"

"Shut. The hell. Up."

Daphanie shot a quick glance at Asher, which was all she had time for before he reached out an arm and physically pushed her back behind him. In her mind, he seemed to grow in size, muscles rippling and easing until she could have sworn he stood at least three inches taller and broader than he had a minute ago. Then the pleats in his coat stretched again, this time actually splitting to accommodate the emergence of a set of beautifully feathered, enormous white wings.

Holy crap.

The wings easily matched her self-appointed bodyguard in height, the folded joints rising over his shoulders to the top of his head and the tapered tips brushing the middle of his calves. When spread, she imagined they would span well over twenty-five feet. How the hell had he kept something like that hidden?

"You will cease this aggression against the human," the Guardian intoned, his voice resonating at a pitch Daphanie hadn't noticed earlier. It seemed to well from not just his body but from the very air and walls around them. It made the bottoms of her feet tingle and she had to fight to keep her gaze from dropping to the floor. That voice had power, even she recognized that, and it wasn't directed at her. She wondered how D'Abo felt. "She has been taken under Guard, and by the laws of the Others you are forbidden from harming her, Charles D'Abo. Leave this place and this girl and abandon all contact with her. This is commanded to you."

For the first time, Daphanie saw the edges of fear crowding into D'Abo's eyes. Caution warred with fury in his expression for several moments, only to be replaced by hatred as he looked away from Asher and focused on Daphanie instead.

"I will raise no hand or *loa* against her," D'Abo spat, not daring to look again at Asher. He directed all his impotent anger instead at Daphanie. She couldn't seem to help the shiver he sent chasing down her spine. "But she will come to what she deserves. Mark my words."

With an impatient gesture to his companions, the affronted man turned and stalked out the club's door. The crowd parted to let him pass.

Daphanie blew out her tension in a long breath. "Well, that was fun. Not exactly what I had planned for the evening, but . . ." Shaking her head, she offered Asher a small smile. "Thanks for stepping in. As scenes go, that wasn't a pleasant one, but I suppose it could have gotten worse. I'm Daphanie, by the way." She held out a hand. "Daphanie Carter."

The man just stared at her, still scowling.

"Right." She dropped her hand and wiped her palm on her jeans. "Well, it was nice meeting you. Enjoy the rest of your night."

So much for that. The big guy didn't seem interested in small talk. Which was a pity, since if small talk led to a little flirtation in this case, Daph couldn't say she would have objected. This Asher guy might be a little intimidating, but he was also smokin' hot.

She turned to pick up the empty glasses she'd set aside during the confrontation. A hand clamped around her wrist to stop her, sending a deliciously rough shiver from her belly to her knees. She glanced up at her rescuer.

"Come with me."

Daphanie frowned. Something was different about him, and it wasn't just that his voice had returned to normal. His expression certainly hadn't softened. And then she realized it was the wings. Or rather, the lack of them. They had disappeared as unexpectedly as they had been revealed, leaving her with the uneasy feeling of wondering if she'd been the only one who saw them to begin with. Maybe she wasn't quite as ready to dive into the world of the Others as she had thought.

When she didn't immediately move to follow Asher, he tugged, gently but firmly, to guide her toward the door. Daphanie shook her head. "Sorry, but I came here with someone. I can't leave without him. That would be rude."

Asher snorted. "If you're referring to the imp, don't worry. Now come with me."

Daphanie dug in her heels and returned his scowl with one of her own. She had to clench her teeth to remind herself that sexual attraction was insufficient reason to overlook boorishness.

"Look, I said thank you for sticking up for me with that bully, but that doesn't mean I'm going to let you do a little bullying of your own. In case you hadn't noticed, I don't like being told what to do. So why don't you let go of my arm and let me go find my friend."

He ignored her and simply began towing her toward the exit. "Your 'friend' is long gone. He skittered away as soon as he saw the first sign of trouble."

That made Daphanie blink. Quigley had just left her? What if that D'Abo guy had really tried to hurt her? What if Asher hadn't stepped in? Who knew what might have happened to her?

"Why, that little . . . imp."

"Exactly." Reaching the club's exit, he pushed her outside and quickly followed, crowding her up against the cement wall at the entrance to the adjoining alley. "So why don't you tell me what you were thinking coming here with him. Are you crazy? Stupid? What?"

Daphanie stiffened. In addition to the conversational skills of a baboon, he apparently had the manners of one, too. Too bad the way he smelled, all warm and rich and elementally male, made her mouth water every time she drew breath. "At the moment, I'm mostly insulted."

"Pardon me. I didn't realize I'd be offending your delicate sensibilities by pointing out the obvious." He glared down at her, his large frame blocking both her view of the street and most of the light from the nearby street lamps and illuminated signage. "Do you have any idea the kind of danger you were just in?"

"The kind I would have been happy to handle on my own." She reached up to push him back a step or two and reclaim her personal space, but something inside stopped her. Somehow she imagined touching this man might be a bad thing for her equilibrium. Instead she folded her arms across her chest and contented herself with shooting him a dirty look.

"On your own?" He barked out a dark laugh, one

with little connection to humor. "Sweetheart, you were about as far from handling that on your own as it's possible to be and still remain standing. Do you even know what that was you were doing such a great job of pissing off?"

"Apparently his name is D'Abo and he's some kind of roaming asshole who doesn't know an apology from his own fat ass," she shot back, beginning to resent this conversation. As attractive as she might find this man, she'd pretty much reached her nightly limit for being condescended to. "In fact, the two of you bear a remarkable resemblance. You related?"

"Charles D'Abo," he informed her with exaggerated patience, "is a witch doctor. He reeks of voodoo, hoodoo, and black magic. I could smell it on him. He was certainly more than you could handle. You'd be better off if you tried a little harder not to make a man like that hate you."

"I don't care how that idiot feels about me one way or the other. I make it a practice not to spend time worrying about men with more arrogance than brainpower."

"Then you might want to change your practices. Men like D'Abo, men like any of those you would find here tonight, any Other you might *ever* find, are not the sorts you want as your enemies."

"Why? Because he might make a little doll in my image and stick pins in it? Let him. I'm not afraid of that megalomaniac."

He leaned in closer. "You should be."

The warm puff of his breath against her skin sent a jolt of electricity through her spine. Daphanie jerked her head back before she could stop herself. Damn him.

"Why?" she demanded, forcing her chin higher. "What's so dangerous about a charlatan with a god complex?"

"What gave you the idea that he's a charlatan?"

She raised her eyebrows. "You mean he's actually a witch doctor? Grass-skirt, bone-through-the-nose, boil-the-white-man-in-a-big-black-cauldron witch doctor?"

"Just how often do you spend your time watching late-night B-movies on television?"

More often than she cared to admit. Especially to him.

"So he really is a witch doctor?"

Asher shook his head. "Did you think I was making this whole thing up? That I had nothing better to do with my night than save the neck of an ignorant human who was too blind to notice when she'd gotten in over her head? Because I assure you, that's not the case."

Okay, that stung. Daphanie knew perfectly well that she *was* ignorant when it came to the Others, but that was why she'd allowed Quigley to bring her here—so she could learn. Having someone throw her lack of knowledge in her face didn't accomplish anything other than making her feel bad. Frankly, it pushed her right to her limit.

Seeing him open his mouth to continue berating her pushed her over.

Boosting herself onto her tiptoes, Daphanie raised her hand and clapped it over his mouth, ignoring the way her palm tingled where it touched his skin.

She leaned in until their faces almost touched and spoke to him very softly. "I don't know if you've noticed, *sweetheart,* but I've had a bitch of a night so far. I ducked out of my sister's wedding reception, I trusted

an imp to introduce me to the wider Others community, I was verbally and very nearly physically assaulted
by a jerk with magical powers, and now I'm being lectured by another jerk who apparently gets his kicks
by taking a baseball bat to the carcasses of deceased
equines."

Asher watched her through narrowed eyes of silver
and gold, but he made no move to tug her hand away
from his mouth. He simply stood, still and quiet, before
her, his chest rising and falling with every breath. She
had to devote a considerable amount of her concentration to ignoring the feel of that breath tickling the skin
of her hand with humid warmth.

"How about this?" she hurried to continue. "What if
I admit that it's true I don't know very much about the
Others, *you* admit that lecturing me is not going to
change that, and we both agree to go our separate ways?
Does that work for you?"

Since it was a yes or no question, she didn't bother to
remove her hand. It had nothing to do with the fact that
the idea of ceasing to touch him made her stomach
clench in protest.

To her surprise, Asher shook his head.

Daphanie frowned. "What do you mean, 'no'?"

He reached up and took her hand in his, carefully
pulling it away from his mouth. But he didn't drop it.
His fingers remained curled around hers and sped her
heart up by at least twenty beats per minute.

"I mean, that's not the way this works," he explained,
his voice soft but implacable. "Weren't you listening
inside? You've been taken under guard. You're my responsibility now. Where you go, I go."

The memory of those huge white wings flashed in Daphanie's mind and she drew back a few inches. "Are you saying you're . . . my Guardian angel?"

His jaw flexed. *"Not* angel. *Just* Guardian."

"There's a difference?"

"Of course."

"And would you care to explain that to—" Daphanie broke off and held up a hand. "No. You know what? I don't really want to know right now. Right now, all I want is to go home, climb into bed, and pull the covers up over my head. Maybe if I say my prayers and I'm really lucky, I'll wake up and find out none of this ever really happened."

Asher just shrugged. "Lead the way."

"Excuse me?"

"Lead the way." He took a full step backward so that he no longer crowded her against the wall and swept his hand out before them. "I'll follow you."

She planted her hands on her hips. "No you won't. I said thank you for helping me out in there, but that doesn't mean I'm going to take you home with me and show you my gratitude. Frankly, it wasn't that impressive a rescue."

He rolled his eyes and took her elbow to urge her forward. "I'm not trolling for sexual favors, human. I'm simply informing you of the way things stand. You are my responsibility now, and I intend to see you safely to your home. As I am not currently aware of that location, you are going to have to direct me."

"I'd be happy to direct you to hell," she snapped. "There ain't no way on God's earth I am telling a total stranger where I live, let alone leading him straight to my front door. I don't care how many good deeds you think you've done me. I don't know you, and I don't need a bodyguard."

"Guardian."

"Whatever. I don't need some strange man to protect me from the boogeyman."

"A bogie would be easier to deal with than D'Abo. They're vicious, but they're not very smart. I think D'Abo is more intelligent than he seems."

Daphanie gritted her jaw until she thought her teeth might snap. "You're missing my point."

"No, I'm ignoring your point, because it's invalid." He halted at the corner and looked down at her. "If you're worried that you don't know my name, it's Asher. Grayson. But whatever you choose to call me, you are stuck with me. I have declared you under Guard, and myself as your Guardian. That is the end of the story."

"And if I don't like this story?"

Again, he shrugged. "Maybe you'll find it grows on you."

Daphanie stuffed her hands in her pockets, partly because she was restless and upset and impatient and needed to move something, and partly to keep from wrapping them around Asher's throat and squeezing.

"Look," she sighed, tired of fighting. "Like I said, it's been a really long night. I am perfectly prepared to admit that when it comes to the Others, I don't know what I'm doing, and you do. I get that. Whatever mistakes I made tonight, I regret, but all I can do is not repeat them. I can't go back and change them. Agreed?"

"Agreed . . ."

He sounded suspicious.

"So the only thing you'd be doing by coming with me is making sure I don't get into any more trouble on the way home, right? But that's not necessary, because I promise to be a good girl. I'll go straight to the apartment, I won't talk to strangers, I won't pass go and collect two hundred dollars. Fair enough?"

He shook his head. "That's the least of my concerns. What's going to happen once you get home? What's going to stop D'Abo from attempting his revenge? Do you think walls can keep out his kind of magic? Or any magic at all?"

"They can if they're warded, right?"

That made him blink. It actually made his head jerk back just a little and a look of surprise settle over his features. "Your apartment is warded? How?"

"I don't know the particulars, because it's not really my apartment. I'm staying at my sister's place while she's out of town, but she mentioned it was warded. That means I'll be safe there, right?"

His frown returned. "That depends on the wards. And who is your sister that she needs or even knows about that kind of protection? You're human. I know you're human."

"And so is my sister," Daphanie explained. Now that he actually seemed to be paying attention, she found she had a lot more patience when it came to answering his questions. "But she's married to a changeling, and she's friends with half the Council of Others, and most of their wives."

"What's her name?"

She hesitated only a second. Surely a man so obsessed with keeping her safe wouldn't have any reason to harm her sister. And besides, by now Danice and Mac would be halfway to their secret honeymoon destination. Even if he wanted to, he wouldn't be able to get to her. Plus, Daphanie had a feeling Mac would tear anyone who tried to harm his new wife into little bloody shreds.

"Danice Carter," she said. "Well, Carter-Callahan now. She recently got married."

As recently as eight hours ago.

"And she knows members of the Council?"

"Regina Vidâme is one of her best friends. Wasn't her husband the head of the Council for a while? And Graham Winters, too. Missy Winters is another of her close friends."

Asher muttered something under his breath.

Daphanie felt a surge of confidence. "So under those circumstances, can we agree that once I get to the apartment, I'll be perfectly safe and will no longer require your . . . Guardianship?"

"You should be safe enough," he muttered with obvious reluctance. "But—"

"Good. In that case—" She interrupted forcefully and held out her hand for the second time in one night. Maybe this time he wouldn't turn his nose up at shaking it. "Thanks for everything you've done. I know you went out of your way to help me, and I appreciate it, whether I needed it or not."

Asher took her hand, but he didn't shake it. Instead, he grasped it firmly in his and used his other to press the button on the pedestrian traffic signal beside them. "Don't thank me yet."

"Why not?"

"Because you might be safe in your sister's apartment, but you aren't there yet, so I'm not through with my everything."

Daphanie sighed and shook her head. She should have known he wouldn't give in easily. "But once I'm inside, you'll go away and stop acting like my babysitter?"

His gaze remained focused on the orange hand glowing on the opposite corner. "Once you get inside the apartment, you'll be able to pretend like I don't even exist."

She could live with that, Daphanie decided. Right now, the important thing was to get home and get to bed. She couldn't remember the last time she'd felt so exhausted.

"Fine," she said with a sigh, stepping off the curb as the signal changed. "Follow me. We'll take a cab to midtown. That will get me home that much sooner."

"You're that anxious to get rid of me?" he asked, shooting her a sideways glance.

"As anxious as I imagine you are to get rid of me."

She quickened her step toward the nearest main avenue, practically dragging Asher along behind her. With her gaze focused on her destination, she couldn't see his face, but she thought she heard him hum something.

Something that sounded almost like . . .

"Interesting."

Four

As humans, we occasionally have difficulty under-
standing the manner in which seemingly old-
fashioned or even antiquated concepts continue to
hold sway in the society of the Others. We might
think terms like "honor" or "vows" or "duty" went
out with the Round Table, but to certain factions
of Others, those words mean as much as a legal
contract.
    —A Human Handbook to the Others, *Chapter Two*

She smelled smoke, both the sweet smoke of burning
incense and the thicker, sharper tang of charcoal. She
felt her pulse throbbing, heard it in her ears, tasted it
in the back of her throat. It grew louder and louder,
increasing in tempo, the rhythm changing and stuttering
until it became the beat of drums. They drove the beat
of her heart, flooded through her body until the rhythm
found her feet and lifted them each in turn. She could
feel the dry grit of dirt beneath her soles, feel her body
bending and swaying to the music of the drums.

*   She felt the cool thickness of humid night air against*
her skin, then the soothing glow of firelight. Then the

air again, fire again, back and forth, each in turn as she twirled and dipped and moved in the dance.

Now the drums beat faster. Voices joined the sound, chanting with increasing urgency, driving the dance, driven by the drums, driven by the spirits. She felt the fullness in her body, felt her tit ange *step aside and let the greater ones in. She could feel the power welling up within her, feel the excitement, the exaltation. She lifted her arms to the roof and gave herself over to the communion with the divine, the dark, the eternal. Only moments, she knew. Only moments and she would be consumed by the power—*

The strident peal of the doorbell intruded like a scream of pain.

Daphanie bolted upright in her bed, her heart pounding and her skin slick with sweat. A bitter, metallic taste lingered in her mouth as she struggled back to awareness. It felt like walking against a fast-moving current. Nothing seemed quite real, quite right. She didn't recognize her surroundings. Where was she? The room looked wrong, smelled wrong. This wasn't her little gatehouse on the canal. Where was she? Why did it smell like her sister's perfumed soap?

Soap tinged with the ashen bite of charcoal.

Fire and amber.

She squeezed her eyes shut and pressed the heel of her palm to her forehead. She felt as if the dream clung to her the same way the smoke did, infusing her hair, her clothes, her pores with an offensive taint. She shook her head, but in the distance, she could swear she still heard the beat of the drums.

Someone pounded on the door.

Throwing back the covers, Daphanie stumbled out of bed, tripping and weaving as she fought her way through an unfamiliar maze of furniture. Even her vision seemed dark and hazy, and the current still pushed against her.

"Who is it?" she called out, collapsing against the bedroom doorframe and giving thanks for its solidity. What the hell was wrong with her? She'd never called herself a morning person, but this lethargic confusion wasn't like her.

"I was kind of hoping you'd tell me that," a woman's voice answered with wary amusement from the next room. "You know, if you'd told me you were going to have company, Daph, I could have rescheduled."

Daph. Daphanie. That was her. She was Daphanie. But who was the woman in the other room? She struggled through the thick confusion. She ought to know that voice. Or did she know that voice? What was that voice . . . ?

"Daphanie?" This time the woman's voice held no laughter. A note of concern entered. "It's Corinne. Are you okay? Is something wrong? Is this guy supposed to be here?"

Corinne.

Daphanie. Corinne.

Corinne. Niecie. Daphanie.

Memory blew in like cold wind, forcing back the fog and slapping her cheeks as if she were some swooning Dickensian heroine. She was Daphanie Carter, artist and blacksmith. Niecie was her younger sister Danice, married just yesterday, and Corinne was their friend Corinne D'Alessandro. She and Corinne had arranged to meet this morning because the other woman was a reporter and she'd offered to do a feature on Daphanie's work for her newspaper.

And the guy in question was her newly acquired barnacle, better known as Asher Grayson.

And he had apparently answered Corinne's ring without bothering to wake Daphanie up.

Cursing under her breath, Daphanie braced a shaking hand against cool wooden molding and pushed herself down the hall to the living room. She could feel herself listing back and forth like a drunk, shoulders bumping into the walls, as she headed toward the sound of voices. Or more particularly, the sound of one voice, deep and low, as it rumbled reassurances at her visitor. The visitor she should have been up to greet.

It took three times as long as it should have to walk the twenty-odd feet, and by the time Daphanie staggered into the living room, Corinne had a look on her face that proclaimed her about sixty seconds away from calling 911.

"Your friend here was just telling me that you're fine, just sleeping, and that I shouldn't worry or scream 'fire' at the top of my lungs to bring the entire building running." Corinne spoke to Daphanie, but she kept her eyes on the figure directly in front of her. A towering, forcefully male figure that Daphanie had hoped against hope was just another character in her strange nightmares. No such luck.

"But I thought I'd just check with you before I took his word for it," Corinne continued. "Are you okay, Daphanie?"

As she asked the question, she shifted her gaze

down and found Daphanie where she had stopped to lean heavily against the back of the sofa.

"Holy crap, Daph! What's the matter? Are you hurt? What did he do to you?" Corinne dropped two large paper bags just inside the apartment entryway and shoved past Asher's physical barricade with the determination of a mama bear. She grabbed her friend by the shoulders, her eyes searching for some sign of injury. "My God, you look like hell!"

Daphanie managed a shaky laugh and used a trembling hand to push her disordered hair back out of her face. "Thanks. That's just what a girl likes to hear first thing in the morning."

"I mean it. Tell me what happened. Did he rape you? Drug you? What?" Even as she peppered Daphanie with questions, Corinne's hand was already pulling her cell phone out of her pocket and flipping it open. "I'm calling 911. Run if you want to, you bastard, but I've seen your face, and I've got friends on the force. The cops will hunt you down like the dog you are. And I'll be right there with them."

Reaching a hand out, Daphanie managed to flip the cell closed before Corinne could complete the call. "No, don't. I'm fine. Asher didn't hurt me. I don't need the police. It's not—There's nothing wrong with me."

"Oh, really?"

"Really," Asher confirmed, shutting the apartment door and turning to face his accuser, who still watched him with unveiled suspicion. "Daphanie is unharmed, as I told you. In fact, as I've taken her under my protection, I can very confidently assure you of that fact, as well as of the fact that she will remain so."

"Taken her under your protection?" Corinne repeated, her voice a mixture of incredulity and disdain. "What are you, the papal see? Daphanie, who the hell is this guy?"

The urge to laugh welled up again. Daphanie might even have given in to it, if she hadn't sensed the sharp note of hysteria behind it. Instead, she groaned. "That's . . . a really long story."

"Well, I'm really curious."

Daphanie sighed. She still felt odd, as if the last vestiges of the dream fog lingered like cobwebs in the back of her mind. But at least she remembered herself now, and Corinne and Niecie and the rest of her family. She remembered the wedding yesterday and the unfortunate incident afterward and the fact that this was Danice and Mac's apartment. They had persuaded her to stay here while they were off on their honeymoon and the place she'd leased for herself was being repaired and repainted. She also remembered her granite-faced, diamond-hard-headed bodyguard.

"Come in and sit down." Daphanie gestured toward the sofa, turning herself toward the kitchen. "But I need caffeine for this. Let me put on a pot of coffee."

"Don't bother. I brought coffee. And breakfast." Corinne retrieved her parcels and herded the other woman with the tenacity of a border collie into the sitting area in the middle of the loft's great room. "Of course, I only brought *two* cups," she added, shooting another glare in Asher's direction.

His expression remained stoic. "I don't drink coffee. I'll make myself tea."

Daphanie watched him retreat to the kitchen and

search out the bright red tea kettle. She admitted to herself that she'd harbored a secret hope that he had been just another figment of her subconscious imagination, conjured up along with the fire and the drums of her dreams. Not only would that have meant she'd dreamed up her very own—stunningly hot—guardian angel, but it would have signified that the whole nasty incident at the nightclub had never happened. If she had her way, a bad dream would explain everything.

Of course, she hadn't had her way since before setting foot in that club last night. She certainly hadn't had her way during the argument outside of it, nor during the trip home, during which she'd been shadowed by the man currently bustling around her sister's kitchen as if he owned the place. Her way would have involved ditching Asher's hovering presence on the curb with the cab, or at the very least in the lobby of the building. She'd certainly tried to make that happen, just as she'd tried to leave him in the elevator, then at the door to the loft, but the dratted man had just bull-dozed his way into the apartment until Daphanie felt as flat as newly leveled concrete.

She couldn't decide what drove her crazier—the way Asher Grayson, self-proclaimed bodyguard and hero-of-the-hour, seemed to get his way through sheer force of will and a complete disregard for the opinions of others; or the way that, despite all her protests and the absolute oddity of being herded and managed by a total stranger, she had never felt the slightest twinge of fear that he meant to do anything other than protect her.

Normally, if a strange man insisted on following her from a club, to her building, and up into her apartment, she'd have had the cops on speed dial before he formed the intent for any of it, let alone before he laid claim to pillows from the spare room and stretched out on the sofa. She'd grown up in Brooklyn, for God's sake; she wasn't some naïve little girl from someplace where no one locked their doors. She locked her door, set an alarm, and took self-defense classes to boot. She didn't trust the average person any further than she could thrown him, but something inside her instinctively trusted Asher.

It made no sense, even less sense than her instant attraction to him. At least that could be blamed on chemistry. Chemistry and the fact that the man had the face of a warrior and the body of a god. Even now, after the arguments and the intrusion and the takeover of her last fourteen hours, she could appreciate that the form inside those battered jeans raised her temperature more than a couple of degrees.

"Just give me the word, Daph," Corinne hissed, jerking Daphanie's attention back to her visitor. She had leaned close under the cover of emptying the bags of bagels and beverages onto the coffee table. "I have my cell right here. I can have the cops here before that bastard knows what hit him."

"No. Corinne, really, no," she repeated, injecting some firmness in her tone this time. "I'm fine. Asher isn't holding me hostage. I just had this really . . . *weird* dream."

"Are you sure? Because you really don't look like yourself, you know."

Daphanie laughed again, helplessly. "Yeah, that's the thing that was weird. In the dream, I wasn't myself. I swear I was someone else entirely."

Corinne paused, looking surprised and confused. "Who?"

"I haven't the foggiest idea." And she meant that literally. "Lord, you must think I'm insane. First you show up and find a strange man answering Niecie's door instead of me, then I stumble out of the bedroom, probably looking like I just escaped from my mad attacker. I'm surprised you haven't given up on the police and called an ambulance to take me straight to Bellevue."

"I still haven't ruled it out."

Daphanie caught her glaring at Asher's back again and sighed. "Let's clear this up again. Frankly, I haven't got the energy today to try to convince a bunch of strangers of my sanity. It's going to be hard enough with you."

"I must discourage you from going anywhere today." Asher stepped into the sitting area, a steaming mug in his hand and a politely implacable expression on his face. "After the events of last night, it would be wisest to remain at home and out of sight, to give the situation time to defuse itself."

"What situation? And who the hell asked you anything?" Corinne snapped, visibly bristling.

"Corinne, take it easy. It's okay. Asher means well—"

"Maybe I'd believe that if one of you explained *what* he means to begin with."

Asher lifted the mug to his lips and eyed Daphanie over the rim. "Would you care to do the honors? I believe I'd enjoy hearing your take on the . . . situation."

Daphanie cast him a dark look—a lot like those Corinne had been sporting all morning—before she turned back to her friend and drew a fortifying breath. "I left the reception early last night."

"Your sister's wedding reception?" Corinne looked nonplussed. "Why?"

Daphanie leaned forward and buried her face in her hands, scrubbing for a moment before she answered. "That's, like, a really long story."

"I'll let you know when I need a bathroom break."

Corinne's expression offered no quarter. Daphanie glanced at Asher, but all he did was lean one hip against the end of the sectional and sip his tea. She was on her own.

"I've been trying to take the whole Others thing in stride, but I guess it shook me up more than I wanted to admit," she explained. Saying that felt like admitting to some great sin, simultaneously a relief and a wrench of shame. "Danice told me that you all found out about it before Reggie even got married. That was at least a year ago, but I had all this sprung on me this week. Whatever promise the Others made Niecie make about keeping them a secret, she damned well took it seriously. And she usually tells me everything. But about this, not a word. It left me feeling totally out of the loop. I came here expecting to hear wedding details and cute new-couple stories, and instead I hear that the world as I know it wasn't really the way I knew it at all."

"Honey, that's how we all felt at first," Corinne said, laying her hand over Daphanie's and squeezing sympathetically. "You should get Reggie to tell you the story about when we first figured out Dmitri was a vampire and decided it was up to us to save her from his evil clutches. She still won't let us live that down."

"But that's the thing." Daphanie knew she wasn't explaining this well, but she struggled to find the words to convey the complex mix of emotions that had swirled through her over the last few days—confusion, disbelief, fear, excitement, betrayal, curiosity. "You all found out together, and you had someone there to explain things to you. You had Reggie and Dmitri, and then Missy and Graham. And now Danice and Mac. But Niecie told me in all the crazy lead-up to the wedding, and now she's gone on her honeymoon, so she can't be here to show me the ropes."

"Well, I'm probably not the best one to ask," Corinne said, "because I'm on the outside looking in myself. But Reggie and Missy would be happy to help you out, and anything they don't know, their hubbies will. Dmitri and Graham and their friends practically run the Others in Manhattan."

"I actually got a head start on that last night. Getting things explained, I mean. That's where Asher comes in."

"Oh, goodie. I was hoping we'd get to that part of the story."

"I went to a club called Lurk. I met someone at the reception. An Other. And while we were talking, he said that Vircolac is kind of like an Others country club—only the rich and famous hang out there. He said the real Others would be more likely to be at Lurk."

" 'He'?" Corinne's eyes narrowed. " 'He' told you that? Who the hell is 'he,' Daphanie?"

"His name is Quigley. He was at the reception trying to scam from the dinner and avoid being seen by my sister. He said he knew her, but she might be mad at him at the moment. I think he called himself some kind of imp—"

"An imp of Satan!" The woman jumped to her feet

and set her coffee aside with a thump. "Daph, Quigley isn't just any imp. He's the imp who led your sister and Mac into Faerie and then abandoned them to be taken captive by the King's Guard. He nearly got them killed."

The fist in her stomach began aiming heavy punches at her sternum. "What are you talking about? Niecie never said anything about almost being killed, or about being taken captive by anyone. What the hell didn't she tell me?"

"Apparently a whole bunch of things, but that's something we can deal with later. Right now, I think you need to tell me what happened last night. *Everything* that happened last night."

And here she had really hoped to forget it. All of it.

"Da-aph . . ."

With a sigh, Daphanie launched into the story, beginning with her first spotting the chubby red hand on top of the table next to hers and ending with waking up to find Corinne at the door and the distinctly grumpy guy with wings still lurking in her sister's apartment. As she spoke, the angry, guarded expression on the other woman's face gradually melted, settling into one of mingled disbelief and grudging respect.

She nodded at Asher. "I guess this means I should apologize for threatening you with the cops. You had plenty of time to hurt Daph if that was what you were after, and the TV is still here, so . . ."

Asher acknowledged the graceless apology with a nod and ignored the rest. "No one owes me thanks. I am a Guardian; Daphanie is human. Protecting humans in danger is my job."

In the bright light of day, Daphanie couldn't decide

how she felt about being referred to as this man's "job," but it didn't feel a whole lot better than it had felt the night before.

"Feel free to give notice anytime," she grumbled. "I didn't ask for your 'protection' and since I don't see the jerk from last night hiding behind the drapes, I think we can assume that I'm safe now."

Asher set down his teacup with great deliberation and leveled those silver-gold eyes on her with serious displeasure. "I was afraid after listening to your version of last night's incident that you weren't taking this seriously enough, and now I'm certain of it. Just because you've been removed from D'Abo's presence doesn't mean you're any safer than you were inside that nightclub."

"How do you figure? Unless you're planning to curse me this time."

Corinne made a strangled sound, but Daphanie was too busy watching Asher's jaw clench to see what might be the matter with her friend.

"I am stronger than temptation, Ms. Carter. I am also a Guardian, and therefore the only thing at the moment standing between you and a serious magical threat."

"Um, I'd like to get back to the serious magical threat thing in a minute," Corinne said, raising her hand tentatively even as she interrupted the conversation. "You might have picked this up from us talking earlier, but neither Daph nor I are what you would call experts in Others identification. So would you mind explaining exactly what a Guardian is, first off?"

Asher shifted his gaze from one woman to the other and sighed. "In the simplest terms, we are a group of defenders whose job it is to protect humans from harm at the hands of the Others. If a human does violence against a human, that's what the police are for. If an Other attacks an Other, the Council of Others can take appropriate action. But humans are so much weaker than the Others, at such a disadvantage against beings who can use magic or enhanced strength and senses to harm them, that the Guardians were created to . . . balance the scales, as it were."

"So are you human or an Other?" Corinne demanded.

"What good would I be if I were merely another human?" Asher scoffed. "Guardians are our own race, created by the first Watcher and bred since then for the sole purpose of continuing our mission."

The man hated explaining himself. It showed clearly in his expression, which Daphanie watched as intently as she listened to his words. She couldn't get over how a face could be simultaneously so blankly grim and yet so easy for her to read. Maybe it wasn't really his expression she was reading, she decided. Maybe it was those changeable silver-gold eyes.

"Oh, right. Daphanie mentioned the wings. I suppose that should have answered the human question, but I guess I'm a little unclear on exactly how you're going to protect her. Or from what."

Daphanie saw a flicker of anger in Asher's metallic eyes and reached out a hand as if she could grab Corinne and yank her back from the precipice. But Corinne was a reporter. She alternately scaled and leaped from precipices for a living.

"I see Daphanie is not the only one who fails to take this seriously."

Corinne shrugged. "I guess I just don't see what the

big deal is. So she got into an argument with this D'Abo
guy at the club. You broke it up, he said he wouldn't
hurt her, and everyone walked away. It sounds to me as
if Daphanie was right in thinking you overreacted."

"Is that so?" Asher's voice had turned silky. Somehow it made Daphanie wary, especially when he turned
to her and arched one imperious brow. "Daphanie, you
mentioned earlier that you had an odd, unsettling
dream last night. Why don't you tell us about it."

There wasn't a hint of question in his tone; it was all
polite command.

"What does her dream have to do with—"

Asher cut her off and gestured for Daphanie to go
on. She wished he hadn't. In fact, she wished she could
forget the dream altogether. The coffee and conversation had all but wiped the last of the cobwebs from her
mind. Just thinking about the dream made her feel
somehow muddled again, as if the fog might begin to
creep back with the memory.

"It was just . . . weird," she began reluctantly. "I've
never had a dream like this before, where I really felt
like I wasn't myself. I mean, I've had dreams where I
wasn't really me. You know, where I was playing some
other sort of character or in some nonsensical situation,
but I've never had a dream before where I felt like I did
in this one. I really felt like someone else, right down to
my bones. The thoughts, the feelings, the way of looking at the world. They were all just . . . foreign. Not me
at all."

She could see Corinne's confused face out of the
corner of her eye, and she could feel Asher's gaze intent upon her, but she didn't look at either of them. The

minute she'd tried to remember, the dream had flooded back and filled her vision.

"I don't know who I was supposed to be. No one was talking in it, so it's not like I heard someone call my name. And I didn't actually see where it was. It was like I had my eyes closed, even in the dream. I could hear things, and smell things, but I couldn't see anything about where I was."

"What did you hear?" Asher asked quietly, forcefully.

Daphanie paused, remembering. "Drums. Not like a drum kit for a rock band, but a lot of single drums. Like in African or Caribbean music, or in a Native American ceremony. There were a lot of people playing drums. And I think some of them were singing in the background, or chanting. But I couldn't really hear the words, just the sound of voices."

"What else?"

She frowned, almost afraid to concentrate too hard on the memory of the thing that had almost taken her over. "That was the main sound. I'm mean I'm assuming there was background noise from people moving around or the fire crackling or whatever, but it didn't really make much of an impression."

"There was a fire?"

"Yeah. Like a bonfire. And it was nighttime, because I could feel the heat from the fire, but on the side that faced away from the fire, my skin felt almost cold."

"Go on. What else did you feel?"

"My clothes. I think I was wearing a dress, something with a full skirt, but not a really long one. A few inches past the knee, maybe. And I think I was dancing. I can remember feeling the skirt swishing around while I moved."

"Do you remember anything else?"

Daphanie shook her head. "Just the smells. I remember the fire and wood smoke, but I smelled charcoal, too. And some kind of incense, I guess. I remember that it smelled sweet and musky and smoky all at once."

Deliberately shaking herself, throwing off the sticky tendrils of the dream-memory, Daphanie wrapped her arms around herself and glared up at Asher. "That was the dream. But I don't see what it has to do with last night."

Asher's brows shot up, but he didn't look surprised so much as he looked like he was intentionally prodding her. "Don't you? You don't see what dreaming of a voodoo ceremony has to do with your encounter with an irate witch doctor?"

Daphanie's heart skipped a beat. She assured herself it was shock. She was just shocked at his assumption. "A voodoo ceremony? What on earth makes you think that was part of my dream? I think it's a pretty big leap from dreaming about wearing a dress and hearing drums to dreaming about a voodoo ceremony."

"And how many voodoo ceremonies have you been to?"

Beside her, Corinne coughed. Daphanie contented herself with a glare. "None, as I'm sure you've assumed. How many have you been to?"

"Enough to make an educated guess about the content of your dream," he replied evenly. "If I'm wrong,

I'll happily apologize later, but in the meantime, it's my job to assume that your dream is evidence of D'Abo's continued interest in you. You have no idea what the man is capable of, but influencing your dream would not be beyond the skills of a powerful practitioner."

Daphanie felt a stirring of unease. "Is D'Abo really that powerful?"

"Do you want to take the chance of assuming that he isn't?"

"I don't want to assume anything, but I also don't want to spend the rest of my life looking over my shoulder and waiting for some crazed witch doctor to jump out from behind a tree and turn me into a toad. I want an accurate gauge of exactly how much worrying I'm supposed to do."

"None," he told her, his voice firm, his tone dismissive. "While you are under my protection, you don't need to worry at all, merely exercise common-sense caution."

"That's not an answer."

Asher looked like he wanted to answer with an attempt at strangulation. Instead, he glared at her and shoved his hands into the pockets of his jeans.

"How. Powerful. Is. Charles. D'Abo?" Daphanie demanded through clenched teeth.

"I don't know."

Daphanie blinked.

"You don't know?" Corinne repeated after a long minute of silence. "You mean you've made all of this fuss over someone who might not be any more powerful than . . . a first-year Hogwarts student?"

Asher apparently got the pop-culture reference. At

least he looked sufficiently unamused for Daphanie to guess that he had.

"No," he bit out carefully. "D'Abo is definitely worth our concern and our caution. He reeked of magic when I saw him last night, all of it dark. That's not something to take lightly. And do I have to remind you that the fundamental truth remains that no matter how powerful a witch he is, *he* is *Other* and *you* are *human*?"

Daphanie and Corinne looked at each other. Corinne pursed her lips.

"There is that," she conceded.

"Thank you," Asher snapped.

"So what we really need to know, then, is who this D'Abo fellow really is and how seriously we should take him as a threat," Corinne continued, nodding decisively. "I know I've never heard of him before today, but I'm not sure that means much. For as many stupid sensation pieces my paper has run on black magic and human sacrifice threatening the very heart of Manhattan, there have to be at least a hundred supposed voodoo temples in the city. There's no reason for his to have stood out."

Asher nodded reluctantly. "I had planned to begin making inquiries, gathering information, but I am reluctant to do so with Daphanie at my side. I can't guess what we could be stirring up, and I don't take chances with the humans in my care."

"Leave her to me."

Daphanie watched in annoyed bemusement as the two people in the room set about planning her day for her.

"I'll take her with me. I'd like to do a little digging

myself, and when it comes to things Other, I always head straight to the source. Daph, go put on some clothes. We'll head over there now."

"Over where?" Daphanie and Asher asked simultaneously.

"The bat cave," Corinne said. "Missy's place."

"Missy?"

"Missy and Graham Winters," Corinne explained to Asher. "I can't think of anyplace safer for Daphanie to be when she's not with you than under the nose of the alpha of the Silverback Clan. Can you?"

Daphanie saw Asher actually mull the question over before he conceded with a sharp nod.

"Plus, Missy's my primary source for this kind of material. I'll ask her about this D'Abo character." Corinne stood and shooed Daphanie toward the bedroom to change her clothes. "And let me tell you, if she doesn't have the answers, someone next door will."

Five

Of course, by saying that the average human has no need to fear the Others, we're not suggesting that nonhumans can't be dangerous. They can be— very dangerous. But if a person minds her own business and makes a modest effort to respect the Others around her, she can be fully confident that she's no more likely to be killed by one of them than by one of her own kind.
—A Human Handbook to the Others, *Chapter Three*

The reason for Corinne's confidence in the knowledge possessed by her friend's next-door neighbors owed a lot to the fact that Melissa Roper Winters lived in the town house directly beside and adjoining the building that housed Vircolac. The club had been established centuries before by ancestors of her husband, and Graham Winters continued to own and operate the venerable Other institution in addition to managing the city's resident Lupine pack, the Silverback Clan. More than once, Daphanie had heard Missy refer to her husband half jokingly as a bit of an overachiever.

Daphanie just called him scary. Almost as scary as the Guardian who had walked her and Corinne to their friend's front door and refused to go any farther than the end of the block until he could see them inside.

Thankfully, Missy informed them that Graham wasn't in when she answered her bell and welcomed both women to her home. Daphanie stepped inside and out of Asher's sight with a mingled sense of relief and . . . loss?

"Well, this is a surprise." Melissa, a petite blonde with sweet features and intelligent eyes, led them into a cozy study and settled them on a luxuriously battered leather sofa. "I figured you'd both be sleeping until noon after yesterday. Especially you, Daphanie. Your mom told me how ragged Danice had you all running with prep work. She said she didn't expect to hear from you anytime before next weekend."

Daphanie shifted uncomfortably. She'd liked Missy from the first time she'd met the woman, but then she couldn't imagine anyone who didn't. Melissa was a kindergarten teacher by training and a nurturer by design. Even before she'd married and started having kids, she'd always struck Daphanie as the maternal type. She was always trying to take care of the people around her, and just being with her made a person feel more tranquil.

Except for right now. At the moment, Daphanie didn't think a baker's dozen of Xanax could offer her tranquility.

"Daphanie has a little problem," Corinne said, cutting straight to the heart of the matter. "We were hoping you could help us figure it out."

Missy cocked her head to the side and frowned. "Oh, no. Of course, I'm happy to help, but I hope it's nothing serious."

Daphanie feared she might choke.

"That's what we're trying to figure out," Corinne continued. "But I can tell you that it all starts with Quigley."

"Uh-oh. That's not a good sign."

"Tell me about it."

"I wish someone had told me about it yesterday," Daphanie said.

Corinne shook her head. "Water under the bridge. The objective now is to figure out what we're dealing with and come up with a plan for damage control."

"Damage control?" Missy's eyes widened and her hand reached out to hover over the phone beside her chair. "Should I call for reinforcements?"

"Maybe later. In fact, why don't we fill you in and you can let us know if we need to muster the troops just yet?"

It was a little surreal, Daphanie decided, to be sitting there listening to someone else recount the events of last night. It felt almost as if she were hearing a story about another woman entirely, instead of a retelling of something she'd personally experienced.

Too bad last night couldn't have been the nightmare and her odd dream the reality. Nothing so terrible had happened while she danced to drumbeats in the firelight, and it had felt so real, she could almost consider it a memory rather than a dream. And it hadn't involved threats, fights, or being intimidated by tall, sexy men with heroic tendencies. That made it tops in her book.

"Oh, my goodness," Missy breathed when Corinne had finished. "You met a Guardian? A real Guardian? I was ready to write them off as a myth. You know, a real myth, not a vampire-slash-werewolf myth. What was he like?"

Corinne threw up her hands. "That's all you have to

say? I tell you that Daphanie here ran off with an imp, mortally offended a witch doctor, and had dreams of performing some weird ritual that were so real she nearly passed out, and all you can ask is what the guy who walked her home was like?"

"Hey, I didn't 'run off' with the imp," Daphanie protested. "You make it sound like we were headed to an all-night wedding chapel in Vegas. I just went with him to a club and let him show me a little bit about the Others."

"Yeah, and he nearly 'showed you' to an early grave!"

Missy held up her hands and scowled at Corinne. "Take it easy, Rinne. I'll agree with you that Daphanie's decisions last night might not have been the wisest ones she could have made, but she looks fine to me. She's here, she's unhurt, and according to what you've said, she's under the protection of a Guardian. Frankly, that's about as safe as a person can get, from what I hear."

"What's that supposed to mean?"

It took an effort for Daphanie not to repeat the question.

"Like I said, I've never met a Guardian, but Graham has mentioned them. From what he tells me, there aren't many left these days. I'm not even sure if he's met one." Missy drew her legs up beneath her and leaned into the arm of her chair. "The louder the community rumbles about the time to Unveil ourselves, the fewer Guardian angels seem to be on the job. Though from what I hear, they're not wild about the angel comparison."

"You might say that," Daphanie muttered.

"Graham says there's nothing religious about them, so that may be what makes them touchy on the subject.

Apparently, they're not sent by God, or anything; they're led by someone they refer to as the Watcher. He's supposed to be the oldest Guardian alive, and it's his job to keep an eye out for humans in danger and to assign a Guardian to protect them if need be."

"That's funny, because I didn't see any winged warriors rushing to the rescue when you and Reggie nearly got yourselves killed." Corinne crossed her arms over her chest and glared.

"Neither Reggie nor I were really in that much danger," Missy said, her tone calm and only the slightest bit reproving. "Besides which, we had Graham and Misha watching over us. I think we were pretty well protected as it was. I gather that the Guardians save their efforts for humans who don't have an advantage like that. In fact, the Guardians supposedly try to stay in the background and only reveal themselves to the humans if there's no other way to help them, so I'm thinking that they generally deal with people who don't know about the Others and may not even realize they're in danger."

"Trust me; I realized it," Daphanie said.

Missy smiled. "From what I hear, I'm not surprised." She hesitated for a moment, chewing her lip. "I'm sorry, but I have to ask . . . did the Guardian really have wings?"

The expression on the other woman's face reminded Daphanie of nothing so much as a little girl about to hear a secret. She couldn't help a soft laugh. "Huge ones. I mean, he didn't spread 'em and fly away or anything, but even folded up, they were enough to give a girl pause. He didn't have them all the time, though. It was like he could . . . I don't know . . . put them away when he wasn't using them. Where he hides them, I can't imagine, but when we left the club, he looked pretty much like a normal guy."

"Hm, maybe I have met a Guardian, then, and I just didn't notice," Missy said. "But as for the disappearing wings, I've learned over the last couple of years that magic can make a whole bunch of impossible things perfectly possible."

Daphanie nodded, then she tried to imagine not noticing Asher Grayson pass by and it was like her brain blew a fuse. The idea just did not compute.

"That's all well and good," Corinne said, leaning forward, "but I'm more interested in hearing about what else the guy can do. I mean, how exactly does he plan to protect Daphanie? Aside from being huge and mean-looking and following her around like her shadow?"

Missy frowned in concentration. "I'm hardly an expert, but from what I can remember, Guardians do have certain powers of their own. Aside from the wings, of course."

"Right," Corinne said. "Because in a hairy situation, he could probably just scoop Daph up and fly her out of danger. Like Superman. Without the tights."

The thought of Asher in skintight spandex flashed through Daphanie's mind and made her draw in a deep breath. A very deep breath.

"They're supposed to be able to identify people at a glance, first of all. Like, they can tell just by looking at someone for the first time if they're human or Other, and even what kind of Other they might be—vampire, shifter, demon, what have you."

Corinne nodded and made an encouraging gesture.

"I think, fundamentally, they view themselves as

warriors, so they're highly trained in combat, and I think I heard something about preternatural healing powers and unusual strength, comparable to a shifter, even. Also—don't quote me on this, though—I think they can absorb a certain amount of harmful magic."

"What do you mean?"

"Like, if someone sent some kind of magical arrow at a human under his protection, a Guardian could step in front and take the damage instead without being hurt as badly as the human would have been. But that might be part of the healing ability." Missy paused, brow furrowed, lips pursed. "That's really all I can remember. Like I said, there aren't a lot of Guardians around, but the stories say that once one has taken a human under his protection, he'll do whatever he has to in order to keep them safe."

"Once a Guardian, always a Guardian."

Daphanie turned in the direction of the door and saw a tall, obnoxiously handsome man with toffee-streaked hair standing in the archway. Behind him was an even better-looking man with dark hair and lightly bronzed skin. Even if she hadn't already known both of them to be Others, she would have assumed it of both. Just like with her new brother-in-law, these two were much too gorgeous to be human.

"Hi, sweetie." Missy smiled at the fairer of the two, her face taking on the kind of glow that Daphanie would have mocked if she weren't so jealous. The woman's love for her husband shone in her expression like a beacon. "Come join us. You didn't tell me Rafe was coming over."

"I dropped in unexpectedly," said the dark-haired

man as he crossed the room to take Missy's hand in his. He raised it to his lips as if it were the most natural thing in the world to kiss the back of a woman's hand like a character from a Jane Austen novel. "You're looking lovely as always, Melissa. You really must leave your brute of a husband and run away with me. I would shower you with diamonds, as befits your radiance."

And somehow he managed to speak like that without sounding like a total prat.

Daphanie shook her head in bemusement.

"Leave my wife alone, you overgrown alley cat," the other man growled, draping a possessive arm around his mate's shoulders. "Go get your own woman."

"Only if one of these two lovely ladies is available. I beg you to introduce me."

Missy laughed out loud while Corinne rolled her eyes. Daphanie merely tried not to let herself be hypnotized by the intensely golden, flirtatious gaze now trained her way.

"Since you've already met both of them, I'd say you can stuff your charm and try it on someone who might not find it insulting," Graham Winters taunted. "Corinne D'Alessandro is one of Missy and Regina's oldest friends, so forgetting her name is about as flattering as complimenting her on how good she looks for her age. And Daphanie Carter is Danice's sister. You met her last night at the wedding reception. So much for Rafael De Santos's famous touch with women."

"Ah, forgive me, ladies," De Santos begged with a grin that could probably charm bracelets. From what Danice had said of him in the past, Daphanie suspected that "charm" was the werejaguar's middle name. "I was clearly ill or suffering from some sort of mental impairment when we were introduced, otherwise I would never have forgotten such beauty."

"Christ, I'm gonna need hip boots if he keeps shoveling this stuff."

Missy elbowed her husband in the ribs hard enough to make him grunt. "Enough of your flirting, Rafe. Tell us what you meant about 'once a Guardian, always a Guardian.'"

Graham had been correct. Daphanie had been introduced to Rafael De Santos during her sister's reception, but the man had been simultaneously meeting about a dozen other people and already schmoozing with five or six more. She supposed that was part of the job of being the head of the Council of Others. She watched as the man settled himself gracefully in the vacant club chair opposite Missy's.

"I meant just exactly that, my dear," he said, speaking to Missy but training that glittering golden stare on Daphanie. "It is not in the nature of a Guardian to abandon a human once she has been taken under his wing, as it were. Especially if there is, perhaps, a lingering threat."

"That's what we've been trying to decide," Missy said. "Whether or not the threat lingers."

"May I ask what sort of threat?"

Corinne groaned and threw herself back into the sofa cushions. "No. I'm not telling that story again. It was hard enough to remember all the details the first time."

"It's not your story anyway," Missy dismissed. "Daphanie, do you mind running through it all again? I'm sure the Cliff's Notes version will do."

Daphanie figured it would have to. Even after retelling and hearing the story retold in the bright light of day, somehow the events of last night seemed less real to her than the events her subconscious had conjured up this morning while she slept. If they'd asked her about the dream, she could have described every detail. About the episode at the club, she could offer not much more than an outline. The events had begun to blur somehow. The only figure she could remember in HD clarity was Asher, and she had to wonder if that was because her hormones played a part in keeping the image fresh in her mind.

And other places.

Forcing eyes of silver and gold out of her mind, she sketched a brief summary of her and Quigley's jaunt to Lurk. She described the encounter with D'Abo, the altercation with the witch doctor and his entourage, and her timely rescue.

When she finished, Graham winced. "I swear, you humans must work at getting into this kind of trouble."

His wife smacked him hard on the leg and scowled. "You can take your idiot Other prejudice and shove it, right alongside Rafe's charm, Graham Winters. Were you listening to the same story I heard? Because it sounded to me like this Charles D'Abo character was the one who started the trouble. Daphanie was the innocent party here. Let's keep that in mind before we open our smart mouths, okay?"

"Obviously Daphanie was not at fault for the altercation," Rafe agreed smoothly, "but the unfortunate truth of our world is that when a human and an Other find themselves at odds, it is the human who faces the greater danger. I doubt that D'Abo is worrying whether he is in continuing danger this morning."

Corinne pounced on the words. "Does that mean this creep really is dangerous? Should Daphanie be worried he might mean that crap about her getting 'what she deserves'?"

"It is hard to say . . ."

"Wait, D'Abo said he wouldn't hurt me," Daphanie reminded them. "He told Asher that himself, so wouldn't that indicate that I shouldn't be worried?"

She hoped she sounded more convinced of that than she felt. The trouble was that she *wasn't* convinced. That was why she'd let Corinne bring her here for answers, instead of relying on the word of a man who seemed to regard humans as beneath his notice. Did that suggest that they were beneath his sense of honor, too?

"Yeah, he said that, but does his word actually hold any water?" Corinne argued. "I mean, what do we know about this guy? Is he the kind who keeps his word, or would he say anything he needed to at the given moment and then forget all about his promise as soon as he got home?"

Missy tilted her head to look questioningly up at her husband.

Graham shrugged. "Don't ask me. I've never heard of him."

"I know his name," Rafe admitted, "but I have never encountered him personally. I cannot vouch one way or another for his sense of honor."

Corinne crossed her arms over her chest. "Well, I'm not inclined to take the word of the kind of jerk who would throw that sort of tantrum over a glass of spilled milk."

"Root beer," Daphanie corrected automatically.

"Whatever."

"I'm not suggesting that anyone take the man's word for his promise. I would be happy to make some inquiries to learn more about him, and I intend to do so immediately." The authority in Rafe's voice assured Daphanie that the head of the Council was definitely a man of *his* word. "In the meantime, however, I have to say that my worries for Daphanie's safety are not extreme. Not only will she now have the Council monitoring her situation, but the fact that she is under the care of a Guardian would make any direct attack on her person next to impossible."

"I wish he'd at least popped in to say hello when he dropped you two off," Missy said. "I would have liked to meet him."

Corinne snorted. "Judging by how hard it was to convince him to let Daphanie out of his sight even while she was here, I don't imagine you'll have to wait much longer for that honor."

The corner of the Felix's mouth curved up in amusement. "I believe Corinne is correct. Guardians do not give their protection lightly. If one placed himself between Daphanie and a threat to her person, she will remain in his charge until a higher authority releases him. Therefore, you may assume he will be around for the foreseeable future."

"A higher authority like what?" Daphanie asked.

Broad shoulders shifted under his elegant silk shirt. "The Watcher, I suppose. But more likely death."

Daphanie squeaked. "Mine or his?"

Rafe chuckled. "Neither of the scenarios you appear to be envisioning. I am uncertain as to the mortality of the Guardians, but I do know they do not suffer from a human life span, so I don't suppose his death to hold the key. And I've never known a Guardian to fail in his duties, so the only death of yours that might apply would be a natural one, achieved after many, many long and healthy decades of life."

Graham shifted on the arm of his wife's chair. "Daphanie, did you say that the name of the Guardian who helped you out last night was Asher?"

"That's what he told me. Asher Grayson." She paused. "Why?"

The alpha whistled. "Because I may not have heard of this D'Abo guy, but I have heard of Grayson."

"Is that good or bad?"

"For you? Good, I'm guessing. How it winds up being for D'Abo will likely be entirely up to him."

Daphanie sighed and leaned back into the sofa cushions. Her adventure in the surreal life didn't look to be ending anytime soon. How was it possible that a week ago today, the most complicated thing on her mind had been reminding herself to drop off her change of address cards at the post office so that her current clients and galleries would know that she was still working and how they could reach her?

What a difference a day makes.

Providing, of course, that day was this past Wednesday, when she'd gone out for Vietnamese with Mac, Niecie, and her parents and sat staring while Danice explained about the Others as steaming drops of beef broth dripped slowly off her noodle-laden chopsticks. A day like that made a hell of a difference. The question left to her now was, what kind of a difference did Asher Grayson intend to make? If any.

"You know, I appreciate the reassurance from you guys. I really do. But frankly, I'm not the kind of girl to put all her eggs in one basket, especially not one someone else is carrying. I'd much rather get a straight answer on whether or not I need to worry about D'Abo. And if I do, what I should be doing about it."

"I wish we could tell you more about D'Abo," Rafe said, "and rest assured that I will make gathering this information my highest priority. But in the meantime . . ."

He glanced at Graham, who nodded.

"In the meantime, I'll get in touch with the Guardians. It can't hurt to have their official approval for Grayson keeping his eye on you."

Daphanie couldn't decide whether that surge of adrenaline in her bloodstream was due to the annoyance of having men she barely knew making decisions for her, or the prospect of spending all this time with Asher Grayson.

Somehow the idea frightened her as much as it thrilled her.

"I don't think I need a babysitter," she protested with a frown.

"Don't think of it as having a babysitter, then," Corinne suggested, her grin turning sly. "Think of it as having really nice scenery. I mean, I did happen to notice—in a purely theoretical way, of course—that Asher *is* pretty damned fine scenery to look at."

"Did you?" Daphanie muttered.

"Based on your descriptions, I think Corinne might have a point." Missy's smile hinted at a certain sense of sympathy. After all, the woman knew all about hot men, judging by the one currently hovering over her.

"No one suggests that you need a sitter," the Felix assured her. "After all, at the moment, we have no evidence that D'Abo does not intend to honor his promise to leave you alone. You were not harmed after you left the club, yes? Nothing unusual has happened since then?"

That question should have been easier to answer. While the foggy remnants of her dream had mostly faded by this point, she still had a hard time believing that conversations like this one made up her new reality. The memory of the firelit dance felt almost as tangible to her.

Daphanie shook her head. "Not unless you count me sitting here right now. Or my developing a craving for milk in my coffee." She quirked a grin at Rafe. "You're not contagious or anything, right?"

The shifter laughed. "I assure you, no. You will catch nothing from me."

"Not even fleas," Corinne taunted. "I hear Missy makes all her visitors wear preventive collars."

Rafe merely glanced at her.

"Don't worry, honey," Missy assured Daphanie, leaning forward to pat her hand. "I'm sure you'll be just fine. There's no reason at all you shouldn't go on with your life as usual. Let us take care of this Charles D'Abo character. That's what friends are for."

Six

While vampires and shapeshifters (particularly werewolves) are easily the most recognizable types of Others, they represent only the tip of the supernatural iceberg. Vampires, as we explored in chapter two, are fairly straightforward creatures, and the shapeshifters featured in chapters three through six are many and varied, but possess commonalities that make studying them a fascinating but manageable task for the average human. When it comes to magic, however, and the Others who use magic, the varieties and possibilities and vagaries are, quite literally, endless.

—A Human Handbook to the Others, *Chapter Seven*

At the moment, it wasn't her friends that Daphanie was worried about. Her friends were kind, funny, generous, supportive, and endlessly entertaining. The man currently glowering at her from the corner of her downtown studio space didn't look very friendly. In fact, he looked irritated. With her. As if she'd wanted him to follow her to the renovated industrial loft where she worked.

That only served to increase Daphanie's own irritation. The last few days had not been the most pleasant of her life. Since Saturday, she'd spent every waking moment trying to find a way to get her life moving back in the direction it had been taking before the incident at Lurk. Or, as she liked to call it, B.Q. Before Quigley.

Of the imp, she'd seen neither hide nor hair since the moment she'd left to fetch his root beer. He hadn't stuck around once the fracas in the club had started, and he hadn't even had the decency to check afterward to see if she'd made it out alive. No wonder her sister apparently had the little creep penned onto her shit list. Daphanie had etched his name on hers in indelible ink, in the number one position.

Number two belonged to the man standing in front of her now.

Since Sunday morning, the man had stuck to her side like a barnacle on the hull of a seventeenth-century pirate ship. She could swear he was giving her a rash.

The problem was that the rash wasn't due to irritation, it was due to the constant hum of arousal that prickled her skin every time he got within ten feet of her. Which meant every damned minute of the day. He was there in the apartment when she woke up, brewing tea and puttering around her sister's kitchen. He was there when she went to sleep, stretched out on the enormous sectional sofa, the remote control in one hand the only hint that he might bear some passing resemblance to a normal man. He was even there in her studio when she tried to work. Like now. And at all of those times, her powers of concentration became extremely hampered by the burning desire to see if his granite-carved lips would soften at all if she pressed her own against them.

As it turned out, Asher Grayson was a hard man to

forget, and trust her, Daphanie had been trying. It seemed odd that other than him, the details of most of the Event had gone a little fuzzy around the edges. The dream she'd had afterward still felt more real to her, though maybe that partially stemmed from having been repeated second for second every night since. But when it came to Saturday, it was like her subconscious only had room for one memory from Saturday night, and for some reason it had chosen to retain the dream instead of the reality.

Except for the reality of Asher. Whether or not he was always near, she couldn't stop thinking about him. Her mind strayed to him when she should be working or sleeping or eating or jabbing herself in the eyes with a fire poker. She couldn't get him out of her head, and maybe that contributed to her peevishness this morning.

"You know, you don't have to just hover all the time. You could . . . I don't know, do something useful. Something at least slightly less annoying."

His glower morphed seamlessly into a scowl. "What are you talking about?"

Her gaze shifted from the short length of mild-steel gas pipe she currently held in one hand to the side of Asher's head. Tempting as the thought might be, she really wasn't in the mood for a fight. Instead, she stepped back from the studio's door and returned to the crate she'd been unpacking onto the enormous carpenter's table in the center of her work area.

"I mean that since Sunday, you've watched me eat, you've watched me read, you've watched me talk on the phone, you've watched me check my e-mail, you've watched me paint my toenails. Hell, you've even watched me watch TV. I'm getting really sick of being watched. And frankly, I imagine you're getting sick of looking at me." She set aside the pipe with several others of the same length and sifted through the packing material for the shorter cuts she knew had to be in there. "So why don't you make yourself useful and help me out here?"

"You want me to help you sort pipes?"

"I just want you to do something other than your garden-statue impersonation. It's driving me frickin' demented."

He remained silent, but she could almost say she was getting used to that. The man was about as talkative as a bedroom slipper. He had a sort of absolute self-containment she both admired and found infuriating. Clearly, he had no problem with silence, no problem being alone. She just wished he wouldn't make her feel like she was alone even when they were in the same room.

She watched out of the corner of her eye as he stirred from his station near the far window and walked through the studio toward her. His haunting silver-gold eyes scanned the space, taking in the stacks of crates yet to be unpacked, the surfaces already coated with oils and metal shavings, the narrow, dirty windows, and the custom furnaces that had been installed against the exposed brick wall.

"I thought artists needed lots of light to work," he said, his gaze finally returning to her.

Damn him. Even his voice made her stomach clench, smooth and dark as Colombian coffee. Why had she wanted him to start talking to her?

"What makes you think I'm an artist?" She struggled to sound casual, wondered if she succeeded. "Most people take a look at my setup and guess demented mechanic."

"I saw the window-box cages outside the Silverback's home. I admired the work. The alpha said you'd made them."

She had. In fact, she had labored for almost a month to create the six intricately worked pieces so that Danice and her friends could present them to Missy for a wedding gift. She'd debated for almost as long as she'd worked, worrying over the motif of moon phases half concealed in tendrils of twining vines. In the end she'd gone with her instincts. The bride had liked them enough to have them mounted on all the ground-floor front windows of her husband's enormous home.

"You're a very talented sculptor."

"Blacksmith," Daphanie corrected automatically. She didn't think of herself in terms of art but of craft. "Sculptors make decorations—things that are nice to look at, but not good for much else. Everything I make has a function. I like things that can multitask."

Which made it doubly confusing to her why she found this single-minded, single-purposed man so damnably attractive. At first, she had clung to the hope that her reaction to him at the club had been a one-time deal, a fluke caused by adrenaline, dim lighting, and the novelty of being rescued by a big, handsome hero. That hadn't lasted past Sunday morning. Every time she looked at him, her stomach recommenced its trapeze lessons. For days, it had felt like a tent at Ringling Brothers below her rib cage.

"I thought blacksmiths made horseshoes."

"Not in the last hundred years." It was her stock answer. She'd gotten that response once or twice in the
past when revealing her profession. "Farriers *fit* horses
with shoes that were most likely mass produced in a
factory using heavy machinery. Some blacksmiths with
specialized knowledge of equine anatomy will work
with farriers to custom make shoes for individual horses
with special needs, but unless you're in England, the word
'blacksmith' only refers to someone who works with and
shapes black metals, like iron or steel. I'm a Brooklyn
girl. What I know about horses I got from reading *Black
Beauty* when I was eight."

"Understood. But you don't need more light to 'work
with and shape black metals'?"

He had finished prowling the room and come to a
stop on the other side of her worktable. He wore the
same black jacket he'd worn on Saturday night, but he
had it open and pushed back so that he could slip his
fingers into the front pockets of his black denim jeans.
With his casually untucked button-down of blue and
black stripes, he looked like something out of the pages
of *GQ*. Daphanie didn't think that was very fair considering her own work uniform of a grungy tank top and
baggy cargo pants, but she had to give him points for
actually paying attention to her minilecture.

She deducted a point from herself for the thrill of
excitement she felt at his showing so much interest in
her work.

She emptied the crate and stacked it on top of the
others at the end of the table. While she did like to
keep a fairly neat work space, at the moment she cared

more about keeping her hands busy. The Guardian's steady gaze made her feel antsy.

"Nope. Bright light actually makes it harder to work. The ability to shape metal depends on bringing the iron or steel to the correct temperature, and the easiest way to tell when it's reached that state is by watching the color—red, orange, yellow, or white. Bright light washes out the color and makes it hard to know when the temperature's right. Indirect light supplemented with artificial light sources work best."

"Then I should call and cancel the window washers who were going to clean off the seventy-five years of grime that's blocking all the light from coming in here?"

"What?" She snapped her head around, inadvertently meeting his gaze and catching the glint of something devilish within.

His serious expression never shifted.

Daphanie blew out a breath. "Nice. You finally open your mouth to do something other than ask me where I think I'm going, and all you can do is mess with me. Can you really not think of any better way to spend our time together?"

Asher tried to read the woman's expression, but he had to admit he wasn't particularly good at interpreting human emotions. Most of the humans under his protection had either been too frightened of the threats to their lives, too grateful for his protection, or too intimidated by his demeanor to express anything more complicated than abject fear and the occasional fit of panic. He could read neither of those things on Daphanie Carter's face.

Nor could he read any indication that she'd meant

her last question the way he'd taken it. As an invitation to share all the many, many ways he could envision spending time with her. Ninety-nine percent of which were completely naked.

Her expression revealed none of the lust that had clawed at his own belly almost constantly over the last few days. In fact, her expression told him little. Her face always had a guarded look to it when she knew he was watching.

That didn't stop him, however, from studying her closely. Maybe if he looked hard enough, evaluated long enough, he could begin to fathom why this ordinary human woman maintained such a hold on him.

Her features couldn't account for it. Though humans might count her dusky skin, dark, slanted eyes, and bladelike cheekbones exotic, Asher had seen more unusual. Hell, he'd seen more beautiful. Her full lips might look soft and lush and infinitely kissable, but he'd kissed hundreds of women. Her slim, curved figure might exhibit surprising strength in the taut, defined muscles of her back, arms, and shoulders, but he'd known female demons who could lift tractor trailers over their heads without mussing a hair. If no one part of her appeared any different or more or better than the thousands of others he'd seen, why in hell should the sum of them have haunted him without respite for the past three days?

Every moment of his time, since that first meeting on Saturday night, the thought of this woman had tormented him. She'd slipped, soft and temptingly bare, into his dreams as he slept. She had whispered in his mind when he tried to eat or read or perform his daily tasks. She had even possessed the utter gall to steal his attention, wholly unbidden, when he should have been focused entirely on his work. Even in his thoughts, the human refused to recognize her place, which was to be nothing more than a job.

That had been his mantra since he'd escorted her home from the nightclub. His job, his purpose, was to protect humans from the dangers of the supernatural world around them and never before had he had the slightest trouble separating his work from his personal inclinations. Could he truly allow a woman—an ordinary, human woman—to undo all these years of discipline and control?

"I've just been trying to be considerate," he finally responded, leaning against the table she had placed between them. Actually, they seemed to have done that by mutual, unspoken agreement, and he couldn't argue with the wisdom of it. "You made it clear that you find my presence to be an intrusion, so I've done my best to be as unobtrusive as possible. I thought that was what you wanted."

That request had even factored into his discussion with the alpha of the Silverback clan. The man had been waiting to speak with Asher when he returned to escort Daphanie home from her visit to the Winters's house on Sunday afternoon. That had surprised Asher for two reasons: one, he hadn't previously made the acquaintance of Graham Winters, let alone suspected the Lupine knew who he was; and two, he hadn't quite known whether he believed Daphanie when she'd claimed a close relationship with so many key figures on the Council of Others. He had wanted to believe it, sure, because it could potentially have made his life easier. Or so he'd thought.

When was the last time he'd been so damned naïve?

Winters's talk had made it clear that Daphanie's close association with the Council only complicated the situation. While it gave her the advantage of powerful friends capable of keeping her out of harm's way, it also made those same powerful friends inordinately concerned with her welfare. And since powerful people rarely had much free time to spare, it made them turn to him to aid in ensuring her safety. Asher could hardly refuse to help. He might not fear men like Graham Winters and Rafael De Santos, but neither were they the kind he wanted to count among his enemies. He felt certain they made much better allies.

"I wanted for none of this bodyguard stuff to be necessary," she grumbled, "but since that's apparently water under the bridge, now I just want to not feel like I'm some sort of strange museum exhibit that you can't decide if you find fascinating or revolting. Or just boring."

If she only knew. He had never viewed Daphanie Carter in terms of a museum exhibit. He was much too aware of her warmth for that. Her warmth, her scent. The sweet, plump curve of her breast beneath her—

He swore silently and hauled back on his libido.

"I think the last word I'd ever use to describe you is boring," he managed, hoping she wouldn't notice the tightness in his voice. "Or did you think my life is more exciting than what's happened to you over the last few days? Because if it were, I'd have worn myself out a long time before this."

She raised an eyebrow. "Am I supposed to be flattered?"

Asher would have been happy to offer her the kind of flattery she wouldn't have to question, but somehow he couldn't be certain of how she would react if he described exactly how enticing he found the firm, lush curve of her ass. He might intend the remark as flattering, but he wouldn't be surprised if she took it as an insult. He found her that confusing.

It would have helped if she'd reacted in any kind of predictable way to him. Somehow Daphanie Carter didn't seem fazed by his default tactic of silent intimidation. Since she hadn't responded to D'Abo's loud and blustery intimidation, either, he supposed he shouldn't have been surprised. Maybe he should just take the safe road and do what she wanted, help her with her metal sorting. At least if his hands were busy, he couldn't give in to the temptation to see if her dusky skin felt as soft as it looked.

He leaned into the table and cleared his throat. Maybe there was another way to win some points here.

"You know"—he shifted and frowned—"I've begun to think . . . perhaps . . . that I haven't exactly been . . . well, that maybe I could have done a little more . . . that I never acknowledged . . . how big of an intrusion this is. On your normal life."

She watched him impassively. "You think?"

"Excuse me?"

"You think this is maybe almost as big a pain for me as it is for you?" she repeated slowly. "I mean, sure you have to spend all your time staring at me sort steel pipes, but I have to put up with being watched. I have to accommodate my life to the presence of someone who doesn't know me, doesn't particularly like me, and has no apparent interest in so much as conversing with me. Do you think that might be a touch intrusive?"

Asher winced. For hell's sake, did she have put it quite so . . . truthfully?

"Yes," he said. "I think it is."

"Hmm."

That was it, the sum total of her response. She met his gaze steadily, her almond-shaped eyes clear and unblinking. She offered him no quarter, no wiggle room, not the barest shred of mercy.

Shit. She was going to make him say it.

Asher ground his teeth together until his jaw muscles screamed in protest. He would never normally use this kind of language, and definitely not in front of a woman, but she'd backed him into a corner. What else could he do?

"I apologize," he finally ground out, the words rolling off his tongue as quickly and easily as stone-cold molasses. He practically had to reach in with his fingers to pull them out of his mouth. He hoped she was happy with herself.

He decided maybe he shouldn't ask her that.

To his surprise, his words had the effect of a magic spell. In an instant, her expression softened, her brown eyes melting like bittersweet chocolate. Her posture shifted, shoulders lowering, muscles relaxing, and her mouth quirked in a smile that conveyed as much sympathy as amusement.

"Apology accepted," she said. "You still with me?"

He stared at her in confusion. "What do you mean?"

"Are you still with me?" she repeated. "Feeling okay? The apology didn't kill you?"

"Very funny."

The smile widened into a full-fledged grin, one that broke over her face like the early morning light, softening and illuminating it all at once. "See, it was at least a little bit funny. And that, my friend, is what I see as your main problem in life: you take everything too seriously. You need to lighten up. Then maybe the idea of admitting when you were wrong wouldn't feel quite so much like unanaesthetized surgery."

Odd, because until this moment, Asher would have defined his main problem in life as being oblivious humans blundering their way through the world of the Others in unenlightened folly.

He probably shouldn't mention that, either.

He watched while she swept the scattered remains of packing straw off the table with brisk, economical motions. She appeared perfectly willing to go about her business and forget both her previous anger at his insults from the other night and her own much more recent insult to him. When would humans begin to make sense to him?

"That is it?" he demanded, stepping around the end of the table and grasping her wrist. She stopped her cleaning to glance up at him. "The apology has been issued and now we forget about it?"

"That's how apologies are supposed to work. If I hung on to being mad at you, what would be the reason for you telling me you were sorry?"

Since he wasn't entirely sure of the reason he'd apologized in the first place, he felt unqualified to answer that question. Hell, at the moment, he felt unqualified for a lot of things, including for dealing with this baffling woman.

"So we go on from here," he said, mind struggling to catch up.

"We go on from here. So why don't you try answering my original question?"

"What original question?"

"Do you think you might be willing to do something more useful and less unsettling than just sitting there watching me all day?"

Ah, that question.

Asher debated the answers he could give her—that he needed to be alert to threats and therefore couldn't let himself get distracted in her presence. That he would be glad to help out as long as she realized that everything else took second place to guarding her. That what he really wanted to do was strip her naked, lay her down on the dusty workbench, and make her scream with pleasure.

Somehow, none of them seemed quite right.

Asher Grayson maintained a strict policy regarding women—he never let any of them close enough to interfere with his work, and he never became intimately involved with humans. The first part stemmed from the fact that as a Guardian, his work wasn't an occupation so much as a part of his identity. He couldn't possibly allow another person, and certainly not a woman, to become as important to him as his own sense of self. The very idea was alien to him.

The second part stemmed entirely from experience. Human women, in his estimation, were too fragile and entirely too young for him. Oh, he cared little for the concept of chronological age; live a couple of centuries and counting the number of one's years started to look a bit ridiculous. No, when he claimed that human women were too young for him, he meant in their souls.

He'd spent his entire existence taking care of humans, keeping them out of trouble, or rescuing them from it when they stumbled in despite his best efforts. They possessed so little awareness of the world around them that he had begun to suspect eons ago that they wore their ignorance as a badge of honor, maintaining the blinders on their eyes because it was just easier to pretend that things like the Others didn't exist. Keeping the supernatural relegated to the world of fairy tales and ghost stories seemed to help the humans sleep at night, but in Asher's eyes it made them look . . . pathetic. Like babies, they felt no need to see the world beyond their immediate surroundings, and the idea of forming some sort of attachment to someone who struck him as little more mature than an infant . . .

Frankly, it wasn't just unappealing; it was downright distasteful.

And yet, somehow, Daphanie Carter made him want to make an exception, to break his own rules. When he looked at her, spoke to her, drew in her scent, he almost forgot she was human. Or else he had stopped caring.

Asher didn't know why the compulsion had the power to drive him forward, but he had to know. He used his grip on her wrist to tug her to the end of the worktable, shifting her around the worn and rounded corner until the scarred wood no longer served as a barrier between them. Now the only thing separating them was space, and he closed that with a single step.

He bent his head toward her and breathed deeply, taking in the subtle scents that clung to her skin—wood and metal, smoke and woman, sweet citrus and the heady, honeyed earthiness of myrrh. He heard a tiny catch in her breath, quick and barely audible. The sound rushed through him, tangible evidence that she shared at least a little of his madness.

The skin inside her wrist felt like living satin beneath his touch. He shifted his fingers and felt her pulse leap. Slowly, he skimmed his palm higher, barely touching, and her skin rose toward him, roughening with awareness. Gooseflesh, it was called, but all he felt was warm, resilient woman.

From beneath heavy lids, he watched her sway closer and exulted. He curved one hand around the point of her shoulder and onto her back, urging her even closer. The other, he lifted and cupped about the nape of her neck, feeling the heavy fall of her ponytail brush against his knuckles. She quivered beneath his touch, and hunger threatened to overwhelm him.

Her breath huffed out, a soft caress against his cheek. He rubbed it against hers, his stubble catching and rasping her smooth skin. His lips brushed the delicate curve of her ear and parted to whisper.

"I can do all sorts of things other than stare at you, Daphanie," he murmured, his voice barely above a whisper. "I could touch you. I could stroke you. I could caress you. Or, I could just do this."

Then he turned his head, aligned her mouth beneath his, and let himself feast.

Seven

For generations, the Others maintained a policy of secrecy, going to great lengths to conceal their presence from the human race. Naturally, this resulted in a rather insular community in which marriages and pair bonds between Others and humans remained rare. While such unions are still considered unusual, it would hardly be accurate to claim they never occur.
—A Human Handbook to the Others, *Chapter Thirteen*

Daphanie felt as if someone had just ignited her forge and laid her out over the heated coals. If the building's sprinkler system were to go off and douse her at any second, she wouldn't even blink, but she suspected she might give off steam.

Come to think of it, she was surprised she wasn't doing that already. Or maybe she was. No way was she going to tear her lips from Asher's long enough to open her eyes and check. Her mama hadn't raised that particular brand of stupid.

The man kissed like a god. Eros, naturally. Or maybe like a devil, because the thoughts he put in her mind with his hard, hot mouth and his warm, strong hands weren't about angels and church choirs; they made her think of dark, humid nights, tangled silk sheets, and the kind of pleasure that made a woman call out to God all the way down the long descent into the inferno.

He didn't just kiss. The word implied a neat and civilized pressing of lips to lips, a temporary joining marked by pleasure and simple contentment. None of that bore even the slightest resemblance to what Daphanie experienced in that moment.

She felt consumed, devoured, trapped by the power of firm hands and intoxicating pleasure. His fingers gripped her only lightly at the nape, more of a caress than a restraint, and his palm against her back urged and encouraged instead of detaining or forcing. The power that held her in place had little to do with physical force and everything to do with desire.

Daphanie hadn't expected the kiss, but if she were to be honest with herself, she would have to admit she'd wanted it almost from the first instant those silver-gold eyes had locked with hers. She almost suspected she'd been waiting for it most of her life.

Fate.

All her life, Daphanie had believed in the power of the universe to guide people toward their destinies. It had guided her into art, into travel, and now into the arms of this man. Who was she to argue with that kind of fortune, when this fortune felt so good?

She lifted herself onto her tiptoes, throwing herself into the kiss with all the exuberance of a cliff diver streaking toward clear, blue water. Like the ocean, he enveloped her. She felt almost as if she were drowning, but she couldn't care. What was breathing compared to the once-in-a-lifetime power of this kiss?

The beat of her heart pounded in her ears, quickened by his touch, heavy, insistent . . .

. . . and coming from the other side of the studio door.

Head spinning, Daphanie tore herself away from Asher's embrace and turned to face the door, staring in confusion at the smooth steel surface.

"Geez, Daph, don't you ever answer doors anymore?" Corinne called from the hallway. "Let me the hell in!"

Beside her, Asher cursed, sharp and low, and she really couldn't disagree with the sentiment. Although she had to admit that the kiss had been headed in only one direction, and without a bed—or even a clean floor—anywhere around, someone would have ended up cursing even more violently sooner or later.

A residual shiver raced across her skin and Daphanie almost laughed. Okay, sooner, then.

"Daph?"

His face cast in grim lines, Asher stepped past Daphanie and yanked open the studio door. On the other side, Corinne stood frozen, her hand raised and curled in a fist in preparation for another vigorous knock.

"Am I interrupting something?"

"You'll have to ask Daphanie," the Guardian snarled, turning away to stalk back to the far end of the studio. "Just think of me as another piece of furniture. I brought a book."

Daphanie made a sound of frustration. For the first time since Saturday night, she'd gotten a rise out of

Asher that didn't involve him yelling at her for wanting to get away from him. In fact, this particular reaction had been all about closeness. Until Corinne had interrupted.

"Your timing sucks," she grumbled under her breath, slumping against the end of her worktable and crossing her arms grumpily over her chest. She glared at Asher's form, perched on a stool at the other end of the studio, a book in his hand and a scowl on his face. He appeared to be ignoring them. Nevertheless, she hoped she'd spoken softly enough not to be overheard.

A sly grin played around the edges of the reporter's mouth. "I'm starting to understand that you might think so. Do you want me to come back later?"

Daphanie glared. "I think it's a little late for that."

Corinne laughed and leaned closer. Her voice dropped conspiratorially. "I'm more than happy to apologize. I won't even argue if you decide you need retribution at some point. But you have to tell me one thing . . . How did he taste?"

Flames shot up the side of Daphanie's neck and bloomed in her cheeks. "What?" she stuttered. "What the hell are you talking about? How the hell would I know? Why would you even ask a question like that?"

"Because I'm a reporter, honey. It's my job to ask questions. And because either that man just kissed the starch out of your panties, or a hive full of killer bees buzzed through here and stung you directly on the lips. Now which one was it?"

Not even willpower could keep Daphanie's knees from buckling as she remembered the power of that kiss.

"God, Rinne, I think he sucked my brain right out of my head," she whispered, fighting the urge to lay said appendage down on the table and savor the coolness of the wood against her overheated skin.

"Oooh, I'm jealous. I haven't had a kiss like that in . . . years." Corinne sighed. "I'm so sorry I interrupted. Want to punch me?"

"Yes."

The reporter laughed. "All right, anywhere but the face. Come on. I know I deserve it."

"Give me a minute to get my strength back."

Corinne's eyes widened. "Wow. That good, huh?"

"You have no idea."

She couldn't, because Daphanie herself could barely grasp the significance of that single, stolen moment. It felt as if her world had tilted and settled into a new alignment. All she could really say was that something inside her had shifted.

But had Asher felt anything similar?

She had to fight not to stare at him across the room. Since she'd just instigated an argument over him doing exactly that to her, it seemed uncouth. Besides, her overloaded mind and senses needed some time to settle down, and staring at his fine body and handsome features wouldn't do much to aid that effort. Better to focus on Corinne and touch base with reality again.

"Whattaya got?"

"Excuse me?"

"Don't tell me you interrupted for nothing," Daphanie groaned. "Please say you had a reason for schlepping out here on this particular morning?"

"Oh, right." Corinne laid a hand on her folder as if

assuring herself it was still where she'd left it. "You have any place to sit in here?"

"Gimme a sec."

Her friend waited patiently while Daphanie poked her head into several open crates until she found what she looked for. She returned a second later with two tall, metal stools that made up for in fire resistance what they lacked in style, beauty, and comfort. She arranged them at one end of the carpenter's table, half facing each other around a blunted corner.

"Voilà," she said, sliding onto one of the seats and focusing on her companion. "Now tell me what's going on. I thought we agreed to postpone the interview for your paper until I got a little more settled in."

Corinne took her own seat and slid her papers closer. She appeared to be guarding them like a holy relic, and Daphanie felt a faint stirring of curiosity.

"We did," Corinne agreed, waving a dismissive hand. "I'm not worried about that. But our powwow over at Vircolac the other day made me curious. A reporter's besetting sin is curiosity."

Daphanie just lifted an eyebrow. She'd heard a lot about Corinne's sins from her sister, and she didn't think curiosity would even rank in the top ten. From what Danice had said, Rinne was a woman who liked men, tequila, and adventure. Not necessarily in that order.

"I've done a couple of articles on witches and psychics in my time," the woman continued, her expression shifting to something intent and glittery as she warmed to her subject. "So I was surprised when this D'Abo guy didn't really ring any bells for me. I know at least the names of most of the so-called magicians the bunko squad likes to target on a regular basis."

"And D'Abo isn't one of those names?"

"No, which made me even more curious, so I decided to do a little investigating."

"I thought Graham and Rafe were looking into D'Abo."

"They are," Asher confirmed.

Hearing his voice come from over her shoulder made Daphanie jump. She'd been trying so hard to focus on Corinne that she hadn't even noticed when he left his perch across the room and joined them at the table.

He took in her glare and shrugged. "If you're speaking of D'Abo, I wish to hear what you have learned."

"Asher's right," Corinne confirmed, "Graham and Rafe are looking into things, but they're going to be looking at this from a perspective of whether or not you need to worry about him—what kind of powers does he have, how strong is he, how often in the past has he been known to swear revenge on people and has he ever followed up on it . . . Those kinds of things."

"But you didn't look at that? That was kind of the info I thought would help me out."

"It will, but I wanted to know who D'Abo *is*. Where did he come from? If he's supposedly so powerful, why isn't he more well-known? Does he have enemies? And if so, how healthy are they?"

Daphanie considered all that and nodded. "Sort of a 'know thy enemy' thing, then."

Corinne nodded. "And thy enemy's enemies."

"So what did you find out?"

The woman's eyes lit up as she flipped open her

folder. "Oh, all sorts of juicy little tidbits." She flipped through a couple of pages and slid out a copy of a black-and-white newspaper photograph featuring a beaming Charles D'Abo flanked on either side by a city councilman and the mayor of New York. "Is this the idiot from the nightclub?"

Daphanie nodded. "That's him. Is he actually friends with the mayor?"

Corinne snorted. "As if. From what I can tell, D'Abo doesn't have that kind of juice in this city. I think this was just a lucky break for him at a fund-raiser for the neighborhood where his business is located. He was standing in the right place at the right time to get some attention."

"Hmm. He seems to have quite a talent for that," Daphanie observed.

"Bitter," Corinne teased, setting aside the photo and pulling out several pages of photocopied newspaper clippings. "Now this is the stuff I found interesting. I definitely wanted to get a look at D'Abo's temple, or whatever you call the place where witch doctors do their voodoo."

"A *hounfort*," Asher said.

"What?"

"It's called a *hounfort*," he repeated. "The ritual space for the congregation."

"Oh, right. Well, I wanted to check out his *hounfort*, if that's really the right name for a former tavern, brothel, and drugstore that now sells charms, potions, and bad incense out the front door while bringing live chickens, the occasional goat, and regular parades of worshippers in the back."

"Chickens and goats?"

"Illegally, of course, but D'Abo is apparently one of the minority of voodoo practitioners in Manhattan who still adhere to the old traditions of the occasional animal sacrifice."

"Yuck."

"Yeah, I have to agree on that one. Apparently, it's something they don't do in front of the 'tourists,' so I haven't been able to find anyone yet who'll talk about those rituals, but I was able to dig up some info about the more public ones."

"And?"

"And they sound pretty standard from what I can tell. Not that I'm any kind of expert on voodoo," Corinne said. "Attendees have a feast, make offerings to the gods or *loa* they intend to honor for the evening, then there's a whole bunch of drumming and dancing intended to invoke the spirits to join the party. The goal is for one of the spirits, at some point in the evening, to take temporary possession of one of the dancers. They call it 'being ridden.' Then the spirit can be asked for advice or favors or blessings or whatever. Different spirits have different personalities and demands that have to be met before they'll appear, so things can vary a bit around the same theme."

In the back of her mind, Daphanie could swear she heard drums, beating out the strange, familiar rhythm of her dreams.

She shook her head to clear it and looked at Asher. "I thought you said whatever D'Abo practiced was some kind of bastardized form of the standard voodoo or Afro-Caribbean religious thing."

"From the few people I've talked to so far, I'm pretty sure parts of it are," Corinne agreed, "but those parts are the ones involving the animals and the stuff not many people want to talk about."

"Oh." A wave of frustrated disappointment swept over Daphanie. Everywhere she went looking for answers these days, it seemed like she only wound up finding more questions.

"Wait," Corinne said, suppressed excitement coloring her voice. "I haven't gotten to the interesting part yet."

"What's the interesting part?" Asher demanded.

"Well, you made D'Abo out to be such an egotist that I expected to dig up lots of stories about how he'd struggled his way out of poverty to build his spiritual empire by the sweat of his brow. Even if it was all a bunch of hokey, it's still what I expected to hear."

"He was 'born a poor black child'?"

Corinne nodded. "Exactly. But that's not what I found. As it turns out, D'Abo didn't so much build anything as he inherited it. Not from his parents, or anything like that, but from the people he studied voodoo with. The temple D'Abo supposedly controls has existed in New York since 1797."

That took Daphanie by surprise. She'd expected the same story Corinne had, all about struggle and sacrifice and building his army of followers from the ground up. After all, it made a guy sound more like a guru if he collected his acolytes based on the power of his words and his personality than if he'd just inherited them from the guy who came before him.

"I didn't think Manhattan had a big nineteenth-century voodoo cult," she said mildly.

"We didn't. We only had one voodoo priestess, who was apparently a transplant from New Orleans."

"Well, of course she was."

"Yeah, D'Abo's temple apparently sprang up around her. He's just the latest head honcho."

Asher nodded. "I think I remember hearing something to that effect."

"So does that mean I don't have to take him seriously?" Daphanie asked. "I mean, if he's more of a figurehead than an actual big, bad muckety-muck—"

"No so fast, grasshopper. Let's not jump to conclusions."

Daphanie battled back her impatience, but she employed not much grace while doing so. "Let's not string along our friends, either."

"Sorry." Corinne flashed an unrepentant grin, but sobered quickly. "I'm not ready to dismiss the guy quite yet, especially not until Graham and De Santos report back. He might not have founded his little army of darkness, but that doesn't necessarily mean he lacks the power to lead it. Besides, I've been thinking about that dream of yours."

Daphanie didn't bother to ask which one. She'd only ever told Corinne about one dream, the one she'd had in the exact the same detail every night this week. She hadn't mentioned that to Asher yet. She didn't even like thinking about the dreams, let alone talking about them.

Asher frowned. "What about Daphanie's dream?"

"I'm not sure. It's just stuck with me, is all, and the more research I've done this week, the more I've started to think that it sounds awfully like an accurate description of one of the ceremonies at D'Abo's temple."

Frowning, Daphanie examined the thoughtful look on her friend's face. "What do you mean? I'm fairly certain that the place in the dream didn't feel like the inside of a building. It didn't even feel like I was in the city. It was more like being out in the middle of nowhere. You know, all crickets and crackling fires. There was no feeling of walls around it. More like . . . I don't know, a tent."

"Well, I don't know either." Corinne shrugged. "I'm just telling you that the more I read about D'Abo, the more I felt like I was reading someone else's account of your dream."

"So, what? You think this guy is somehow . . . controlling my dreams?" She felt Asher lay a warm hand on her shoulder and found herself leaning toward him, absorbing the comfort.

"I think that's unlikely," he murmured, his tone soothing. "If D'Abo had that ability, I imagine he would already have sought some greater action than just the dreams. He would have influenced you in some other way, and I see no evidence of that."

Corinne huffed out a brief sigh. "I've gotta say, I'm relieved to hear that. In circumstances like this—meaning anything having to do with the Others—I get a little suspicious about stuff. I don't know what D'Abo is capable of. Magic is still almost as new to me as it is to you. But if Asher says you're okay, I'm going to take his word for it. Still, if I were you, I just think I'd keep my eyes open."

Daphanie pulled a face. "Even when I'm asleep."

Asher squeezed her shoulder reassuringly. "Don't worry. That's my job, remember? I'll make certain nothing happens to you. Trust me."

Daphanie nodded, then found herself going very still inside her own mind. She did trust him. The knowledge hit her like a sledgehammer to the forebrain, but it was there, solid, instant, and undeniable. She trusted Asher completely. After just a few short days of sitting in his glowering presence and wishing him to Hades, something inside her had decided to acknowledge that she felt safe with him. She knew in her core that he would never do anything to harm her and would, in fact, do everything in his power to protect her.

The surety of it nearly sent her reeling.

"You shouldn't listen to me anyway," Corinne said, her eyes on Asher's quelling expression. "I have a natural predisposition toward paranoia. Plus, I'm a reporter. I think everything is a conspiracy. But honestly, I was just trying to help."

Daphanie forced herself to focus on her friend and nodded. "I know you were. And I do appreciate it. Like you said, I'm better off knowing what I'm up against."

"Just remember, you're not up against anything alone." Corinne gathered her papers back into their messy pile and flipped her folder closed. She nodded toward Asher. "In addition to the big guy, here, you've got me and Missy and Graham and Rafe and the whole crew on your side. And I'll keep digging, too. Something is nagging at the back of my mind about this whole situation, and I just can't put my finger on what it is. I hate that feeling. Which means I'm not going to let this drop until I figure it all out."

"Thanks."

Corinne dismissed Daphanie's word with a wave of

her hand and stood to make her way out. "Don't thank me. This is what friends do."

Daphanie slipped out from under Asher's hand and walked her friend toward the door. "Still—"

"Of course, friends also tell each other all the juicy details about their sex lives. Especially when they involve big, strong men with faces like Renaissance sculptures and asses you could bounce a quarter off of."

Daphanie caught her friend's wiggling eyebrows and shoved her playfully out the door. Even as she shot a quick glance over her shoulder to see if Asher had overheard. His expression remained as bland as ever. Which told her nothing.

"As if," she teased back, keeping her own voice hushed. "Go get your own sex life, D'Alessandro, and stop trying to live vicariously through mine."

"Oooh, so you and the Yummy One have a sex life? Already? Damn, girl, you work almost as fast as I do!"

"Ha! Wouldn't you like to know. Good girls don't kiss and tell." And with that, she closed the door in the other woman's face, still grinning.

Determined to get the last word, Corinne laughed at her through the thick layers of steel. "Maybe not," she called, her voice muffled but clearly intelligible. "But bad girls have more fun!"

Eight

In the end, every human being needs to make a choice: do I continue to live my life the way I've always lived it and simply keep my distance from the things and creatures who frighten me? Or do I take a chance and see where this new adventure of a life among the Others will lead me?

—A Human Handbook to the Others, *Conclusion*

She kept her eyes closed and her head tipped back toward the apex of the tented ceiling, showing the loa *no fear and no shame. Again, she smelled incense and charcoal and the sweet, earthy scent of burning tobacco. Her people offered only the finest, grown not two miles away in the English's cherished fields.*

Her pulse throbbed, filling her head and trickling down the back of her throat like the rum she'd taken in Their names. Her heart beat louder, tempo increasing, urgency rising as the rhythm of the drums drove them all faster. Her feet pounded against the cool earth, the grit of dirt clinging to her soles. It was a new feeling for her, this cool, dry earth, different from the rich delta soil she'd been used to, but the dirt didn't matter.

Neither did the air matter, cooler here, thinner, for all the complaints the white men offered when the summer sun beat down on them. They were weak. They would not have survived in the thick, tropical humidity on which she had suckled. At home, fire had been a gateway and a duty, but here, the glow of firelight became a thing of beauty, a necessity that kept the biting chill from drawing her away from Their arms.

Now the drums beat faster. Voices sang louder, driven by the drums, driven by the spirits. In the morning, the farmers and traders in the town at the tip of the island would whisper of dark rituals and dangerous spirits in the distance, and she would laugh, knowing the truth would only frighten them more than their ignorant speculations.

She felt a familiar rush of fullness within her. Her gros bon ange *began to shrink, making room to let the greater Ones in. She could feel the power welling up within her, feel the excitement, the exaltation. She lifted her arms to the roof and gave herself over to the communion with the divine, the dark, the eternal. She felt His* ange *settle over her like a heavy weight, thick and ancient with power, and when her eyes snapped open, they were His eyes, dark with menace and bright with intent.*

Nous sommes au ras au ras, chère. J'vas t'donne tous la puissance, tite fille, *His voice whispered in her head,* et nous avons choquer le ciel, non?

She laughed, loud and long, and the sound made the drummers stutter in their blows.

Daphanie sat bolt upright in her sister's bed, her

sheets and tank top soaked with sweat. She scrubbed at the skin of her arms, trying to rid herself of that feeling of heaviness, but it didn't shift. It clung to her like oil, coating her from the inside out. It wasn't just her body that felt heavy, but her soul.

She couldn't stay where she was. She felt tainted and she needed to get away. From the bed, from the dream, from herself. Throwing back the sheets, she scrambled to her feet and stripped off her clothes as if they'd been splattered in blood.

God, she needed air.

The thick fog of the dream stayed with her, a feeling she'd come to both know and dread over the past week. Every day for seven days she'd woken with this hazy, unclean feeling, and her nerves suffered for it. Every day she woke feeling a little heavier, a little less herself, and tonight, the one-week anniversary of her night at the club, she was ready to tear off her own skin to make the sensations go away.

She needed air.

Not stopping to think, Daphanie grabbed her sister's cotton robe from where it hung on the back of the bed-room door. She was already halfway through the great room as she dipped her arms in the sleeves, and she barely had it belted closed when she pushed open the door at the back of the kitchen and stepped out onto the rooftop terrace built above the apartment building's lower wing. She hadn't even glanced toward the sofa where Asher habitually slept. She just needed to get out.

She hurried over to the low wall facing the street and drew in great gulps of cool night air. Her hands trem-bled as she pressed them flat against the granite surface, and her eyes fixed sightlessly on the light traffic moving twelve stories below.

Daphanie, she chanted to herself over and over. *Your name is Daphanie. You're a blacksmith. You're a human being. It was only a dream.*

The problem was, it had never felt like a dream.

Even the first night, the sensations of dancing to the beat of drums in a tent on the edge of nowhere had felt more real to her than the polished wooden floor of her sister's swanky new apartment. It had been bad enough then, when all she'd dreamed of was a little dancing, but every night since, it had only gotten worse.

At first, the dream had progressed with glacial slowness, advancing one footfall at a time so that the first couple of nights she hadn't realized it was advancing at all. But by Thursday, the feeling of anticipation had built to a fever pitch, and last night she'd finally understood that in the dream, the woman she was had been inviting some sort of spirit to possess her.

Tonight, she'd felt the first touch of that foreign presence within her body and the memory of it made her want to vomit.

It had been dark, black, inside her, a feeling of corruption and vice and bone-deep malice Daphanie had never experienced before. It had threatened to consume her, but the Daphanie in the dream had gloried in it, had invited it in and welcomed it, even as she understood the evil it represented. The Daphanie in reality couldn't even begin to comprehend that, but to the Daphanie in the dream, the spirit, the dark thing inside her, had represented power.

For the first time in her life, Daphanie finally

understood the concept of selling one's soul to the devil. She felt as if hers was gone and the devil now crawled underneath her skin.

"Are you all right?"

She choked back a hysterical laugh.

The voice behind her was soft and deep, low and familiar. He stepped out of the shadows of the small, private terrace and stood close enough that she could feel the heat radiating from his body and seeping through the thin fabric of her borrowed robe.

"I'm fine."

If you called feeling like a stranger in your own skin "fine." If "fine" meant feeling as if she were still walking around in the dream. Or as if the dream walked in her.

Her hands clenched on top of the wall, the rough stone scraping across her skin as her knuckles curled. She flinched when his big, warm hand settled on her shoulder.

"You don't look fine."

This time she did laugh, and the sound rang with bitterness and fear. Was it hers? Or the dream's? Did not being able to tell make her a lunatic? "That's what I admire most about you, Asher. You're just a fucking charmer. You just take my goddamned breath away."

He turned her to face him and studied her expression. "What's wrong?"

She tried to tug away from him. "Not a thing. Everything is just frickin' peachy."

Asher held firm. "Everything is very obviously not fine. You look like you've seen a ghost."

"Well, I haven't." She'd *felt* one, maybe, but she hadn't

seen one. Her eyes had remained closed for almost the entire dream. What she'd seen when she opened them . . .

It hadn't been a ghost.

"I can honestly say, I didn't see a bloody fucking thing. Satisfied?"

"No."

"And isn't that sad for you."

Daphnie knew she was acting like a brat, but she couldn't seem to do anything about it. She wasn't acting like herself, not thinking like herself. Her body didn't seem like hers; her words didn't seem like hers.

God, what the hell was *wrong* with her?

She jerked away from him and stalked back toward the kitchen. God, she didn't want to go back inside, but she couldn't stay out here with him. The dream still buzzed in her head, crawled under her skin, and knotted her stomach. She felt like all she had to do was close her eyes and she'd slip right back into it, right back into the grasp of that other self. Of that heavy, black soul that had settled over her.

"Daphanie."

He caught up with her in two long strides and tried to make her face him. When she shrugged in an attempt to slip out from under his grip on her shoulders, he stopped trying to turn her and simply wrapped his arms around her from behind. He tugged her back against him and leaned his head close to hers until his breath fluttered against her cheek.

"Tell me. What happened?"

She couldn't help it. She melted against him. His body drew hers like a lodestone, softening her bones, relaxing her muscles. Every lean, hard plane of him conformed to her softer curves. They fit together like two halves of a whole and the sensation made her want to weep in joy and frustration.

"Tell me."

Oh, how she wanted to.

She wanted to pour her heart out to him. She wanted to tell him every new detail of the dream, but something inside her rebelled at the idea. Her mind screamed that if she spoke the words aloud, it would only give the things inside her more power; it would send the blackness seeping deeper into her soul, make the taint more permanent. She couldn't speak of it.

All she could do was lean against him, trying to absorb his strength through her skin, as her eyes drifted helplessly shut.

Asher felt the change in her.

Actually, he felt both of them.

The first made something inside him roar in triumph as she relaxed into his embrace. She softened against him, letting him press her closer to his body, letting him support some of her weight. She felt heavy, not physically—he could have lifted her in one hand without noticing—but mentally, emotionally. Psychically. Something was eating away at her from the inside and he wanted to demand that she tell him what it was. He couldn't fight it unless he understood it, but she guarded the truth from him with a wary sort of ferocity.

She didn't trust him completely yet, and while he understood it, it nearly drove him mad.

"Tell me," he urged, curving his body around hers, trying to shelter her from the demons in her own head.

He felt her tremble. He watched her profile as her eyelids dropped, shuttering their velvet depths, and that's when he felt the second change overtake her.

Her body shifted. Instead of relaxing into him, her muscles took on a subtle tension. She no longer felt soft in his arms, like a sleepy child, but sinewy and strong, like an anaconda, all muscle and predatory instinct.

Tension flooded through him.

"Daphanie?" he inquired cautiously.

She rotated slowly in his arms, a move that originated in her hips, which she swiveled against him, deliberately dragging her soft warmth over the vulnerable and suggestible flesh between his legs. He hardened helplessly and cursed.

Her eyes still closed, she tilted her face toward his. The smile on her full lips made him simultaneously horny and horrified. He watched in frozen fascination as she strained upward, pressing her breasts against his chest, taking every opportunity to wriggle and sway against him. She felt like sex in a nightrobe, but he sensed something very wrong in the sightless face below his.

Her hands slid into the close-cropped hair above his nape and tried to drag him toward her.

"Come, *cher,*" she purred in a voice replete with seduction and devoid of Daphanie. "*Donnes-moi le bec doux.* Just a li'l sugar, baby."

Asher nearly choked on his tongue. The words were so foreign, so unexpected, he didn't even recognize her as she spoke. And he certainly hadn't expected her to revert to speaking in some odd form of French.

He reached behind him and grasped her hands to drag them away. Something was very wrong.

"Stop it, Daphanie," he ordered, deliberately making his voice sharp and raspy. Or maybe that was a byproduct of his involuntary arousal. His mind might understand that this wasn't like Daphanie, but his cock didn't seem to care.

He drew her hands out to the sides, but she continued to lean toward him. "Open your eyes."

She collapsed against his chest, rubbing hard little nipples against him provocatively. His shirt and the thin fabric of her robe provided a woefully inadequate barrier between them.

Her lips drew together in a pout, one that only served to make them appear more luscious and more kissable. "Don't be so mean, *bébé*," she purred. "Just a little kiss . . ."

Asher opened his mouth to repeat his demand that she open her eyes, but she was faster than he'd expected.

The moment his lips parted, she lunged forward, striking like a snake. Her lips landed on his before he was even aware of her movement, her tongue sliding wetly into his mouth to tangle with his.

Shock cost him a precious second of reaction time and when he finally grasped her torso to put her away from him, she had already wrapped herself around him like an octopus reeling in its prey. She had propelled herself upward so that her legs wrapped around his waist, her thighs bracketing his hips and her groin rocking indecently against his involuntary erection. Her arms clung to his shoulders as if locked in place, her fingers digging into his scalp as she seemed to try to devour him whole.

For the first time in his life, Asher thought he might

begin to understand how a woman felt when subjected to an unwanted sexual advance. He'd wanted Daphanie from almost the first moment he saw her, but this was not Daphanie. It didn't feel like Daphanie, didn't even taste like Daphanie. Instead of the sweet, honeyed kiss he remembered, this woman tasted of bitterness and rage and malice.

He tore his mouth from hers and tightened his hands around her ribs until he feared injuring her, but that was what it took to pry her off him. He looked down into her beautiful face, now contorted into an unrecognizable grimace of fury, and whispered a grim apology.

Then he struck her with a precisely measured blow to the bundle of nerves at the base of her ear and caught her as she crumpled.

Scooping her up in his arms, he headed into the kitchen and out the apartment's front door. It was past time to find out what had been bothering Daphanie Carter, because he had a sneaking suspicion it had just tried to bother him, as well.

Nine

Possession—a state in which a person's mind, body, and/or soul are controlled by a foreign entity. This control can be exerted either externally (through psychic or magical influence) or internally (by a noncorporeal entity entering and inhabiting the body of another being). Possession can occur either voluntarily or involuntarily.

Most humans tend to associate the concept of possession with the classic horror film The Exorcist, *in which a young girl is possessed by a demonic force. In actuality, possession can be accomplished by any of a number of different Others, of which demons are only one example.*

—A Human Handbook to the Others, *Glossary*

Daphanie regained consciousness slowly. First she became aware of an acute throbbing in her head, then of the sound of voices nearby speaking in hushed tones. She had to struggle to make out what they said.

". . . good you brought her here . . . did the right thing . . . just wondering who to call . . . and the Council . . . not exactly on the friendliest terms."

Daphanie thought she recognized the voice, but her intellect hadn't quite caught up with her consciousness. She couldn't quite conjure the correct face or name for the speaker. It was a man, though. She could tell that much.

". . . hit her so hard?" This time a woman spoke, the voice soft and concerned, and also discernibly scolding. ". . . probably feels like her head is exploding."

The woman had that right. Daphanie couldn't remember the last time her head had ached so badly. Of course, she also couldn't recall what had happened before she'd begun to regain consciousness a moment ago, so maybe that didn't mean much.

"You weren't there," another man said, sounding at once defensive and apologetic. "I tried being gentle, and it didn't work. She wasn't herself. No human woman I've ever met has been that strong, blacksmith or no."

The woman sighed. "I know, Asher, I'm sorry. I'm just worried. What you described was definitely not like Daphanie. We need to find out what's going on."

Missy. The woman speaking was Missy.

The realization brought a flood of relief. She hadn't lost her memory. It was all coming back. Thank God.

"I'll make some calls." It was the first voice she'd heard again. Graham. He sounded thoughtful, and maybe a little bit concerned. "Maybe Rafe can pull some strings. The witches may not like us much, but they can't completely ignore us, either."

"Thanks." She heard cloth shifting and felt Asher's presence move above her. "Shouldn't she be waking up by now?"

"She may be—"

"I'm awake."

The words emerged with a distinct croaking sound, but at least they made sense. At the moment, that seemed like an accomplishment.

"Here, drink some water," Missy urged, and Daphanie felt the cool, smooth rim of a glass press against her lips.

She raised her head a few inches and sipped gratefully. Her mouth had been so dry.

"How are you feeling?" Asher asked, and she could hear the guilt and concern underlining his normally impassive tone.

"Like I just got whacked upside the head by a baboon who outweighs me by a hundred pounds or so." She opened her eyes the barest slit and looked up at him. "How are you?"

Missy snorted. Asher just laid his hand over hers for an instant and squeezed gently.

"Let Missy take care of you," he urged. "Graham and I will be back as soon as we can."

Daphanie watched him leave with a frown on her face. "He couldn't at least have given me a clue what's going on?" she demanded peevishly of no one in particular.

Missy answered anyway. "Go easy on him."

Daphanie turned to scowl at her, the expression turning into a grimace as her head protested, joined swiftly by her stomach. "Easy? The man hit me. He knocked me unconscious."

The words held a lot less heat than they might have, and Missy must have noticed.

"And he feels terrible about it," she said. "Although, from what he said when he brought you inside, it doesn't sound like you gave him much choice."

Daphanie forced her eyes fully open and looked around the small, tastefully decorated bedroom. "Where's here?"

"Our house. Graham and I were sound asleep when someone started pounding on the front door. At four-fifteen in the morning," she added wryly. "I think he would have knocked the darn thing down in another minute. Luckily Graham didn't even stop to put on clothes before he went to answer it."

Daphanie frowned. She was pretty sure he'd been dressed when he and Asher left the room together.

Missy grinned. "Don't worry. I always make him dress for company. He's perfectly decent now."

From what she'd seen of her friend's husband, she suspected he was more than decent even stark naked. Maybe especially stark naked. She might have suffered a head wound, but she wasn't dead. She also wasn't injured badly enough to make the mistake of offering that opinion out loud. The alpha and luna Silverbacks had a reputation for mutually jealous natures.

Instead, she asked, "Asher brought me all the way over here?"

"*Carried* you all the way over here, looking ready to tear the building apart with his teeth if we didn't get you help."

The revelation sent a wave of pleasure coursing through Daphanie, and she had to work to beat it back. She disguised her reaction with a huff. "Maybe if he hadn't knocked me out, he wouldn't have had to bother you trying to get me medical attention."

Missy looked at her oddly. "He didn't bring you here for medical attention, Daphanie. Do you remember seeing a red cross anywhere on our front door? If you'd needed a doctor, he would have taken you to a hospital."

"Then why am I here?"

"You don't remember?"

Unease crawled through Daphanie's stomach, but whenever she tried to turn her thoughts back to the hours earlier, it was like trying to sift through quicksand.

"I remember I had another dream," she admitted with reluctance. "A pretty bad one. At least, I remember feeling freaked out when I woke up. I went outside to get some air. I think Asher was there, lurking, like usual." Her brows drew together and she shook her head slowly. And carefully. "But no, I don't remember. Did he tell you what happened? Did I get hysterical or something? I know the dream's had me on edge the last few nights . . ."

"Daphanie. You nearly raped him."

Her heart and stomach clenched in unison and she gazed at Missy with wide, bruised eyes. "What?" she whispered.

The luna's face filled with sympathy and her words were soft, but they still slashed at Daphanie like razor blades.

"Asher said he tried to talk to you after you went out on the terrace," Missy explained quietly. "He could tell that something had upset you, but you didn't want to talk about it. You tried to shake him off and go back inside, but he stopped you. He literally had to restrain you to keep you from running. Then he said you just . . . went a little crazy."

Daphanie buried her face in her hands as the barriers erected by her subconscious came crashing down, allowing her to see what she would have preferred to forget. "Oh, God."

A gentle hand settled on her knee. "You kissed him. He tried to stop it, because he knew you weren't thinking straight, but—"

"I crawled all over him," Daphanie breathed, bile creeping up into the back of her throat. "I frickin' climbed him like a jungle gym. Oh, my God, Missy, what the hell was I thinking?"

"It doesn't sound as if you were thinking."

Daphanie's head shot up at the sound of an unfamiliar voice. The last thing she wanted at the moment was for someone else to hear all about her humiliating behavior. In truth, she wanted nothing so much as a shower hot enough to scald her skin, a loofah the texture of sandpaper, and about a gallon of the kind of soap that surgeons used to scrub in before an operation. Nothing less would ever make her feel clean again.

"Who is she?" she hissed at Missy. Had they called for a shrink? Would that be such a bad thing?

The woman didn't even blink at Daphanie's rudeness. She stood in the door to the guest room looking dignified, gentle, and maddeningly serene. It made Daphanie feel even dirtier. And crazier.

"Daphanie, this is Erica Frederics." Graham ushered the woman into the room with his hand at her elbow, but he watched Daphanie carefully. "Asher and I asked her to come over for a few minutes to talk to you."

"Do you really think this is the best time?" Daphanie almost choked on a laugh that had very little to do with humor and an awful lot with incipient hysteria. She really needed that shower, before she snapped and startled babbling fit for Bellevue. "Maybe we can do this later. Like tomorrow. Or next year."

Asher stepped in behind them and fixed his gaze on Daphanie's face. "You need to talk to her," he said calmly.

"I don't—I don't think this is the right time. I should put some clothes on and go home." Daphanie scrambled from the bed and tugged at the hem of her short robe—or rather, her sister's short robe. She gave a brief prayer for the floor to swallow her up, to no avail. "I'm totally disrupting Missy's day. And taking over her and Graham's house. That's so rude. I'll just leave."

"Going home isn't going to make you feel any better," Erica said. She sounded just like she looked, like an aging hippy, but her voice contained a backbone of steel that Daphanie hadn't expected. "The thing you're running away from is attached to you. Wherever you go, it will only follow."

Daphanie froze, caught in the act of yanking open a drawer in hopes of finding one of the changes of clothes she had heard Missy was famous for keeping on hand, in case of emergencies. This felt like an emergency to her.

The woman reached out a hand and Daphanie flinched, but the hand never touched her. It hovered four or five inches from her skin while Erica examined her through narrowed eyes.

"It's incomplete," the woman continued. "Something is keeping it in check, but it feels stronger than it should be, given the tenuous attachment. You won't be able to shake it easily."

Daphanie's gaze flew to Asher. "What is she talking about?"

"Erica is a witch." It was Graham who answered her question, his voice surprisingly gentle for the impatient, forceful man she knew him to be. "Asher suggested that he thought you might be under some kind of magical influence, and I seconded the opinion. It looks like Erica agrees with us."

The woman nodded. "It's undeniable."

Daphanie felt a surge of something, but whether it was fear or hope, she couldn't decide. She didn't like the idea of being under some kind of spell, but if someone could figure out what it was, maybe they would be able to get rid of it.

She gave the witch a longer look.

Erica Frederics appeared to be in her late forties or early fifties, in that sort of late-afternoon period after adulthood has had time to settle in but before age has bothered to make an appearance. She had long, thick hair the sandy apricot color that some redheads turned on their way to gray. In fact, she already had plenty of gray mixed in, and she didn't bother to try to hide it, letting her waves hang freely almost down to her waist. Her skin was lined, but subtly, and a certain heaviness had begun to creep in around her jawline and at her middle. She wore a long tunic over a long, loose skirt, but Daphanie got the impression the clothing had more to do with comfort and habit than with a desire to conceal her thickening figure.

In all, the woman looked exactly like what she was, a middle-aged earth mother with a talent for reading faces and a gift for nurturing.

She scared Daphanie almost shitless. "What are you talking about?"

"There's a shadow on you," Erica answered, bluntly but not unkindly. "Something black is trying to attach itself to your soul. It has a foothold, but it's tenuous. Whoever placed it there will be unsatisfied. They'll try for something firmer."

"Who will? Attached how?"

The witch smiled, serene and sympathetic. Daphanie couldn't decide if she found that comforting or maddening. "I'm not certain yet. May I?"

She reached out once more, stopping again a few inches from touching Daphanie's face, but this time she clearly wanted to continue.

Daphanie found herself nodding.

Erica's hand settled on her face as lightly as a butterfly. The tips of three fingers glided to rest against her cheekbone and the woman stared deep into her eyes.

The witch's eyes, Daphanie noted, were hazel, a deep, mossy green ringed in smoke and turning a bright golden copper just around the pupils. They looked like little bits of the forest floor, and something told her they held just as many secrets.

A frown flickered over Erica's face. Her lips parted and she blew out a deep breath, exhaling steadily while the tips of her fingers began to quiver. When she flinched, Daphanie felt a little electrical shock, as if she'd just crossed a winter carpet in thick wool socks.

"Black as death," the woman murmured. "There's something very dark at work here, Daphanie Carter. You need to take care."

Daphanie had been prepared to scoff at the witch's evaluation. After all, what had she said that any so-called psychic with a crystal ball and a booth at Coney Island couldn't have repeated? But somehow, she found she couldn't be dismissive, not so much because of what Erica said, but because of the secrets flickering wildly behind her eyes.

"You shouldn't be alone," Erica concluded, dropping her hand and stepping back from Daphanie. "This will work faster on you, gain more power, if it finds you alone."

"She won't be alone. I'm staying with her, and believe me, from now on, she's not getting out of my sight. This is not going to happen again."

The witch half turned to smile ruefully at the Guardian. "Nothing is going to happen again, Mr. Grayson. What's going to happen already has. At this point, it's just a matter of degrees."

"What do you mean?" Daphanie demanded.

Erica sighed. "You've been cursed," she said bluntly. "Someone has used magic to try to influence your behavior."

"Yeah, well, it sounds like last night, it actually worked."

"Not completely. You did no one any harm, from what I hear. Not even yourself. No, I don't think that last night was the end goal." She shook her head. "There is something larger at work here, but whatever happens next won't be about gaining something new; it will be about strengthening the charm that's already been laid."

Daphanie felt her mouth tighten. "I don't think 'charm' is an appropriate description for whatever this is. 'Charm' makes me think of leprechauns and fairy godmothers, not voodoo priests who want me dead."

"Voodoo?" Erica sounded startled.

"What? Didn't Asher mention that was what started all of this? I pissed off some witch doctor, who apparently seems to be having trouble getting over himself."

Erica shot Asher and Graham a disgusted look. "No, they left that little detail out. Huh, men."

"Does it change things?"

"It most certainly does. Voodoo is a highly sympathetic form of magic. It relies heavily on the use of objects and tokens to effect change in the material world. Hence the famous voodoo doll. A curse laid by an ordinary magic user can be broken by any other practitioner, provided an equal or greater amount of will is used to effect the change. A voodoo curse is significantly more complicated." She eyed Daphanie. "Do you know if this witch doctor has anything belonging to you?"

Daphanie snorted. "Hardly. The man isn't exactly on my Christmas list."

"Well, make sure it stays that way," Erica advised. "That's probably why the link is as weak as it is." She saw Daphanie's puzzlement and explained. "Like I said, voodoo uses objects to magical purposes. The dolls in particular are linked to the person they're meant to represent through the uses of that person's possessions, usually stolen. A practitioner of voodoo might steal a woman's scarf, for instance, or a man's handkerchief and use the fabric to make the doll's clothing. Some of the person's energy is tied up in his or her possessions and that helps to forge the link so that the actions performed on the doll are experienced by the intended victim.

"That's what makes the voodoo curse so hard to lift. Because there is a physical object linked to the victim by magical energy, that object must also be destroyed in order for the spell to be broken. Devious people, voodoo priests. The _houngan,_ or white magicians, are difficult enough, but the _bokor,_ the ones who practice on the darker path, are even worse."

"You mean someone out there might have a doll that looks like me and be sticking pins in it to make me act like an idiot?"

Erica smiled. "It's possible, but it would be unlikely unless the _bokor_ had something of yours to bind the doll to you. Something you've had for a long time and used or worn frequently is usually preferred, because the closer it is to you, the more of your energy it will have stored."

"Like I said, I haven't exactly presented any witch doctors with tokens of my favor—"

Daphanie broke off, her skin going cold.

While it was true she hadn't given any scarves or hankies away lately, or suffered any unexpected thefts, she had nearly forgotten that something _had_ been taken from her. Last Saturday night.

"What?" Asher demanded, reading her expression and stiffening. "What are you thinking, Daphanie?"

"Last week at the club," she said weakly, her hands

nervously tightening the sash on her belt. "It was such a little thing, I didn't even really think about it."

"What happened?" he snarled.

"One of D'Abo's little flunkies, the one he tried to sic on me. I forget his name. But before you were able to reach us, the guy tried to grab me. He missed, so I just forgot about it. Only he didn't really miss. He tried to grab my wrist and he grabbed the hem of my top instead. All he got was a tiny little strip of fabric. I was so relieved he didn't hurt me and so angry about the whole incident that I completely forgot about it."

Asher swore, long and low, and Erica looked uncomfortable.

"This is . . . unfortunate," the witch murmured.

"It wasn't like it was a favorite top that I'd had forever," Daphanie struggled to reassure them. "It was fairly new. I just bought it a couple of months ago. I think that was only the second or third time I ever wore it. That means it wouldn't have a lot of juice, right?"

Erica nodded. "Theoretically, that's correct, but it would still be something, especially since you were wearing it when it was taken."

A growl rumbled through the air. Daphanie glanced at Graham, but he only looked grim. No, it was Asher doing the growling. He looked ready to grind someone's bones to make his bread.

"It's good that it wasn't something you were more connected to," the witch hastened to reassure them. She'd realized who the noise was coming from, as well. "In fact, that's probably the reason why I detected so much weakness in the attachment. The curse can't take hold with so little of you to feed its power."

"Then I'm safe."

Erica's lips compressed in a grim line. She shook her head. Daphanie already hated when she did that.

"You're not at immediate and dire risk, but I wouldn't call you safe," she corrected. "The weakness of the curse prevents your enemy from certain, more immediately dangerous acts, but what Asher described to me as having happened earlier tonight is a fairly good illustration of the fact that you're not out of danger."

Daphanie gave a growl of her own, this one fueled mostly by frustration. "So what do I do? Sit around and wait to see if something worse happens? Go knock on D'Abo's door and demand he give me my scrap of fabric back? What?"

Surprise flickered across Erica's expression. "D'Abo? Charles D'Abo? Is that who threatened you?"

Daphanie nodded. "Why?"

The older woman shook her head. "I'm simply surprised to hear that. He is not one I would immediately have guessed would cause trouble for someone like you, especially considering those you number among your friends. He's widely viewed as more cow—er, more cautious than that."

"Well, I doubt he knew who my friends were when I spilled a glass of root beer on him."

"Is that what started all this?" Erica sounded bemused.

"As close as I can figure."

"Odd. Oh, not that D'Abo would make a fuss over something so trivial," she assured her, "but that he would cling to it for so long. I wouldn't have guessed him to have that long of an attention span."

"I guess I made an impression."

"I would say so."

"The question stands, though," Daphanie persisted. "You've said the curse is already on me, so I have to figure out a way to get rid of it. Or at least keep it from making me do the wacky."

Asher touched her hand with his. "I will be with you at all times. You will never be alone, never be left unprotected. I'll watch over you as you sleep, if that's what it takes."

Daphanie rolled her eyes. "Fat lot of good that's going to do. You can't beat up a curse, Asher. Whatever is affecting me isn't something that will care if I have a live-in bodyguard. It needs to be removed."

"Of course it does, but I'm afraid that removing the curse is not within my power." Regret filled Erica's tone, but somehow, that failed to make Daphanie feel any better. "Voodoo curses are tricky, and definitely not part of my area of expertise."

"Who do we need to talk to, then, to get the curse removed?"

Asher's fingers curled around Daphanie's and squeezed with gentle reassurance. He asked the question automatically, as if there were no question that he was in this with her, that there was a "we" fighting this thing, not just a "her." Her heart clenched again, but this time the feeling didn't stem from fear. In fact, it might have even caused her a flutter of nerves. But in a good way.

"I'm afraid that the surest way to remove a voodoo curse is to confront the priest who laid it." Erica's expression filled with sympathy, and Daphanie had to bite back a curse.

Wasn't that just the way of things?

"Right, because I'm sure that the people who like to lay curses are always just happy as hosannas to remove them when asked politely."

"I didn't say it was simple. I said it was sure."

Asher squeezed her hand, cutting her off from speaking again. "If that is what needs to be done, then that's what we'll do."

He looked down at Daphanie, and she could see that in spite of his customarily austere expression, his eyes watched her softly. With this man, she realized, the truth was always in the eyes.

"The sun is rising even as we speak," he said, raising his head to glance out the window where the sky had indeed begun to pinken with morning light. "You need to get some more sleep, but later today, we will go and beard the lion in his den. Apparently, he did not understand when I told him that I had taken you under my protection. I believe it is time to enlighten him further."

When spoken in that silky, menacing tone, the term "enlighten" took on an entirely new meaning, one Daphanie suspected might involve a great deal of pain.

"You'll take me to D'Abo's temple?" she asked. He might have used a plural pronoun, but in Daphanie's experience, when alpha males used the term "we," it was always better to confirm they hadn't been speaking with the royal "we."

He hesitated. "You are under my protection, Daphanie Carter. It is my duty to take you wherever you need to go."

As answers went, that one made perfect logical sense.

So why did it leave Daphanie feeling so entirely unsatisfied?

Ten

In the human world, the term "alpha male" is often used to refer to a man with a certain sense of arrogance, machismo, and natural command. In the world of the Others, alpha is a formal title reserved for the male head of a Lupine pack.

Of course, that doesn't mean certain Other men don't have plenty of arrogance, machismo, and command of their own.

—A Human Handbook to the Others, *Chapter Three*

Asher spent most of the morning feeling restless and dissatisfied. While Missy had finally prevailed upon Daphanie to get a couple more hours of sleep—mainly by having Erica Frederics dose her with a potion guaranteed to keep her from dreaming—he had been left at loose ends, with nothing to do but watch the clock and twiddle his damned thumbs.

"For the sake of the bloody moon, Grayson, if you don't stop that infernal pacing, I'm going to have your liver for lunch."

Asher turned to the Silverback alpha, who sat sprawled in a battered armchair lazily flipping through the channels on a wide-screen television, and glowered. "You had lunch an hour ago."

"Yeah, but I'm a fan of alliteration, and 'lunch' and 'liver' both start with *l*."

"What about dinner?"

"The only body part I could think of that starts with *d* is 'dick,' and there's no way in hell I'm going to threaten to eat any man's dick."

Asher resumed pacing.

Graham growled. "Seriously, dude. You're driving me nuts. If you're just going to spend the damned day dying to get your hands on D'Abo, why don't you go get it over with? I'll even ride shotgun. Anything to get you out of my damned house."

Asher paused for a moment, then continued pacing toward the far side of the room. "I promised Daphanie," he mumbled.

Graham lifted a hand to his ear. "I beg your pardon?"

"I promised Daphanie I'd take her with me," Asher bit out, fixing the alpha with the dirtiest look he could manage. "I can't go without her."

"Ohhh." Graham smirked, drawing out the word and embuing it with worlds of meaning, all of them snide. "You promised the little human girl you'd do whatever she asked you to. Now I understand." He held up one finger, like a maître d', and adopted a snooty tone of voice. "Pussywhipped, party of one, your table is now available."

"Fuck you."

"Very eloquently put." The alpha continued to grin

at him. "I didn't think you Guardians were allowed to get involved with humans."

"I'm not involved with Daphanie," Asher protested with a growl. "But there aren't any laws against it."

"Ahhhh, so you *checked*!"

"Asshole."

"Puppy."

"I'm not involved with D—with the human." Asher caught himself and tried to infuse his voice with conviction. All the conviction the rest of him lacked. "I don't *get* involved with humans. I protect them; it's my job. Which is why I know that they're too ignorant and too fragile for any other kind of relationship."

Graham nodded, pursing his lips around a smile. "Yeah, I know. I told myself the same thing before I met Missy. Hell, after I met her, too. Right up until I realized she smelled just like warm, ripe peaches."

"She smells like myrrh," Asher murmured before he could catch himself.

Graham pretended not to hear. "I mean, I'm the first to admit that part of Lupine culture can seem . . . primitive to outsiders. We're not exactly sweet, fluffy lapdogs, after all. I knew perfectly well that no human woman would be strong enough to deal with our traditions. I mean, can you imagine a human woman running through the woods on a mate hunt? She'd be dead meat."

"Exactly." Asher nodded in agreement. A Lupine mate hunt was notoriously savage. In it, all the unmated members of the pack gathered in a rural or wooded setting and at a predetermined signal, the female would flee, leaving the males to give chase. When a male caught his chosen partner, he would mount her and take her right there, cementing their bond as a mated pair in the most primitive way possible. The idea of a human woman in that situation didn't even bear consideration.

Until Asher glanced over and saw the grin threatening to split the alpha's face in two.

Wait a minute. Hadn't he heard a rumor that Missy Winters had been forced to run in a mate hunt before she married Graham because of some sort of challenge to his authority over the pack? She had apparently made it through just fine.

Asher cursed. "This is an entirely different situation."

"Right." Graham nodded. "I mean, Melissa was a sweet, innocent kindergarten teacher who had spent her whole life putting other people before herself when I met her. How could your independent little Amazon of a blacksmith ever live up to that kind of feminine ferocity?"

"I hate you," Asher muttered.

"Back atcha, my brother."

"It *is* a different situation. No insult intended, but you're Lupine and your wife is human. The difference in your expected life spans is negligible. When Daphanie was born, I had already celebrated my five hundred and twelfth birthday."

"You should meet a friend of mine," Graham suggested. "You might have heard of him? His name is Dmitri Vidâme. His wife is a real firecracker. Not to mention being just shy of a millennium his junior."

"You can't use that comparison. A vampire has the option of offering immortality to his mate. I can't make Daphanie a Guardian. It doesn't work like that."

"No, it doesn't. But does that mean it can't work at all?"

"Can you think of a way it would?"

Graham threw up his hands. "Look, it's not my job to find a way for the two of you to be together. I've got enough on my plate without adding 'matchmaker to the Others' to my résumé. All I'm saying is that it's ridiculous to pretend you're not in love with the woman just because that would make your life easier."

"I never said I was in love with her."

"You never said you have balls, either, but I thought that was a pretty obvious one."

Very few things in this world irritated Asher more than arguing with someone who possessed the unmitigated gall to be right.

The question now was, as Graham would likely put it, what the hell did Asher intend to do about it?

Clearly Asher intended to spend the day pissing her off, Daphanie decided. By the time they left the Winters' house, she had noticed that he seemed to have a talent for it.

"I want to go home," she had repeated at least twenty times while they had discussed plans for the day. "I refuse to confront D'Abo wearing borrowed clothes."

"What's wrong with your clothes? They look fine to me."

Daphanie had glanced down at herself, at the baggy gray sweatpants that refused to stay up above her hip bones despite repeated tightening of the drawstring at the waist, and the virulent green T-shirt with the huge, yellow smiley face placed strategically across her tits.

Although since the damned shirt was so tight on her, the smiley face's expression had strayed disconcertingly close to a leer.

"Fine in what sense?" she'd demanded.

"Fine in the sense that they keep you covered and protected from the elements. What the hell else are clothes supposed to do?"

She had rolled her eyes. "God, you are such a man."

He had stared at her impassively.

She'd tried again. "Look, while I'm grateful to Missy that she was able to provide me with anything at all to wear, these are not the clothes I would choose to have on when I confront the man who's trying to kill me." To be honest, she wouldn't have worn those clothes to confront so much as a mirror. She'd heard lots of stories about Missy's store of emergency clothes, but she had never been told those clothes were donated by people with such a mean streak.

"Why does it matter what the hell you're wearing? You're going to an occult store, not a fashion show."

"And no one will take me seriously if I show up looking like a blind ragpicker!"

While she couldn't claim that Asher had ever quite grasped her point, he had at least given in. But he did manage to sulk during the entire cab ride to Mac and Niecie's apartment.

In a manly sort of way, of course.

He followed her from the cab into the lobby of the building, or maybe stalked after her would be a more appropriate description. She supposed she should be grateful he restrained himself from stomping.

She wished to God she could understand the man,

but she'd never met anyone more baffling in her entire life. Part of her wondered if it had more to do with him not being human, or not being a woman.

He simply baffled her. One moment he was treating her like a burden, an onerous chore he couldn't wait to see finished and off his hands, and the next he was cradling her against his chest and roaring out a demand that the alpha of the Silverback Clan do something to save her from some sort of evil curse. At least, that was how Missy had described it.

Daphanie had seen for herself, though, how one moment he could look at her as if she were a buzzing insect he longed to swat, and the next minute, his eyes could blaze with concern. Or desire. Earlier that morning, during that predawn conversation, he had squeezed her hand tenderly and looked ready to battle the entire world on her behalf, but since she had joined him in Missy and Graham's TV room after waking for the second time, he'd been staring at her as if trying to decide in which of a thousand different ways he would finally choose to be rid of her.

Was it too much to ask for a little consistency?

All Daphanie could say for sure was that if fate really had brought them together, it had a pretty sick sense of humor. Why bring together two people so obviously not meant to be together?

Well, if she were honest, Daphanie had to admit she wouldn't object to the idea of having Asher Grayson as her lover. What sane woman would? The man was hot enough to singe her retinas, and only a dead woman could have missed the jolt of electricity that passed between them every time they touched. The chemistry clearly worked. What worried Daphanie wasn't the chemistry.

It was her heart.

She knew instinctively that Asher Grayson could break it without even half trying. In fact, she very deliberately refused to look inside that pesky little organ for fear she would learn it was already too late for her. Just because she had always believed in love at first sight didn't mean she could afford to have it happen to her. Especially not now.

Her mind remained on her six-foot-plus problem as she led him off the elevator and down the hall to Niecie's apartment, so it took her a full minute of standing in front of the shattered door with her key out and ready before the reality of what she was looking at sank in. When it did, her stomach turned over.

"Oh, my God," she breathed, taking an instinctive step back.

Asher lifted her bodily and set her aside, cursing softly as he placed himself between her and the ransacked apartment. "Wait here," he snarled, placing a palm in the center of her chest for emphasis.

Daphanie didn't think she could have moved if she'd tried.

She stood frozen, watching in numb horror as Asher made an efficient sweep of the apartment. Daphanie could see that the great room was empty, but Asher checked closets and cabinets, under furniture and down the hall where the bedrooms and bathrooms were located separately from the main space. When he returned, his face looked hard and grim and Daphanie wished she could feel the same. She was too busy being horrified.

"They're gone. Probably long gone," Asher said, the corners of his mouth drawn straight and tight. "Come inside. You need to look around, see if anything's missing."

She shook her head and remained where she was. "How could I tell? They're not my things. They're Niecie's." Horror gave way to guilt. "Oh, my God, what am I going to tell Niecie? She was doing me a favor, letting me stay here, and now look what's happened! How am I going to tell her?"

Asher stepped back out of the apartment and took her hand, squeezing gently. "This isn't your fault," he insisted, his voice low and reassuring. "Your sister will understand that."

"Not my fault?" Her voice sounded hollow and incredulous, just like she felt. "Of course it's my fault! Why else would someone do this? I mean, it's obvious this wasn't a robbery. The television is still here, all the stereo and computer equipment. Hell, Mac must have thousands of dollars' worth of gadgets and surveillance equipment here that he uses in his business . . . Whoever was here wasn't looking to fund a drug score."

"You don't—"

"He was looking for me."

She felt Asher stiffen beside her. He said nothing, but she knew she was right. This had been done to hurt her, not her sister. Niecie was the innocent party, the injured one, and Daphanie would have to live with the fact that this had only happened because of her.

Asher drew her forward gently. "You have to go in and check. Daphanie. You need to tell me if anything is missing."

She dug her heels in and shook her head. "I told you, how would I know?"

He remained gentle but implacable. "You need to check."

Reluctantly, she unlocked her knees and allowed Asher to lead her into the chaos.

The intruders had done a thorough job. Every drawer and cabinet had been emptied, every table and chair overturned. The cushions had been yanked from the sofa and tossed aside, some of them with huge holes rent into the fabric. Papers had been scattered and shredded, picture frames and pottery smashed, dishes broken.

Daphanie choked back a hysterical laugh. "It doesn't even look like they were trying to find anything. It just looks like they wanted to destroy it."

Asher didn't speak, but he didn't have to. She knew he agreed with her. The purpose of this break-in had been at least as much to hurt her as to find whatever they'd been looking for.

"I don't see anything obviously missing," she said, picking her way carefully through the wreckage, "but like I said, how could I tell?"

"I'm less worried about the things in here," Asher admitted. "I agree they weren't after your sister's belongings. Which is why I want you to check the bedroom. You need to make sure none of *your* things are missing."

For a moment, Daphanie just frowned at him. It took several seconds for his meaning to sink in, for her to remember what Erica Frederics had told her.

A practitioner of voodoo might steal a woman's scarf, for instance, or a man's handkerchief and use the fabric to make the doll's clothing. Some of the person's energy is tied up in his or her possessions and that helps to forge the link so that the actions performed on the doll are experienced by the intended victim.

Daphanie felt herself go pale. "Do you think . . . ?"

Asher urged her forward. "Go look."

The bedroom looked like a replica of the great room, only in miniature. Even the mattress had been knocked askew, hanging drunkenly off one end of the bed frame.

Daphanie felt her heart clench. She hated the idea of someone having invaded the apartment this way, not for her own sake, but for her sister's. Danice didn't deserve to have her things pawed through, her mementos broken, her belongings disarranged. She should never have invited Daphanie to stay.

We'll be out of town for three weeks. Trust me, you'll be doing us a favor, Danice had said, her smile radiant with excitement and love for her soon-to-be-husband. *If you don't stay here, we'll just have to have someone else come in to water the plants, bring in the mail, keep things looking lived in. C'mon, Daffy. Say you'll stay. You can even use our room and sleep in the big bed. The guest room is full of boxes and wedding presents, anyway. We're still only three-quarters unpacked.*

God, Daphanie did not want to look at the guest room. She thought seeing her sister's wedding gifts broken and violated would just kill her.

She stared down at the floor, at the clothes emptied from her still half-packed suitcases strewn all about, through watery eyes. "I don't know . . . I don't see—I . . . I can't tell."

"Keep looking."

His voice sounded so gentle, as if he knew how hard this was and he hurt right along with her. But he remained insistent.

Daphanie shook her head, but she kept looking. Slowly she made her way across the floor to the closet—a single one of Mac's dress shirts hung lonely and forlorn on its hanger—then on to the master bath. Tubes and bottles and lotions and creams lay scattered across the floor and counters. Her own bottle of shampoo—which she perpetually forgot to replace the cap on after she used it—had been knocked into the tub, the contents spilled out into a pool of pale, aromatic green. A container of powder had broken and dusted every available surface with fine grains of dusky tan. Daphanie's hairbrush lay drunkenly in the sink, shed hairs clinging to the bristles.

"I don't know," she said softly, almost despairingly. "I don't see anything . . . But I just don't know."

"All right." Asher laid an arm across her shoulders and guided her gently back toward the apartment's entrance. "You've seen enough. Let's get you back to the Winters'. I need to let Graham and Rafe know what's happened, and Missy can keep an eye on you while we go and take care of this once and for all."

Daphanie jerked to a stop in front of the upside-down coffee table. "What? No!"

"No?"

"No. I'm not going back to Missy's," Daphanie insisted, trying to figure out what had ever made him think she would. "I need to stay here. Someone needs to start cleaning up this mess, and then I need to figure out a way to explain it to my sister."

Asher's mouth hardened. "If you think I'm leaving

you here alone to deal with all this, you're crazy. I'll find someone to come over and clean it up, but you are not staying here alone. Hell, after this, you'll be lucky if I let you go to the bathroom alone."

"And you'll be lucky if I don't kick your balls up into your sinuses," she shot back. "Let me tell you, I'm getting real tired of you managing my life for me, Grayson. I'm a grown woman, I'm a capable woman, and I can decide whether or not I want to spend the rest of my damned life hiding in my sister's friend's house."

"I'm not asking you to hide, damn it. I'm just asking you to stay safe!"

Daphanie's eyes narrowed and she drew herself up, even standing on her toes to give her a couple of extra inches of height. She glared at Asher and used her finger to prod his chest for emphasis.

"Stop trying to fob me off on other people like I'm a problem you can't wait to get rid of," she hissed. "You want me safe, you can damned well keep me safe yourself. And if you don't like that idea, you can just kiss my brown ass. How would you like that, Mr. High-and-Mighty Grayson?"

He didn't answer. Not unless you counted a suppressed roar as an answer.

A suppressed roar and the wildest, hottest kiss Daphanie Carter had ever experienced in her independent, adventurous life.

Eleven

Mating rituals among the Others vary as much as they do among humans—the modes and methods may change, but the end result is always very much the same.
—A Human Handbook to the Others, *Chapter Fifteen*

Asher thought his head might explode. Either one of them. It was a toss-up which would go first. With Daphanie Carter, the possibilities were simply endless.

He hadn't intended to kiss her again. In fact, he'd made a vow to himself stating exactly that. In spite of his conversation with Graham, or maybe because of it, he had come to realize how ill suited he and the human really were for each other. He might . . . harbor feelings for the woman, but he knew perfectly well that to act upon them any further would be folly.

As he had told the alpha, he had been more than five hundred years old when Daphanie was born. Part of being a Guardian was the ability to suspend aging. It would be difficult to battle demons and fiends and other assorted threats against humanity, after all, if one had to worry about advancing arthritis or the inevitable decline of muscle strength inherent in the aging process.

Once Guardians reached full maturity and took up their duties under the auspices of the Watcher, they ceased to age, remaining forever at the height of their physical powers for the entirety of their careers. Asher, then, could conceivably live, quite literally, forever. How was he supposed to reconcile that with loving a human? With watching her slowly fade, year after year, into old age, infirmity, and finally death?

If he were a vampire, he could share his immortality, and he knew that if that were his situation, he wouldn't hesitate to bind Daphanie to him for eternity. But he wasn't a vampire, and Daphanie had never said she wanted to be with him, let alone be with him forever.

When their lips met, he knew he didn't care.

She flowered beneath him, responding to the anger and frustration and desperation in his kiss as if she understood every nuance of the emotions. Instead of shrinking from him, shunning him for his aggressive ardor, she met it, pouring her own heat and passion into the embrace. Her arms lifted and clasped around his neck, her body bent and pressed against him, and her tongue tangled with his as if she could fit herself to him so securely, she could prevent ever coming dislodged.

Gods, how he wished that were possible.

His hands slid down her sides, yanking her even closer, adjusting her hips against his until she tilted her pelvis to provide a natural cradle for his arousal. He shuddered at the utter perfection of the fit and moved his hands behind her to cup the lush, firm cheeks of her ass in his palms.

She felt like heaven and tasted even better. He wrenched his lips from hers, ignoring her petulant whimper, and skimmed his mouth over the sharp angle of her cheekbone, the round curve of her face, and down the slender length of her throat. He drew hard on the smooth skin, taking her flesh in his teeth and testing its resiliency. She shuddered wildly in his arms, and he felt an instinctive kinship with every vampire in existence. He would have given anything for the ability to draw her inside, to consume her and feel her very essence sink deep into his bones.

He had never, ever, wanted a woman this badly. Wanted *anything* this badly.

Her head fell back on a whispered moan and for the second time in twelve hours, her legs twined around his hips and drew him closer to her heated center. This time he had no desire to fight it. This time, he used his grip on her bottom to help her, to lift her higher until the fly of his jeans rode tight against the sweatpants' seam between her legs. He even pressed himself home more securely and brought his mouth back to hers for another ravenous kiss.

He wanted to sink into her. He wanted to throw her to the paper-strewn floor and take her right here, right now, in a frenzy of need. He wanted to scoop her up and whisk her back to his home, to lay her out on his bed and feast on her for hours. He wanted anything and everything, and he feared he would lose his mind if he didn't get it. He needed to decide.

She decided for him.

With one hand, she cupped the back of his head, holding him to her as she continued to strip away his sanity with her hot, eager mouth. With the other, she traced a burning path down his chest and abdomen, inserting clever fingers between them until she could flick open the metal button at his waistband.

Pop.

He could have sworn he heard the disc jump free of the hole. His breath froze in his chest and he wrenched his mouth from hers again, this time not to taste her honey-sweet skin but to look into her eyes and see in them a desire as fierce as his own.

Pop.

The second button on his fly opened and the strength of his erection began to force the opening. Her gaze burned into his, brown irises nearly swallowed whole by yawning, black pupils.

Pop.

Another. One more and he'd be free. One more and she would be able to take him in her hand and bend him entirely to her will.

He almost couldn't bear the anticipation.

Pop.

His world distilled into that single sound.

Time froze, his breath stilled, his pounding heartbeat slowed to a sluggish, drawn-out thhhuuuh-thmmmp. A smile coasted across her lips, one lush millimeter at a time. Her hand moved just as slowly.

Her fingers closed around him like a revelation, slim and hot and unbearably eager. They pressed him into her palm and took him in an infinite instant from suspended yearning to instantaneous, breathless urgency. And she accompanied it with a low, wicked chuckle.

Asher growled in response.

To hell with his bed. To hell with any bed. He had to have her now. He had to get inside her before his heart gave under the strain. He had to get inside her before he went utterly, irredeemably mad.

His fingers flashed into action, tugging and tearing at her clothes, glorying in the sharp sound of rending fabric and the dewy warmth of smooth, flushed skin. She laughed again and stroked him, her palm sliding and squeezing from root to tip, drawing forth a bead of eager fluid. Her thumb swept across and rubbed the moisture into the head of his penis, sending every one of four thousand nerve endings screaming with the agony of pleasure.

She was trying to kill him. He had to have her before she succeeded.

He tipped her to the floor, remembering only at the last minute that she was human and fragile and managing to twist their bodies so that he landed beneath her, cushioning her fall. She barely blinked, just grabbed his waistband in both of her hands and yanked the stiff denim down over his hips. She stared down at him, her gaze hungry and intent, and he could swear it felt like a thousand volts of electricity coursing though his body.

He twisted again, this time bringing her beneath him. Rough hands stripped away the remaining scraps of cloth, leaving her bare and heated and reaching for him. How could he possibly deny her?

He roughly kneed her legs apart and settled into the cradle of her hips, hissing at the sensation of his shaft riding in the wet furrow between. Daphanie only lifted her knees higher until she could plant the soles of her feet against the top of his ass.

Damn, she bent like a gymnast, shifting and curving and twisting to fit every possible inch of skin against skin. He felt as if he were wearing her, and it still wasn't enough.

Using the leverage afforded her by the positioning of her legs, she braced herself against the bottoms of her feet and pushed against him, her hips nearly lifting both of them off the carpet of rough wool and paper. Asher slipped his arms under her knees, letting them rest in the crooks of his elbows as he braced his hands against the floor and rose above her.

It was time to stop playing games.

He saw her eyelids drift lower and bent his head. He grasped her lower lips between his teeth and nipped sharply. A warning. Her eyes flew open and he could see her register the intent in his gaze. Heat flared between them and she managed a short, jerky nod before he flexed his arms, pressing her knees higher. He held her pinned with his body and his gaze as he fit himself against her entrance and began to press forward.

Her breath caught in her throat, tangling on a moan and threatening to choke her. She kept her eyes open wide and locked with his, but he could see the strain of it on her brow. He knew her lids wanted to close, wanted to block out the distraction of sight in order to concentrate wholly on the miraculous pleasure of their joining. But Asher would not allow it. He wanted to see every nuance of the act reflected in her face. Even as her gaze went blind and unfocused, he could see how her pupils dilated further, opening wider and wider even as her body did the same.

She felt like bliss.

Her body closed around him like a soft, wet furnace, burning along every last inch of his flesh until he had sealed them completely together. Her sightless eyes stared up into his and he wished she could understand the excruciating, mindless pleasure it gave him to be inside her. Finally inside her.

He had waited for this since the dawn of time. No haven like this had ever existed, no place so hot and perfect and wholly, deeply his. He wanted to stay this way forever, locked together, united and complete.

But need laid a whip against his back and drove him recklessly onward.

He wasted no time with subtlety. There would be other chances for that, other opportunities to love her slowly, gently, to savor each shift of skin, each sigh and moan. Another time, he would be able to tease her with a slow, drawn-out rhythm, a slow, powerful tide gliding endlessly in and out of her tight, gripping warmth. But not now.

This time he balanced on the edge of madness and all he could do was race closer to the precipice, driving her ruthlessly on before him.

He withdrew from her in a sharp, ruthless move that left her crying out his name. A quick twist of his hips, a press of his shoulders, and she opened wider, lifted her hips higher to bring him back in line with her aching need. He paused for the space of a ragged breath.

Two.

Three.

And just as her lips began to tremble on the verge of begging, he threw himself forward. Into her. Into passion. Into a pounding, driving rhythm that had nothing to do with tenderness and everything to do with desire.

Daphanie sobbed and gripped his shoulders. He could

feel her muscles straining beneath him, feel her short, neat fingernails digging hard into his flesh, looking for some kind of grip to steady herself against his ruthless hunger. He had her bent nearly doubled back on herself, offering her no leverage, no power, no choice but to submit, to allow him to take her in whatever way he chose.

His demons chose to be ruthless.

Her breath tore from her throat on short, raw cries, too muffled for screams, too sharp for moans. Her hands slipped against him as sweat beaded on her skin and his, and her whole body rocked and quivered, trapped between his unyielding body and the unyielding floor.

Something inside him screamed at him to stop. He was too rough, too bestial. He was hurting her. She was fragile, sweet, human. She deserved better than this. She deserved to be made love to, not ravaged on the floor in a red-hazed fury of lust. The internal voice nagged at him persistently, protesting every time he thrust himself forcefully into her tender, swollen body.

But conscience didn't stand a chance against the heat and glory of frantic, animalistic sex.

At least he knew she wouldn't have to suffer his attentions for long. Already he could feel pleasure rising, heat and tension gathering low in his spine, at the nape of his neck, at the base of his balls. He could feel himself approaching flashpoint and could feel his woman shaking and sobbing beneath him. He needed her with him.

With a low snarl, he adjusted his hands for better leverage and hunched his back, shifting the angle of his penetration until he could feel the head of his penis riding hard against her internal walls on each brutal stroke.

She choked on a scream, neck arching, head snapping back until she broke their shared gaze and struggled frantically simply to draw breath. Asher swore graphically and shifted. He grabbed the back of her head, his fingers tangling in her hair as he forced her face back to his. Her leg slipped up over his shoulder, sending him a fraction of an inch deeper, and the added sensation threw her over.

She screamed and sobbed, her eyes wide and fixed on his, her consciousness clearly elsewhere, focused entirely on the fierce internal contractions milking his cock. She squirmed, trying to get away from him, to escape the continued assault of his brutal thrusting against agonizingly sensitive flesh. He pinned her in place and only moved faster, increasing the pace until he thought his heart would explode from the strain of holding back his climax.

He didn't want to come. He didn't want to stop moving, stop claiming her, stop forcing her to physically acknowledge the intensity of what lay between them. His body, however, reminded him that in the end he was only a man.

Her tight, spasming heat finally overcame him. His head tipped back on a roar, every muscle tensing, threatening to snap his body in two as he poured himself helplessly inside her.

His last thought, before he collapsed on her in a sweaty, inconsiderate heap, was that the decision had clearly been taken out of his hands. It was no longer a matter of whether or not he should allow Daphanie Carter a place in his life.

She had already taken up residence in his heart.

Twelve

Psychic phenomena, it is important to realize, have no direct link to the Others. While some species of Others might possess talents of a psychical nature, it is equally true that humans may be born with—or even, in rare cases, acquire—similar gifts. Such abilities may include telepathy, clairvoyance, mind reading, telekinesis, psychometry, mediumship, precognition, and many other fascinating skills.

It is also interesting to note that while humans have been forced by the Unveiling to accept the presence of supernatural creatures in the world, some remain reluctant to acknowledge the possibility of ordinary humans with supernatural abilities.

—A Human Handbook to the Others, *Chapter Nineteen*

It took at least an hour for Daphanie's heart to start beating again, and another few minutes for Asher to get her settled comfortably, if limply, in the center of his big, wooden bed. She barely remembered the trip from Niecie's apartment. She felt a twinge of dread wondering if he meant to have another go at her, because she was fairly certain a second round would have killed her, but thankfully he simply climbed onto the mattress beside her and gathered her to him until she slept.

She slept deeply, waking only once after several hours when she felt his warm length shift away from her and slide from the bed. She must have made a sound of distress, because she had a dim awareness of him murmuring something against her ear, pressing a kiss to her forehead and ordering her back into sleep.

She had no trouble obeying.

It was too bad he didn't instruct her not to dream.

Again, she found herself in the now familiar tent in the woods, only this time she could see the old, stained canvas. Her eyes, this time, were open. She looked around the moderate space, noting the dozen people gathered around a long plank of wood near the tent's entry flap. The board had been balanced between a couple of logs to create a rough sort of table and piles of food and drink had been stacked atop it. People stood there, talking, laughing, eating, the air thick with a sense of anticipation.

She shivered, still unused to the cool of the night air. Back home, no one shivered in summer, unless they shivered in fear. Even in total darkness, back home the heat kept a body and soul together. She supposed she could have worn something different, put a heavy wool pelisse over her loose white blouse and skirt, but that would have restricted her movements, and a restricted woman couldn't dance. The colorful turban she had wound around her head would at least keep some of her heat in. And once the drums started beating, she knew she would never feel the cold.

At the other side of the tent stood the pé. She gazed at the altar with satisfaction, noting the flowers and candles, the jumble of beads, bells, amulets, stones, rattles, and even bits of precious money. Rum and food lay there, too, soon to be offered to the hungry loa.

She herself had provided the tobacco, traded with a white farmer in exchange for a taste of her black ass. She didn't count the cost. Sex, after all, was the readiest kind of coin she had, and the one she'd traded in the longest.

At the center of the peristyle, their temporary, secret hounfort, the center post doubled as the poteau mitan, because in trying times, compromises had to be made. Nearby, though, the fire already burned, and in her pocket, she felt the weight of the farine guinée *she would use to trace His* vévé *in the dirt. Tonight, she could call Him from the crossroads, and he would come to her. Once He came, he would give her His power and Manon Henri would live long enough to revenge those who had wronged her. She would live long enough to reclaim her rightful place as Queen of the new world, the most powerful mambo who had ever called the names of the ancestors.*

Manon Henri would live forever.

Daphanie woke almost gently this time. She didn't bolt upright in a panicked sweat, didn't feel her muscles twitching in response to the lingering beat of drums. This time there had been no drums. This time, the ritual hadn't yet started. She should feel relieved.

Instead, she felt chilled all the way down to her bones.

No fog followed her into consciousness this time. Her mind was clear, her senses sharp, and her soul weighed down with a black, oily film of evil.

Daphanie trembled and pulled the thick down duvet up around her ears as she stared into the dimness of the unfamiliar room. She knew exactly where she was; she remembered Asher carrying her here yesterday evening, after that ridiculous bout of sex on her sister's floor, but she had been too overwhelmed and too exhausted to make note of her surroundings.

Now she was too frightened.

She didn't want to move. Something inside of her screamed that if she moved, the spirit directing those movements would not be hers. If she moved, she suspected that her fingers would trace strange symbols on the walls and floor. Her feet would move in swift, stomping patterns across Asher's floor, and she would speak a strange kind of French, using words she had never heard during her year in Paris, or the weeks winding her way through the Languedoc. If she opened her mouth, her voice would call out a name she couldn't even bear to let her mind acknowledge.

Something, she knew, was very, very wrong.

Daphanie trembled, feeling suddenly and utterly alone. She strained to listen to the sounds of the quiet apartment, hoping to hear Asher's soft footfalls, or the rattling of dishes, or even the tinny voices of a television set in the other room. Nothing. The place was silent, eerily silent. A kind of silence that made her wonder hysterically if the dream had really ended, or if this was just another scene, another facet of the nightmare that had become nearly as familiar as her own name.

Daphanie Elizabeth Carter.

Manon Séraphine Henri.

Which one was she?

Which name was hers?

A hysterical giggle boiled in her throat.

God, she really was losing her mind. Not that it wasn't becoming a little crowded in there. Oh, she knew she was Daphanie. She knew her name and where she'd been born and where she grew up and who her parents were. She knew where she'd gone to school and who her friends were and what was the name of the President of the United States. She even knew what day it was.

But she also knew that in the back of her mind, something unfamiliar crouched. Something that hadn't been there before. Something she recognized but didn't want to engage with.

Something that scared the shit out of her.

The shrill ring of the telephone split the silence and made Daphanie jump. She contemplated yanking the covers up over her head and hiding, but she was afraid to be alone even in a soft, stifling cocoon.

She heard another ring and gritted her teeth. She didn't have to answer. After all, it wasn't her phone, and Asher must have some kind of voice mail service. But what if it was Asher calling her? She had no idea if he'd thought to bring along her cell phone when he'd carried her out of Danice's apartment.

Turning her head, she glanced warily at the bedside table. An old-fashioned desk phone in dignified black occupied one corner. She thought she could just reach it.

A third ring. Carefully, Daphanie snaked her hand along the sheets, keeping it under the covers for as long as possible before darting it out and snatching the receiver from the cradle. She tugged it beneath the duvet with her.

"Hello?"

"Daph?"

"Corinne?"

There was a brief pause. "Yeah, it's me," the woman said. "Sorry, you just sounded really weird for a minute."

Daphanie gave another short laugh. "Really? Imagine that."

"Daph, are you all right?"

"Oh, you could say that." Shifting the blankets to answer the phone had left a gap in the edge of her cocoon, and Daphanie shivered as a tendril of cool air reached her. "How did you know I was here?"

"At Asher's place?"

Daphanie hummed.

"He told me. I was with Missy when he stopped by to get Graham. On their way out, he told us that if we needed to reach you, to call his number. I thought I'd check and see if you wanted some company. We all heard about the apartment, so I thought you might need a distraction."

She frowned. "Why was Asher picking up Graham? Where did they go?"

"To talk to D'Abo." Corinne sounded surprised that Daphanie would ask. "Since you had to deal with the break-in yesterday instead of tracking him down, Asher said he wanted to take care of it this morning."

"Is it morning?"

"It's ten forty-five." Another pause. "Daphanie, are you sure you're okay? You don't sound right. Do you need me to come over there?"

Part of Daphanie wanted to say yes, to beg the ever confident, ever capable Corinne to burst through the door and come save her, but that was her cowardly voice. The rest of her knew that the only way to deal with the thing that scared her was to confront it head-on. Just a few more minutes under the covers and she would do it. She swore she would.

"No, don't bother," she said, trying to inject some confidence into her voice. "I'm fine. Just a little muzzy. I only woke up a few minutes ago."

"Really? Are you sick? I'll come over. I'll stop at Sarge's and pick up some matzo ball soup."

"I'm not sick, and you don't need to come over." Daphanie debated with herself for a minute and then decided it was better to know than not know. "You could do me a favor, though."

"What do you need?"

"Would you be willing to do a little more research for me?"

"Oh, honey, research is my middle name! My bread and butter. My raison d'être." She mangled the French while Daphanie tried not to wince. Not because of the pronunciation, but because of the memories of mangled French in her dreams. "In other words, be happy to."

"I, um, I heard a name that I wondered about. Like, maybe if it had any connection to this whole voodoo thing."

"Let me grab a pen." Papers rustled, then Corinne grunted. "Okay, lay it on me, my friend."

Daphanie gritted her teeth against the lingering taste of corruption and spat the name into the phone. "Manon Henri."

Silence met her revelation.

Daphanie felt her stomach flutter. "Corinne? Hello? Are you still there."

"Oh, I'm here," the other woman said on a stilted laugh. "You're kidding me, right? Manon Henri? I told you about her days ago."

"No you didn't."

"Yes I did," Corinne insisted. "When I gave you what I found on D'Abo. Manon Henri is the voodoo priestess who moved here from New Orleans and founded the temple D'Abo now runs. That's where you got her name, right?"

Daphanie only wished that were true.

"No, you never mentioned her name," she said. "You told me about how she founded D'Abo's temple, but we were too busy talking about him. You just kind of glossed over the woman."

"Then where did you hear her name?"

"In my dream."

Corinne swore. "Don't fuck with me, Daph. You'd have to have some kind of psychic thing going on to know something like that from a dream."

"Trust me, I'm pretty sure I'm not psychic, and I'm positive I'm not fucking with you. The dreams I've been having are about Manon Henri."

"This is too weird."

Daphanie snorted. "Tell me about it."

"Shit. I already told you what I know about Henri, Daph. She came here from Louisiana around 1795, she founded a voodoo temple with an official start date of 1797, she died. Fast-forward a couple hundred-plus years and in comes D'Abo. That's the story."

"Which is why I need you to dig deeper. Why did she end up in New York? What kind of person was she? How old was she when she died, and how did it happen? How well-known was she in Manhattan, and what did she do while she lived here?"

"Just the basic outline then," Corinne quipped.

"I know it's asking a lot, but it's . . ." She sighed. "I can't tell you why, but I just have a feeling that for some reason, she's important to what's going on."

"Despite having been dead since before the Civil War."

"Despite that."

"All right," Corinne agreed. "Give me some time, and I'll see what I can find out."

"Thanks. I appreciate it."

When she hung up, Daphanie spent several minutes staring at the phone and remembering the scene in her dreams. She had meant what she told her friend. Somehow, Manon Henri was the key to this whole mess, Manon and the dream.

Now if only Asher would come back so she could tell him all about it. Or so *he* could make *her* forget all about it. At the moment, Daphanie didn't think she could afford to be picky.

Thirteen

There exists a curious similarity in the role that reputation and perception play in the social hierarchies of both the human and the Other world. Obviously, the perception of an alpha's power governs his ability to hold onto his position within the pack in the same way that a politician's efficacy or moral authority can govern his ability to hold onto his office.

In no other group, however, does reputation and perceived power seem to have a greater positive or negative effect than among magic users (i.e., witches, sorcerers, voodoo priest/-esses, summoners, etc.). In fact, there is some speculation among outsiders (magic users being by and large notoriously secretive and insular) that the level of fear and respect accorded to a magical practitioner may actually enhance or diminish that person's natural power.

—A Human Handbook to the Others, *Chapter Seven*

The jingle of the bell perched atop the door announced Asher's entrance into the small retail space. The scent of herbs and incense immediately greeted him, and behind him, Graham gave a small, choked cough.

"La Société de Bon Anges, Charles D'Abo, *houngan*

& prop.," just off Delancy Street, turned out to be quite stark and sparsely stocked compared to what Asher had expected. The interior and shelves had all been painted white, and most of the shelves were pushed back against the walls on three sides of the modest room. Books, candles, decorative items, stones, poppets, and bundles of herbs took up most of the display space, lending small bits of color and interest.

On the right side of the room, a nicked and worn-looking glass counter ran most of the length of the space, with the shelves behind it stacked with uniform, clear glass jars, each bearing a neatly hand-printed label in black marker on white paper. The jars appeared to contain various amounts of herbs, spices, and resins, presumably for magical rather than culinary purposes. Inside the counter, two shelves offered up a variety of jewelry, baubles, magical tools, and small colored cloth bags.

Opposite the counter, two ancient chairs with worn and faded cushions flanked a low round table about eighteen inches across. In one of the chairs, a young Latina woman sat poring over a book. She looked up when the men entered and offered a blank and expressionless stare.

"Can I help you?" she asked in a voice devoid of either interest or enthusiasm.

"I'd like to see Charles D'Abo," Asher informed her.

"Sorry, you can't."

She bent her head back to her book.

Behind him, Graham snickered softly. Asher sent him a glare, mostly out of a sense of obligation, because he understood the sentiment. She hadn't sounded very sorry at all.

Still, Asher wasn't in the habit of allowing himself to be dismissed by rude human teenagers (O the redundancy!). He leaned forward and adopted a more menacing stare.

"I want to see D'Abo. Now."

This time when she looked up, the girl blinked. But she still shook her head. "H-he's not here," she stammered.

He dug for patience. "When will he be back?"

"N-no, I mean, he's not here. At all." She swallowed. "He never came in today. No one's seen him."

This time, when Asher frowned, it wasn't for effect. What did she mean, no one had seen him?

"Did you expect him to come in?"

"Sure. He comes in every day. Even when the store's not open, he at least goes to the *hounfort* to work. He's a very busy man, you know, and very powerful. Someone is always seeking him out for advice or magic or to learn the ways of the *société*."

"She sounds like a damned recruitment poster," Graham murmured behind Asher's back. "Is this a temple or a cult?"

"Does there have to be a difference?"

Asher agreed that the shopgirl sounded as if she'd memorized her answer from a proselytistic tract, but at least her eyes weren't empty. She had the look of a true believer rather than a zombie minion.

"Has anyone tried getting in touch with him? Called him at home, gone to see him?" he asked her.

"I tried calling the number on the side of the register." She waved at the counter and the ancient electronic cash register perched on top. "But no one answered. No one in back seemed to know where he was, either, but they told me not to worry. They said he has been under a lot of stress lately, with almost constant attacks from his enemies. He probably stayed home to rest."

Asher could only assume that "in back" referred to the *hounfort,* the home of the temple where private ceremonies, rituals, and magics were performed. It surprised him that no one in the whole building knew where D'Abo was.

It also irritated him. He wanted to know where the man was at all times so he could ensure Daphanie's protection.

"Wow, brainwashed *and* dumb as a brick," Graham muttered under his breath. "If that's a sample of the caliber of the man's followers, I say we leave him to his own devices. With stupid like that, this group's gotta be its own worst enemy."

The shopgirl appeared not to hear.

Asher was hard-pressed not to agree.

"But did anyone go to check on him?" he persisted. The last thing he wanted was an unaccounted for D'Abo. If the man had changed his routine or gone underground, he might have done so in order to concentrate on his plans for Daphanie.

"No."

"I feel the need to apologize to bricks."

Asher ignored the alpha. Personally, he couldn't decide if she was a victim of stupidity or a terminal lack of personality.

"Then give me his home address," he ordered. "*I* will go and check on him."

The girl blinked. "Oh. No, I don't think I can do that."

He tried a glower. "Why. Not."

She shrank back a little, but she didn't change her answer. "Because. That might make the *houngan* angry. I wouldn't want to make him angry."

Asher leaned down, trapping her against the back of her chair. He gave her a moment to absorb his presence, then asked, very, very softly, "Do you want to make *me* angry?"

The girl squeaked in terror.

Graham laid a hand on his shoulder. "Back off before her head explodes."

Asher shot him a killing glare.

"You're not getting anywhere," the alpha pointed out, "and I just got a text message from Rafe." He waggled his cell phone under the other man's nose. "He wants us to meet him back at the club *tout de suite*."

Asher straightened slowly, barely noticing when the girl's eyes rolled back in her head and she slid bonelessly out of her chair and onto the floor.

"Why?" he demanded.

Graham rolled his eyes. "How much information do you think he packed into a text message? Let's get out of here so we can find out."

"I took the liberty of asking an acquaintance to look around the Callahans' apartment," Rafe informed them when they had gathered in Graham's office on the ground floor at Vircolac. "I thought he might be able to find some clue as to the identity of the burglars and their motive for striking."

"Didn't we already know that?" Graham asked. He sat behind his desk, his legs outstretched and his booted feet propped on the cluttered surface. He also kept a weather eye on the open door to ensure his secretary didn't catch him at it. "It was D'Abo and his minions and they were looking for something he could use against Daphanie. Something to strengthen the curse he put on her."

"Ah, but if it was D'Abo looking for something to use against Daphanie, why was nothing taken?"

"Do we know for sure nothing was?" Asher demanded. "When I asked her if she could see anything missing, she said no, but she was hardly in a state to swear to it. She was too shaken up."

"Perhaps that is true, but I suspect her first inclination will prove to be correct. It would have been much easier to remove a small item belonging to Daphanie and slip out of the apartment unnoticed. Exerting that sort of destructive effort seems excessive."

"Unless they did it to scare her. If that was their goal, I can vouch for their success." Asher's hands clenched into fists on his lap. He would never forget the look on Daphanie's face when she first glimpsed the chaos in the apartment. She had looked so lost. Hurt. It made him want to hurt whoever had given her that look. Hurt them until she smiled.

That she wasn't the type to smile at another's pain didn't really matter to him. It would make *him* smile.

"Do you think that was the goal?" Graham asked. "I got a glimpse of the place, and you're right that it looks like it cost someone a lot of trouble. That wasn't five minutes' work. Whoever was in there took his time about it."

Rafe nodded. "I think it was part of the objective, yes. But I believe there was more to it. I don't believe the intruder was there looking for an item of Daphanie's clothing. I believe he went there for *her*."

Asher went blank.

Graham's feet thumped onto the floor and he leaned forward in his chair. "You think D'Abo went there to try to get to Daphanie directly?"

"Is that not what you would do?" Rafe asked. "If you had a desire to seek revenge on someone, would you break into her home to grab a hair ribbon in hopes of causing her some magical distress? Or would you hope to grab the enemy herself?"

"Of course I'd go after her," Graham said. "But I'm Lupine, not some kind of witch doctor. I don't believe in wasting time on this sort of thing."

"What man does?"

Asher stood so fast, his chair toppled backward, crashing to the floor with a reverberating thump. "I have to get back to my place. I left her there alone. I thought she'd be safe because of the wards, but her sister's apartment was warded, too, and that didn't stop them there."

Rafe rose and stepped into the Guardian's path. "Relax, my friend. I have already seen to your woman. I posted guards at the door to your home as well as on all the streets leading up to it. She is well protected."

"By whom? What kind of guards? Are they any good?"

The Felix's mouth quirked. "Ask Winters. They come from his security force."

Graham rolled his eyes. "Of course they do. Hey, my pack is your pack, compadre. Feel free to reassign my guards anywhere you like. In fact, why don't you just give them all the month off with pay? Clearly, I can foot the bill and deal with the inconvenience."

"It is unbecoming of you to whine," Rafe said. "You were unfortunately away from your office when I realized precautions needed to be taken." He paused and grinned. "If it's any consolation, I consulted with your wife before I spoke with Logan, and she gave me her blessing to make whatever use of your security that I needed."

"Yeah, I feel so much better now," the Lupine grumbled.

"Feel free to take it up with her."

Asher relaxed just a fraction at the news that Logan Hunter headed up Daphanie's guard. He didn't know the Lupine well, but he did know that he held the position of beta to the Silverback Clan and chief of security for Vircolac and the pack's other, more private, concerns. If Asher couldn't personally be with Daphanie, at least he could trust Hunter to protect her with his life.

Rafe turned back to Asher. "Rest assured, I would never take risks with another man's mate, Guardian. She is as safe as we can make her. For the moment."

"But we need to make her safer."

"Exactly. In my opinion, the only way to make her wholly safe is to remove the threat against her."

"That's what we were planning to do," Graham said.

"That's what we went over to D'Abo's temple to do—to remove him. Only it turns out the bastard wasn't there."

"And no one seemed to know where he's gone. I tried to get the address of his home out of one of his minions, but she refused. I was unable to press her further because Graham interrupted to tell me you'd texted."

The alpha snorted. "You were unable to press her further because you'd already pressed her so hard she passed out. When we left the shop, she was drooling on the linoleum."

Asher shrugged. He didn't much care about details.

"I admit, I am not surprised to hear that," Rafe mused. "I suspected he might prove hard to find after I heard of what my acquaintance found at the Callahans' apartment."

Asher sharpened. "Why? What did he find?"

"He found this." Rafe reached into the pocket of his trousers and came out with a string of large beads carved from a variety of different woods, ranging in color from the pale cream of maple to the violet of purpleheart and the dark brown of walnut.

"I recognize it. It's D'Abo's." Asher frowned, an uneasy feeling needling him. "He wore it at the club the night he and Daphanie had their confrontation."

Graham snorted. "It must have fallen off while he was ransacking the apartment, and he didn't notice. Very clumsy of him."

Rafe pursed his lips. "I suppose that is a possibility. A *slim* one. But I do not think that is what happened."

Asher reached out and took the necklace from the Felix. He examined it closely, stretching the circle around his spread fingers. Still that sense of wrongness prodded at him.

"Where did he find it?" he asked, glancing up to meet Rafe's sharp, golden eyes.

"On the living room floor, just to the left of the entrance. A sheet of paper lay half over it, but it wasn't hard to spot. He found it just like that." Rafe nodded to the piece significantly.

"Just like this . . . ?" Asher repeated, rolling the words over in his mind while he stared at the unbroken circle of beads. It took only a few seconds, and he swore like a dockhand.

Rafe nodded. "This is what I said when he handed it to me."

Graham just looked confused. "What? Have the two of you developed a secret language? What the hell are you talking about?"

"Rafe's . . . acquaintance found it *just like this,*" Asher repeated, holding the necklace aloft. "Look at this part right there. There's a clasp on it. The necklace isn't big enough for D'Abo to pull on and off over his swollen head. He has to put it on by fastening and unfastening the clasp. And the clasp is fastened. There's no way this necklace just fell off of anyone."

The light dawned in the alpha's face. "Holy shit. So that means someone left it in the apartment on purpose."

"Planted it," Rafe said firmly. "Someone deliberately planted the necklace so that we would assume D'Abo had been the one who was there, the one who ransacked the place."

"Okay, that part I get, but why bother? Who else were we going to think did it? No one but D'Abo has any reason to want to harm Daphanie." Graham looked at Asher.

"And yet D'Abo is missing."

Rafe nodded, his eyes glinting. "Exactly. I think someone is deliberately trying to confuse us. Whether it is D'Abo or someone else, and I begin to lean toward the idea of someone else at least playing a role, our adversary wants to ensure that our little mystery remains a puzzle to us."

"He can want whatever he damned well pleases." Asher balled the necklace up in his fist and shoved it into the pocket of his coat. "I intend to find out what's going on and put a stop to it. For Daphanie's sake."

Fourteen

If there is one generalization that can be applied to the Others in regards to the relations between the sexes, it is that Other men have never made the mistake of underestimating the power of a woman.

It is likely the reason they were not wiped out centuries ago.

—A Human Handbook to the Others, *Chapter Two*

Daphanie took the news with surprising calm, more than Asher expected he had exhibited. She just curled her fingers around the cup of tea she had poured for herself and watched him with bruised eyes. She hadn't slept as well as he'd hoped she would. In fact, she looked like she hadn't slept in days.

"If it's not D'Abo who laid this curse on me, who could it be?" she asked.

She looked like a child curling up on the bench at the table in his breakfast nook, her feet tucked beneath her and another pair of ill-fitting sweats clothing her. This time they were his and both shirt and pants bagged on her hopelessly, despite her having rolled up hem and cuffs half a dozen times each.

"I think I can safely say that I don't make a habit of pissing off people with magical powers." Her lips curved at her own humor, but the expression didn't reach her eyes.

"Of course you don't," he said, reaching out to seize one of her hands, tangling her finger with his. They felt cold in spite of the warmth of the tea. "You're not the one who caused this, and whoever is behind it, we're going to find them, and we're going to stop them. Understand?"

She nodded, and her smile this time was almost genuine. She lifted their joined hands to her mouth and kissed the back of his knuckles. By the time she lowered them back to the table, the smile was gone.

She was beginning to worry him. During this past week, he'd seen the shadows beneath her eyes begin to bloom and her skin grow a little paler, but he'd put it down to her not sleeping well. After all, it couldn't be easy to rest when he knew she continued to have the dream of the ritual in the firelit tent. That was why he'd left her sleeping when he went out to seek D'Abo. He'd wanted her to regain a little of her energy, hoping it would make her feel more like herself.

It hadn't worked.

He squeezed her hand. "You look tired. Do you want to take a nap?"

She eyed him over the rim of her cup. "I suppose that depends."

"On what?"

"On whether 'nap' is a euphemism."

He chuckled. "And if it's not?"

"Then I'm not interested."

He scooped her up and settled her on his lap, tea and all, bending to press a kiss to her forehead.

She scowled up at him. "Cut it out."

"Cut what out? Kissing you?"

"Kissing me like that. I'm not a child, and I'm not fragile. You can stop treating me like I'm going to break if you touch me the wrong way."

He bit back the urge to tell her he feared exactly that. Had she looked at herself in the mirror today?

"Did I treat you like I was afraid to break you last night?" he asked instead, his voice dropping to an intimate rumble.

The smile that bloomed across her face almost took his breath away. "No, you didn't," she purred, leaning against him. "And it was wonnnderful."

He chuckled. He'd given himself a few tense moments last night, thinking he might have hurt her, in spite of the obvious pleasure she'd taken in their joining. It felt good to hear she'd enjoyed it.

"Now if *that* was what you meant by napping . . ." She leaned up to nip at the end of his chin, her quick tongue soothing the minor sting. "In that case, I would be very interested."

Asher glanced down at her, seeing the light flush desire had brought to her cheeks and feeling a surge of mingled relief and tenderness. Gently, he plucked the mug from her grasp and set it aside.

"It wasn't quite what I meant," he murmured, gathering her closer and brushing his lips gently once, twice, across hers. "But I think I should be able to come up with something to interest you more than sleeping."

She purred her agreement against his throat and let him lift and carry her through to the bedroom.

Last night, he had tripped Daphanie and beat her to the floor—literally. But tonight, he had something else in mind.

He set her gently on her feet beside his bed. The sheets were still rumpled from when she'd risen late that morning, but he had more interesting things to think about than her housekeeping habits. Like the warm, slumberous look in her dark eyes, or the pink flush of desire climbing up from the neck of her borrowed sweatshirt, heating her skin.

In silence, he stripped her of her clothes, leaving the garments crumpled on the floor as he lifted her and placed her gently in the center of his mattress. He pulled the tangle of bedding aside, shoving them down to the foot of the bed with the duvet to give himself an unobstructed view of her naked body.

Her dusky skin glowed, all coffee-and-cream silk, against the navy cotton of his sheets. His eyes slid over her, slowly, hungrily, from her delicate toes—the nails painted a glittering bronze—up her surprisingly long legs to the neat tangle of dark curls between, over the gentle curve of her belly and the lush flare of her hips to the sweet, soft weight of her breasts. Her nipples tightened under his gaze, hardening to rosy brown points and making his mouth water for the taste of them. One more item he'd rushed past last night, and he added it to the list of things he meant to savor this time.

Raising his gaze to hers, he saw her tongue dart out to moisten her lips and felt his own curve in response.

Oh, yes, this time he had a very, very long list. And

he intended to accomplish every single item on it. Even if it took all night.

Daphanie shivered under her lover's gaze. Whether it was from the chill of being naked in the cool dark of his bedroom, or from the anticipation, she couldn't tell.

It didn't matter, anyway. Judging by the look in his eyes, Asher would warm her up soon enough.

She watched as he straightened and began to shed his own clothes, his eyes never leaving hers as he dealt with buttons and zippers. Last night they'd each been in too much of a hurry to spend much time looking at each other, but tonight Asher moved slowly, deliberately, and she was grateful for the opportunity it gave her to feast her eyes on his masculine beauty.

She'd never seen a man like him, not in all her thirty-one years. He could have modeled for a Renaissance sculpture, all hard planes, graceful lines, and lean, powerful muscle. Except for his sex. She couldn't imagine a fig leaf in the world that would serve to cover his impressive erection.

Free of confining fabrics, he joined her on the bed, crawling over her like some great jungle cat, straddling her thighs and settling back on his haunches so that she felt like nothing so much as a plate of delicacies spread out for his enjoyment. He certainly eyed her with an appropriate hunger.

"You're not touching me," she pointed out, her skin tingling in anticipation.

"Oh, but I'm making plans," he purred, smiling like a Cheshire cat. "I don't want to rush this. I want— No, I *need* to take my time."

She forced out a nervous laugh. "Fine, but I'm not getting any younger here."

Something dark and raw flickered behind his eyes, but it was gone before she could remark on it. Then he leaned forward and pressed his lips to hers and she couldn't remark on anything at all.

He kissed her unhurriedly—a new experience between them—his mouth settling over hers in degrees, warm and inquisitive. His lips nudged hers, searching for the perfect angle, and when he found it, she could feel him sigh against her.

She recognized that sigh. It was a breath of utter contentment, of perfect peace, and her soul echoed it in secret tones.

She tried to part her lips, to draw him deeper, but every time she attempted it, he drew back until their mouths barely touched, making her whimper in frustration until she realized that if she didn't press, if she let him set the pace, he would give her what she wanted.

What she needed.

Daphanie let herself sink back into the mattress and back into the kiss. Asher murmured his approval against her lips, his tongue darting out to trace the seam between them. She struggled not to hurry but to savor the teasing, ticklish caress. He repeated it a second time, a third, and then nudged her lips more firmly and invited them to part and allow him entrance.

He snuck in like a thief, soft and quiet and unexpected. She would have thought he would slide deep, let his tongue tangle with hers and steal the last coherent thoughts from her head; but instead, he dipped in only shallowly, exploring the inner surface of her lips, the tender skin just behind her upper teeth, the very tip of her tongue, all with a thoroughness that threatened to drive her mad. If he maintained this pace, morning would come and go and come again before she felt him inside her, and she knew her heart couldn't take that kind of torture.

She needed him now.

He must have sensed the fraying of her nerves, because he gave her just enough to have her head spinning and her heart leaping and an entire kaleidoscope of butterflies fluttering madly in her stomach. His tongue slid along hers in a slow, leisurely tangle just as he lowered his body to hers, pressing skin to skin all along the tense, shivering length of her.

She moaned aloud at the minute culmination. If she'd had the strength, she would have laughed at the idea that he could make such a simple, preliminary step in the act feel almost as intense as an orgasm. She recognized it as a talent, but when all this was over, she thought she would have to kill him for it.

At least now she could feel him. The heat of his big body warmed her, and she could feel the proof of his need pressing against her belly. Now, she could tell exactly how much he wanted her, how difficult it must be for him to seduce her so slowly, and she appreciated the strength of his resolve.

She also determined to break it by any means necessary.

Daphanie stretched beneath him, slowly, sensually. She pressed her softness against him, reminding him of the plump pillows of her breasts, the warm welcome of her thighs. She felt the answering stutter of his breath, the increased heat of his kiss, and gloried in it.

His hands traced her curves, and she wrapped her arms around his shoulders. By mutual accord their lips parted, his to trace a lazy path down her throat and over her breastbone, hers to whisper his name in a sweet rush of need.

His mouth slid over the curve of her breast to close around the peak, and she moaned a shivering sound of thanks. She rubbed her hands over the taut muscles of his back and shoulder, drawing him closer.

Her legs parted to twine with his and she realized as he slipped naturally between them that the sense of competition had dissolved in the sweet haze of togetherness. They each worked toward the same goal, the same end. She wanted to feel him become part of her; he wanted to make her a part of him. No one needed to win tonight, because there was no way either of them could lose.

He drew at her breast with strong, rhythmic pulls, but the pleasure of it didn't spur her to desperation; it settled over her in a glow of contentment. She tilted her hips, not to beg him to enter her, but to savor the knowledge that he would and to enjoy the feel of him, thick and heavy against her. She could love him this way all night. All day.

All her life.

Even as the thought slipped into her consciousness, he slipped into her body, as soft and easy as morning. He released her nipple and trailed his mouth across her chest to the other, curling his tongue around the neglected tip and drawing it inside. Daphanie crossed her ankles behind his back and drew him deeper.

They moved with a dreamy, thoughtful rhythm, not racing toward climax but gliding toward it, drifting like leaves on a current, content in the knowledge that pleasure waited for them, even as it encompassed them on the journey.

Daphanie shifted her hands and cupped his cheeks in her palms, drawing him away from her breast until she could press her lips once more to his.

The kiss tasted of communion, felt like a benediction. Asher tasted of tenderness and joy, affection and hunger. She poured the emotions back into him, even as her hips rose and fell to meet his easy rhythm.

The pleasure built not in waves or in increments, but as in the slow, steady trickle of water filling a vessel. Daphanie was the vessel, and in moments she felt the pleasure overflow into ecstasy.

She heard Asher groan, felt him go still above her, felt his muscles quiver and his heart stutter as he emptied himself inside her. A soft cry tore from her own lips, half sob, half clear, ringing note of joy.

Her last thought before she slipped into sleep was that if she really were going mad, she hoped that God would leave her this one memory to sustain her. She knew she could live on it for the rest of her life.

Fifteen

The number of professions occupied by Others in our society never ceases to amaze most humans, to wit . . . all of them. Name a human occupation and you will be guaranteed that an Other has performed it, and is likely performing it somewhere right this very minute. Others are and have been doctors, lawyers, teachers, and clergy; artists, artisans, laborers, and servants. They have built buildings and composed symphonies, shoed horses and written novels.

You see, the desire to have a profession, a purpose, is one of those basic instincts that drives all sentient creatures. Why should the Others be an exception?

—A Human Handbook to the Others, *Chapter Two*

Daphanie woke feeling refreshed, even if she had the vague impression that the dream had visited her at least briefly during the night. She could discount that, because it had remained on the edges of her mind, kept at bay by the twin forces of exhaustion and Asher's warm body beside hers.

By the time she'd had a shower—made doubly

relaxing by the addition of playful, soapy sex—and wolfed down a surprisingly tasty omelet, she felt ready to take on the world. Or at least a few feet of iron pipe.

"If I don't get into the studio, I'm going to wind up pitching myself out a window," she warned Asher, conscious of the look of displeasure he'd donned when she'd brought up the idea. "I'm not the kind of person who can stand to sit around twiddling my thumbs and waiting for stuff to happen. I need to keep busy."

He did not appear sufficiently moved, so she tried another tactic.

"Besides which, I have orders to fill," she pressed. "I accounted for getting nothing done last week because of the wedding, but I was planning to be back at work yesterday. I can't let myself fall behind. It's not like I have a staff I can delegate to."

Guilt, she had always found, was a great motivator.

Asher gave in with a sigh, but he didn't bother to try looking happy about it. "Fine, but you're not going to spend any time in that studio alone. I'm coming with you. I'll give you four hours, but that's all I can spare. I have things of my own to do today."

What, did he have a Guardian clock he needed to punch?

"Eight," she insisted. This was her job they were talking about.

"Five."

"Seven," she wheedled, throwing him a cheeky grin. "And I'll throw in oral sex."

She thought she saw his mouth twitch.

"Six. And that's final." He pushed away from the

breakfast table and reached for her hand to accompany her to the door.

"Six," she agreed as she led the way out of the apartment. "Plus the oral sex."

"You drive a hard bargain."

If he thought she drove a hard bargain, he hadn't seen anything until he glimpsed her with a hammer.

When they got to the studio, she cleared off the one chair she kept for occasional exhausted collapses, pushed him into it and ordered him to stay there, out of her way. Then she fired up her furnace, stoked the forge, and set out to melt her troubles into malleable, white-hot iron.

Daphanie hadn't worked much in front of observers since college, but she found Asher's presence in her studio to be unobtrusive and surprisingly pleasant. He obeyed her by keeping out of the way, sticking to his chair and occasionally asking the kind of intelligent and concise questions she never minded answering. Otherwise, he occupied himself quietly with a book he pulled off her small shelf of reference materials. She found his choice interesting. Instead of paging though a technical manual on the workings of a forge or the fundamentals of a smith's craft, he chose a study of the blacksmith artists of West Africa's Mandé people. Like herself, he appeared less focused on *what* went into working metal and more concerned with the why.

It made her smile.

She smiled for a good two hours. It took nearly that long for the coke to heat to her satisfaction and for her to arrange the coal layers around it just the way she wanted them. The first fire in a new space was critical in her mind, and she wanted this one to be perfect.

When the coke glowed at just the right color and the heat blasting off the hearth made her think of the outer circles of hell, Daphanie reached for her tongs and thrust a short length of pipe into the forge.

God, she loved her work. She loved watching the cold, hard steel begin to stir like some magical creature previously frozen in place by an evil spell. She loved the way it began to color, like a blush creeping into its cheeks, the way it seemed to reach toward the hearth as heat stretched and expanded it. More than once she had ruined a piece and had had to start over because she got so caught up in the sight of the changing metal that she let it go past the workable state of orange-yellow and straight to nearly liquid white.

Today, she very consciously monitored herself along with the pipe, drawing it away from the forge and onto her anvil just as the edges of the glowing portion began to lighten from brilliant orange. She worked quickly to establish the basic shape for one of her organic candle holders. She used the hardy hole in the anvil to brace the hot end of the pipe and set her weight into the lever end, forcing the steel to bend in a short, fluid curve. As it cooled, she added a half twist, then deepened the curve before plunging the whole thing back into the forge to reheat.

She worked steadily for another hour, pausing occasionally to swipe her arm across her sweaty forehead or to chug from the bottle of water she kept ready on the worktable. The heat was ferocious, in spite of the high ceilings of the converted industrial space. Even with the industrial ventilation fans churning full blast, sucking hot air away from the forge as fast as they could manage, the heat was intimidating. The fans couldn't hope to keep up with the output of the glowing coke; all they could do was keep the temperature down far enough that it didn't threaten to scald the inside of her lungs when she stood waiting for the steel to heat and reheat.

The few friends who had ever asked to come and see Daphanie work had never asked more than once. Most people couldn't take the sweaty, dirty atmosphere of a working smithy, but Daphanie gloried in it. In her uniform of tank top and loose-fitting, lightweight trousers, she was in her element, and her element was fire.

She felt the glow from the hearth heating her cheek as she gripped the wolf jaw in her gloved hands and watched the half-formed candlestick slowly begin to glow red again. She could feel the sweat beading on her brow, sheening her cheeks, trickling down her nape despite the ruthlessly high, tight ponytail she always wore while she worked. For an instant, she remembered the heat of another fire on her skin and she dropped her tongs on a strangled gasp.

Asher reached her before the sound of the metal tongs bouncing off the brick of the forge and the concrete of the floor even had time to echo in the large space.

"What?" he demanded, his eyes and hands running swiftly over her. "What happened? Are you hurt? Did you burn yourself?"

Daphanie shook her head frantically. She opened her mouth and tried to tell him, but no sound came out.

Her muscles spasmed, jerking her in his grasp like a marionette, and she felt a surge of terror as a familiar, sickening haze began to blanket her mind.

No! she tried screaming, but the desperate cry remained trapped in her head. In the studio, the only sounds came from the forge and the fans and Asher urgently demanding to know what was wrong with her.

She didn't *know* what was wrong. It felt like she was being dragged bodily back into one of her dreams, but that was impossible; she wasn't sleeping. She was wide awake, perfectly alert and perfectly aware of her identity, her work, her lover watching over her in a vain attempt to keep her from harm. The dream wasn't supposed to come to her like this, wasn't supposed to *be able* to.

Daphanie's mind screamed those very words even as the haze clenched around her mind like a malevolent fist and dragged her consciousness beneath a thick, oily pool of black oblivion.

"Daphanie!"

Asher had never known terror like the sight of this woman convulsing in his arms. He gripped her above the elbows, watching helplessly as she shuddered. Her eyes rolled back in her head, the warm brown disappearing and leaving behind only blank, eerie whiteness. Her head snapped back so hard he thought he heard a tendon ping like a rubber band, pulled and released too quickly.

"Daphanie, wake up! Do you hear me, Daph? Snap out of this!"

He shook her, too afraid to be gentle, but she took no notice anyway. She flopped in his arms like a rag doll, and he felt his heart squeeze in his chest until it had no more room to beat. What the hell was happening here?

He lifted her clear of the floor and began to carry her to the chair he'd just jumped out of. He'd left his jacket there with his cell phone in the pocket. All he could think to do now was set her down and call 911. That's what you were supposed to do when a human had a seizure, right? Call emergency personnel, rush to the hospital, and wait while modern medicine and pharmacology made everything all right again.

That was the way this worked, wasn't it?

He made it barely two paces back to the huge carpenter's table when Daphanie's eyes flew open and she stiffened in his arms to the rigidity of a wood plank. For a long, tense moment she stared at him, her almond-shaped eyes drawn unnaturally wide with absolutely no sign of Daphanie discernible in their velvet brown depths.

Asher swore, his breath catching in his throat. Instead of Daphanie—warm, funny, fierce Daphanie—something cold and brutal stared out at him. His heart sank.

"Fils de putain!"

With a feral snarl, the Thing that wasn't Daphanie sprang at him, teeth snapping at his throat. The move took him by surprise, so much so that he almost didn't pull away in time. He'd expected a struggle to get free, not an immediate and lethal attack. He grunted and shoved the Thing away from him with enough force to send it slamming back into the side of the worktable.

The Thing barely paused to register the impact. It just hissed and screamed and launched itself at him again.

Shit, what the hell was he supposed to do now?

Asher darted to the side, flipping his arm out to catch the Thing in the chest and knock it onto the floor. It sprang up again like a damned Weeble, but this time it hesitated, giving Asher an actual second to think. One glance at the Thing's achingly familiar face was enough to tell him that Daphanie no longer occupied the shell facing him. Something else had taken her place, and that something wanted him dead. He had no trouble with the concept of defending himself, but he found he had a *lot* of problems with the idea of hurting Daphanie in the process, even if it was only her body and not the real her.

Damn it, he'd grown pretty frickin' fond of that body recently, and he wanted to see it given back to the soul it belonged with so he could express that fondness again.

He had to find a way to stop the Thing without permanently harming the woman he loved.

And wasn't it a fine time for his subconscious to let loose with that little bit of news?

The Thing and Asher eyed each other for several tense minutes, neither ready to make the first move. But Asher had love and patience on his side, and the Thing consisted of nothing but fury and hate. In the end, it inevitably struck first.

Asher saw it before it happened, knew, from the way the Thing tensed, what was coming. He betrayed not a flicker of surprise when the Thing shot a hand out behind it, grabbed a solid length of pipe from the pile on the table, and held it aloft as it threw itself at its enemy's head.

Asher's hand shot up, his fingers wrapping around

the creature's wrist and preventing the blow from falling. His arm trembled, making him blink. He hadn't expected the Thing to be so strong. Daphanie was far from weak for a human, but she was only human, and a woman; the Thing that had taken over her body possessed easily three times the strength to go with its burning malevolence. Asher actually had to exert himself to keep the pipe from splitting open his skull.

Enough. He had to get this under control before one of them got hurt. If it was him, he wouldn't live to tell about it; and if it was Daphanie, he wouldn't *want* to live. It was time to get this done.

With a grunt, Asher straightened his spine and flexed his shoulders, feeling the blades shift and bend to make room for what was to come. He felt the unpleasant pull of skin splitting and the burning sensation of his wings emerging from his back, the muscles and tendons cramped from disuse. It always felt like waking a sleeping limb to free his wings after he'd kept them hidden. The appendages prickled and burned as he spread them and gave one sharp flap to get the blood circulating.

Then he gripped the Thing by the throat with his free hand and lifted them both from the studio floor.

The Thing within Daphanie hissed and struggled, but Asher's grip compressed her windpipe, slowly cutting off its supply of oxygen. He clenched his teeth at the sight of his woman struggling for air. He wanted to release her or soothe her or breathe for her, but instead he continued to squeeze, exerting very careful pressure until the Thing dropped the pipe to claw at the hand around its throat. Asher heard the clang of the metal hitting the floor and eased his grip just enough for the Thing to draw breath.

Then, before it could recover enough to go for him again, he shifted his grip to compress her carotid artery until Daphanie's body went limp against him.

Asher returned them to the floor with a thump, pressing Daphanie against his chest with one arm and reaching for his cell phone with the other.

Damn it, that was the second time he'd had to knock his woman unconscious. If it came down to a third, he was going to get very cranky.

Sixteen

Common signs of possession include speaking in tongues (i.e., any language not known by the victim in life); feats of unnatural strength; unnatural signs of aggression; violence toward close friends, family members, spouses, or children; rapid, drastic, and unexplained changes in core physical appearance (eye color, facial features, skin color, or condition), and the occurrence of unexplained phenomena in the victim's presence.

To quote one expert on the phenomenon, "There are a lot of things to look for, but when it comes right down to it, you just know it when you see it."

—A Human Handbook to the Others, *Glossary*

Rafe and Graham took the news calmly, but with a good deal of obvious unease. Asher couldn't blame them. This time he might have phoned a warning, but it was the second time he'd carried the same unconscious woman into the alpha's house in less than a week. She had regained consciousness once, only briefly, long enough to open her eyes and gaze unseeingly up at her concerned friends. Asher had been relieved not to see the malevolent force that had last occupied her gaze, but frightened not to see any sign of Daphanie, either.

Missy sprang immediately into action, tucking Daphanie's still unconscious form into the same bed she'd occupied a few days before and sitting vigil by her side while they waited for Erica's return.

The witch took one look at the insensible woman and grasped the silver amulet she wore around her neck.

"This isn't good," she whispered.

Asher resisted the urge to mention that he'd already figured out as much.

"We need to know exactly where we stand, Erica," Rafe said, his tone as grim as Asher felt. "What's happened to her?"

Erica laid a hand across Daphanie's forehead. Asher already knew the skin felt clammy and feverish and that she seemed to quiver constantly, a sort of low vibration, like a tuning fork run amok.

"It's much stronger than before, the curse. This has taken on characteristics that make it very nearly a form of possession."

"What is that supposed to mean?"

"Possession traditionally refers to a foreign entity taking up residence inside another person's body," the witch explained. "There are many forms of the phenomenon, from something as subtle as hearing a voice in the back of one's head to a host's complete psychic and physical transformation. But the form most people think of is one in which the foreign entity completely takes over the host's consciousness, basically assuming control of that person's thoughts, feelings, and actions."

"I'd say that's a pretty good description of what happened at the studio."

"Yes, but you said that when she stirred after you brought her into this house, she didn't renew her attack on you."

"No. She didn't renew anything. She just lay there. She opened her eyes, but it was as if she weren't there."

Truthfully, it had looked almost as if no one were there, and that scared Asher more than anything.

"Exactly. That's very significant," Erica said. "The type of total submersion of the host personality and the violent outburst you describe would normally be the hallmarks of a traditional possession, but we already know that what is affecting Ms. Carter is more akin to a curse."

"Do we know that for sure?" Missy asked. "Is it possible that we might have been mistaken before?"

Erica shook her head. "I don't believe so. I can feel the taint of the magic in her. It's definitely a power rather than an entity that is affecting her."

"What difference does that really make?" Asher asked. "Either way, some outside force is making her do things she wouldn't normally do."

"It makes a great deal of difference. Because it is a curse and not an entity possession, it won't be dispelled with an exorcism. If it were that easy, I would already have begun a ritual to drive the entity out. A curse is much more complicated, and a voodoo curse such as this one still requires that you find the *bokor* responsible for laying it and destroy whatever object he has attached to Ms. Carter's spirit."

Rafe's mouth tightened. "Believe me, Erica, we have

been working quite diligently to accomplish that very thing."

"Good, but you must work faster. I would say the good news is that she's fighting it, but a battle like this can cause almost as much harm as the possession itself, if it goes on too long."

"How long is too long?" Asher demanded.

Erica shrugged. "It's difficult to say. Such things depend on the individual. A weak person can be depleted in minutes; a strong one could last days."

"Daphanie is strong," Graham vowed, clapping a hand on Asher's shoulder. "You know she is."

He did. But then, the force possessing her was strong as well. The question was, which would prove stronger?

"What can we do?" Missy wanted to know. Always practical, she focused on Daphanie's immediate needs. Asher felt a rush of gratitude.

"Keep her warm. Keep her hydrated." Erica hesitated. "I wish I could offer something more, but none of my potions or protections can do anything with the curse as long as the _ouanga_—the power object—is still out there."

She left a subdued group behind her in the little guest room.

"I think our search for D'Abo just took on a new urgency," Graham murmured, his eyes fixed on Daphanie's still form.

"But what if Rafe is right and D'Abo isn't the one behind this but is being used as a dupe to throw us off the track?" Asher could barely speak, but he forced the words out from between clenched teeth. He felt helpless and hobbled, unable to save his woman, unsure he even understood *how* to save her. It made him want to rip something into pieces.

Small, bloody pieces.

"Even if I am right, I still believe finding D'Abo is our best chance to discover the identity of our mastermind," Rafe said. He turned a serious expression on Asher, and when he spoke again, his tone had taken on the solemnity of one speaking a vow. "We will find him, Asher. And when we do, we will see that he pays for what he is doing to your woman. You have my word."

Asher gave a small, viciously controlled nod. It never occurred to him to contradict the Felix's calling Daphanie "his woman." What point was there in denying the truth? Their relationship may have begun as one of a Guardian protecting a human, but he believed that the events of the night before demonstrated how far past that things had gotten.

He pushed the memories from his mind. If he let himself linger on the feel of Daphanie in his arms, he would be too distracted to do what needed to be done to keep her safe.

He looked at the Felix calmly. "How do we find him?"

"You and Graham have already been to his place of business without success, so I suggest we begin at his home."

"We tried to get his address from one of his employees, but no dice," Graham said. "I checked the phone directory and tried a few search sites online but no luck. D'Abo is apparently a man who values his privacy."

"Give me a moment."

Asher watched while the Felix drew a cell phone

from the pocket of his trousers, flipped it open, and punched in a number. "Hello, my friend. I will apologize in advance for my rudeness, but I'm feeling a bit pressed for time. I had hoped you would be able to provide me with a piece of information."

There was a brief pause. "Nothing so complicated. I need an address, a home address, for an individual with some concerns for privacy. Charles D'Abo."

Asher looked at Graham and raised an eyebrow. The alpha shrugged.

They both waited.

"Thank you, *compadre*. I owe you one." The Felix flipped the phone closed. "Four eighty-nine East Eleventh Street."

Asher just stared.

"Apartment three A," Rafe added helpfully.

"How did you do that?"

"I didn't. My friend did."

Graham cursed. "Misha. Damn it, I should have known."

"Yes, but I did, so all is well," Rafe said. "Dmitri Vidâme. There is no information he cannot get, except for that which he already has at his fingertips."

"And he got D'Abo's home address that quickly?" Asher asked in disbelief. Hell, if he'd known the information could be had in the space of seconds, he would have had it by now. There was more to the story than money, though he knew Vidâme had a lot of it. If not most of it. "That's impossible."

"Not for Misha," Graham said, his tone distinctly envious. "One of the hobbies he apparently picked up over the last thousand years—well, okay, the last thirty—was computer hacking. And it turned out he had a talent for it, plus enough money to buy the kind of machines that make the guys who run supercomputers turn a little green. I should have gone right to him. It would have saved us a lot of time."

"There is no point rehashing our decisions," Rafe said. He slid his phone back into his pocket and waved toward the door. "The important thing is that we act on the information now that we have it. Gentlemen?"

Asher held up a hand. "Just a minute."

Turning back to the bed, he nodded at Missy. "Would you be willing to stay with her until she wakes? I don't like that she's still unconscious, but I don't want to delay, either. If we were to miss a chance to find D'Abo . . ."

Missy smiled and shooed him away. "Don't worry. I'll take good care of her. You heard Erica; Daphanie is a fighter. I know she'll be fine. And I'll be with her when she wakes up. I'll tell her where you went. In the meantime, you just go find this D'Abo character and put a stop to this. It's the best thing you could do for her. For both of you."

"Thank you." Asher leaned down and pressed his lips to Daphanie's clammy forehead, tasting the salt of fevered sweat, even though her skin felt chilled through. It frightened him.

"I'll be back soon," he whispered, tucking a strand of hair behind her ear. "I promise."

Then he straightened, gave Missy a last brief look of thanks, and followed the others out of the room. He didn't care if he had to tear Manhattan down brick by bloody brick. He *would* find Charles D'Abo, and when he did, no power of man or Other would stop him from killing him.

That was another promise, one he made to himself.

"We should probably have a plan," Graham said as they stood outside the small condo building gazing up at the third-floor windows. "One that goes a little further than just knocking on the man's door, waiting until he answers, and then telling him to knock it off."

The sun had just begun to set, painting the block with alternating splashes of golden light and dusky shadow. Asher wished it would just go dark already. He was guessing that the designation "3A" indicated that D'Abo occupied the building's front apartment, which made it a lot trickier to go with his original inclination, which was to spread his wings, lift himself through the air, and launch himself through one of the available windows. He would have the man's throat in his hands in a matter of seconds. Less than a minute after that and it would all be over. Daphanie would be free of him, and of the bloody curse.

Provided that he and the others were incorrect in suspecting that someone else was involved in the curse laid on Daphanie.

Damn it, so much for his preferred plan.

"I agree that merely asking the man to desist from bothering Daphanie is unlikely to meet with success," Rafe agreed, jingling the change in his pockets as he gazed up at the façade of the building through narrowed eyes. "However, I have not yet discarded the idea of approaching him head-on with a brisk knock on his door."

"Come again?"

Rafe looked back at his companions. "At the moment, we find ourselves in a unique position. D'Abo is by all accounts an intelligent, if fatally arrogant, man. He knows that a large number of people in the community heard him make threats against a human woman at a club last week, but since then, Daphanie has not seen him, nor sensed his presence, and no one else has reported seeing him near her. Unless he is the figure behind the attacks, he should be completely unaware of their occurrence. That gives us the chance to gauge his reaction when we ask him if he is behind it."

"His reaction will be to deny it," Graham protested. "You pointed out that he's not an idiot, and besides, you're the head of the Council. He wouldn't admit it to you if he'd done anything."

"Yes, but you will be able to examine his expression, his mannerisms. Men often end up betraying themselves in the little things when they take it upon themselves to lie."

"What if he denies his involvement and he's telling the truth?"

"Then we play to a different advantage. We let him know that we believe someone may be framing D'Abo for the attacks. An innocent man would appreciate the warning and might be able to provide us with some idea of who could bear a grudge against him strong enough to make him want to share that theory. It is a win-win situation."

" 'This word . . . I do not think it means what you think it means,' " Graham quoted.

Asher couldn't help agreeing, for more reasons than that *The Princess Bride* was one of his favorite movies.

The alpha persisted. "You're forgetting about the third possibility. What happens if he is lying about not being involved, and we have reason to believe he is lying. Do we show our hand and expect him to experience a change of heart leading to a confession?"

"Of course not. If he is lying and we all agree that he is lying, then that casts matters in an entirely different light. If that turns out to be the case—"

Asher finished the thought. "If that turns out to be the case, I'll kill him."

Seventeen

Most Others possess senses infinitely superior to those of us humans. Vampires have acute night vision, naturally, and astonishingly good hearing. The sidhe of Faerie are said to have a sense of taste so acute that they can taste a drop of poison in a cask of wine. But it is usually shapeshifters who take the prize as the most well rounded of the super-sensers. Like their animal counterparts, most shifters have increased powers of hearing, sight, and smell. A famous story tells of how one particular Feline shifter in Lithuania smelled Napoleon's army coming before the French had even crossed the Vilnus.*

—A Human Handbook to the Others, *Chapter Four*

**Ed's note: Never mention this story to a Lupine shifter unless one is prepared to listen to an hours-long dissertation on the superiority of the Lupine over the Feline sense of smell.*
> —A Human Handbook to the Others, *Chapter Four, footnote*

As it turned out, D'Abo had nothing at all to say about Daphanie's troubles. It was hard for a man to speak when his tongue had been cut from his mouth.

Rafe and Graham had smelled the blood almost at the same time, before they had even reached the building's second-floor landing. Asher saw them stiffen and exchange glances, heard them curse, and watched them sprint halfway up the next flight of stairs before he knew what was happening. He continued in ignorance until he skidded to a halt behind the others and saw Rafe finesse the door open with his elegant hands and a set of stainless steel lock picks. Clearly there was more to the Felix than met the eye.

He saw the blood the instant the door swung wide. It would have been impossible to miss. The place looked like the set of a horror movie, one of the slasher flicks that owed less to the psychology of fear and more to the liberal application of corn syrup and red food dye. The apartment didn't smell like sugar, though.

It smelled like death.

The three men stepped inside and shut the door behind them. Better not to alert the neighbors or the police until they'd had a chance to look around. The human authorities would only complicate matters.

The apartment opened out of a compact entryway no more than three feet long, leading directly into a small living room. The white and exposed brick walls were decorated with an eclectic mix of African and European art, personal photographs, and ribbons and smears of cast-off blood.

Charles D'Abo lay on his back in the center of the floor, his legs resting on a printed black-and-white area rug and his torso on the gleaming, golden hardwood. His eyes were open and staring, his lips parted as if in a silent scream. Blood had spilled from each corner, leaving him with a macabre red smile painted nearly from ear to ear.

"We're late," Graham growled, his nostrils flaring as

he sorted through the mingled scents of blood, fear, and human waste. "The blood's cold. He's been dead for hours."

"I suspect since last night." Rafe crouched beside the body and examined it impassively. "The blood is congealed where it's puddled on the floor and the spots on his clothes are mostly dry."

Asher bit back a scream of frustration. Every step he'd taken in this thrice-damned mess had ended up being three steps behind, and now here was their best lead lying dead and silent on his living room floor. It made him want to kick something. He contemplated the body, but he thought Rafe or Graham might start to question his sanity if he went around assaulting the dead.

He assaulted the sofa instead.

"Fuck, *fuck*, *FUCK*!"

"My sentiments exactly," Graham said, his gaze flickering around the otherwise empty room.

"This is certainly not what I'd hoped for," Rafe admitted, pushing to his feet, "but I think that—"

"Wait." Graham held up a hand and his eyes narrowed. "There's something odd about this. Look around you. What *don't* you see?"

The other men frowned and reexamined their surroundings. The apartment appeared small, but comfortable, the decorating casual, the condition scrupulously neat. If it hadn't been for the body and the spattered blood, Asher might have called it immaculate. There was no clutter, no discarded drinking glasses, no knickknacks collecting dust. It could have been the apartment of a banker just as easily as that of a voodoo priest.

Asher cursed. "You're right. There's nothing here. The man would have to keep *something* in his apartment, wouldn't he? Especially something that vital."

Rafe threw up his hands. "All right, I give up. I don't see it. Metaphorically as well as literally. What are you talking about?"

"There's no magic here," Graham pointed out, gesturing to the one, lonely bookcase, its shelves packed quite unoriginally with books and two small but flourishing potted plants. "I don't see a single ritual tool. Not even a candle. Some of the art looks African, but it doesn't even look Afro-Caribbean. There's no personal altar, no charms, no voodoo dolls. Just a lot of empty space."

"In other words," Rafe mused, "it looks like the apartment of someone not really all that interested in voodoo."

"Exactly. It's barren of magical items. I'm certainly no voodoo priest, but I've been in the apartments of a handful of witches in my day, and more than one summoner. Every one of them had an altar for her personal use. Every one of them scattered candles around like they thought electricity was just a passing fad. Every one had at least one piece of art with a magical theme, and every *single* one of them had bits and pieces of their craft lying here and there among the rest of their belongings. But the best-known voodoo priest in Manhattan, a man who runs his own temple with more than a hundred active members, doesn't even have a biography of Marie Laveau on his bookshelf?"

Asher's lips tightened. "And he winds up dead in said apartment with his tongue cut out. Someone wanted to make an example of Charles D'Abo."

"Probably the same person who wanted us to believe that D'Abo was the man responsible for the break-in at Daphanie's sister's place."

Graham shook his head. "See, that's the part that doesn't make sense to me. Why go to the trouble of planting evidence of D'Abo's guilt, and then kill him? Why dispose of the cover he just established for himself?"

"Maybe D'Abo knew too much and was killed to ensure his silence," Rafe speculated.

"Hence the missing tongue? I don't buy it."

"And your theory?"

"What? I look like Sherlock Holmes to you?"

"There is always the possibility that the murder was unplanned," Asher said. "Maybe the killer didn't come here to kill D'Abo, but they had an argument and things got out of control."

"Out of control accounts for a dead body," Rafe allowed, "but not the removal of a man's tongue."

Asher stepped closer to the body and tilted his head to the side, considering its position and appearance. "Are you confident we can rule out some sort of magical motivation?"

Rafe hesitated, then shook his head. "I'd never claim to be confident about matters of magic. I don't know enough about any of it. The witches in this city have historically been reluctant to share their secrets with the rest of the Others."

Graham snorted. "The witches in this city have historically been reluctant to *associate* with the rest of the Others."

"I notice that did not prevent you from entering

several of their apartments over the years," the Felix
pointed out.

Graham grinned unrepentantly. "Hey, that was strictly
PM. Pre Missy."

Asher tuned out their banter. Not because it offended
him for the two men to express a sense of humor in
front of a dead man; Asher was a pragmatist who realized that humor made an effective coping mechanism
when finding oneself face-to-face with death, one he'd
used a time or two himself. But because his instincts
whispered that the body had more to tell them.

He paced a slow circle around the corpse, letting his
eyes drift over it from several different angles. In death,
Charles D'Abo lacked the energy that had made him such
an impressive figure in life. The last time they had met,
D'Abo had been healthy and arrogant and surrounded by
obsequious toadies ready to serve his every whim and
agree with his every pronouncement. Somehow the pride
that had made him so obnoxious had also served to make
him appear strong and vital and powerful.

Now, he just looked ordinary, like a million other
light-skinned black men struggling through late middle
age. Asher would have put his age at around sixty, perhaps a few years younger. His jowls had begun to sag
and his hair to thin. His barrel chest drew attention
from the fact that his belly hung over his waistband, and
his brightly patterned, African-inspired clothing had
hung loosely enough to conceal the fact that his legs
were almost spindly and covered with a map of dark
spider veins.

He really looked only slightly more like a voodoo
priest than Asher did, the Guardian decided.

Another step between the body and the sofa brought Asher even with the dead man's right shoulder. He paused to examine the way D'Abo's arm had been bent at the elbow, fingers curled toward the palm and turned down against the patterned rug. The black-and-white stripes framed the hand in stark contrast, their regularity broken only by a tip of white protruding less than half an inch in the vee between thumb and index finger.

Bending at the knees, Asher crouched beside the body and reached out to nudge the hand aside with the backs of two fingers. Beneath where it had lain sat a small piece of white paper folded twice to form a square not more than an inch across.

Graham and Rafe broke off their banter and stared.

"Well, I'll be damned," the alpha breathed. "I totally missed that."

"As did I," Rafe echoed. "What does it say?"

Asher shrugged, but his pulse raced and the skin between his shoulder blades itched the way it always did before something significant happened. He reached for the paper, his fingers jerking when a shrill beep reverberated in the quiet room.

"Sorry," Graham said, reaching into his pocket. "That's me."

He flipped open his cell phone and frowned at the screen for a second. When he looked up, his expression was inscrutable and his tone firm.

"Grab the paper and let's go," he ordered. "That was Missy. Daphanie is awake."

Eighteen

Zombies, rest assured, are a work of fiction, the stuff of Hollywood legend. At least, the ones you're thinking of are.

The type of zombie that exists in the real world is not a reanimated, rotting corpse with a taste for human flesh and warm brains; it is the product of a specialized form of necromantic magic practiced by a subset of voodoo priests known as bokor. *The* bokor *creates a zombie by driving a person's soul from his or her body using a combination of powerful spells and potions and imprisoning it in a secret location. The victim's body can then be controlled by the* bokor *and used as a mindless slave.*
—A Human Handbook to the Others, *Chapter Sixteen*

Daphanie woke with an aching head and a complete inability to move. She could breathe, she could hear and see and smell, and she could blink her eyes. Anything more was impossible.

Quite naturally, she panicked.

The first thing she did was scream, long and loud and in a key sharp enough to shatter glass, but the only sound in the room was the muffled tick of the grandfather clock in the hall and the slow, steady sigh of breathing, her own and someone else's. Every few minutes a quiet rustling would indicate the turn of a page in a book, so Daphanie knew she wasn't alone.

She tried to turn her head to see who was with her, but all the determined straining in the world shifted her not a fraction of an inch. She couldn't even make her eyes move and glance to the side. Her gaze remained fixed on the attractively plastered tray ceiling. Its blankness seemed to taunt her.

Panic welled again, and Daphanie beat it back. It hadn't done her any good the first time; she didn't see how it would help now. Panic never got anyone anywhere. She needed to think. What did she know?

From the calm quiet surrounding her, she knew no one else was aware of her situation. She had friends, after all, who would spring immediately into action if they had the faintest idea that something was wrong. Even now, one of them sat patiently at her bedside, passing the time by reading a book and waiting for Daphanie to waken and speak to her.

She inhaled deeply, or at least she tried. The breath came in at the same rate and the same depth as all the others, but by concentrating on it she thought she could smell a faint hint of vanilla. Missy always smelled like vanilla, as if she spent all her free time baking sugar cookies and frosting cupcakes. So Missy was the one reading beside the bed. She at least knew that.

She also knew from the ceiling and from the presence of her friend that she was back at the sprawling town house next to Vircolac. She'd woken up to that ceiling before, recently, when Asher had carried her to the alpha and luna's home after her attempted sexual assault. Since the last thing she remembered this time was being in her studio with Asher, she had to assume that there had been another . . . incident, and he'd carried her here again. She really wished that would stop happening.

Daphanie didn't have to be able to look around the room to know that Asher was not present. She would have felt him if he were. She had developed an acute awareness of him, always knowing when he was nearby, not from his scent or his heat or the feel of his gaze on her, but from the way every nerve in her body seemed to wake and flex and stretch itself in his presence. At the moment, her nerves lay quiet. No Asher.

What else did she know?

Reluctantly, Daphanie began to review the more disturbing information.

She knew that something had happened at the studio. The details eluded her, but she had the impression of her vision blurring, of a disturbingly familiar thick fog creeping over her consciousness. She remembered the feel of her tongs and hammer in her hands and the pleasure of working with hot steel and good company. She remembered the rush of fear when the fog had begun to descend. Fear and confusion that the familiar enemy would strike not in sleep but in the middle of an ordinary day. Then, abruptly, a thick shroud had blanketed her consciousness and she remembered nothing else.

Until she woke up now, frozen and helpless in her borrowed bed.

Once again, she fought to keep the terror from overwhelming her. It would be so easy to sink under the weight of her own fear, but that felt too much like giving in. She refused to do it. After a week of having her own mind and body hijacked by dreams and seizures and the whims of megalomaniacs with a penchant for playing with dolls, she had grown tired of being toyed with. Giving in to the panic would be just another example of the ways in which she no longer controlled her own consciousness. She'd be damned if she'd let that happen.

Of course, lying trapped and immobile did a pretty good impression of damnation. Daphanie couldn't imagine a more tormenting experience of hell.

Missy sighed softly and turned another page in her book. Daphanie concentrated on the reassuring knowledge of her presence to help her focus. While her friends were with her, she knew she had hope. They wouldn't let her stay like this forever. Even if she couldn't open her mouth and tell them what was going on, in a little while, Missy would check on her and realize that something was wrong. All Daphanie had to do was last until then.

She knew Asher would return soon, as well. His absence could only mean that he was out there working to save her. Even if he didn't know she had woken up paralyzed and frightened, he would be working to handle what he did know—that D'Abo had laid a spell on her, that the spell had caused strange dreams and even stranger losses of consciousness, that the witch doctor needed to be found and forced to lift the spell. And if Asher had to use excessive force, beatings, and physical abuse to make that happen, he would do it.

Daphanie even hoped he would enjoy it. At the moment, she'd love to indulge in a little physical violence of her own. She'd love to do anything that involved turning her head or flexing her little finger. She wanted to *move*.

Instead, she heard Missy do it. Her friend flipped her book closed with a soft thump and leaned forward in her chair. Daphanie could tell from the way the air shifted and the scent of vanilla momentarily intensified.

"Oh, good, you're awake," Missy said, and Daphanie could hear the relief and pleasure in her tone. "How are you feeling? Do you want a glass of water?"

More than she could possibly express, but of course, she couldn't express it. All she could do was lie there.

"Daphanie?" Missy prodded. "Are you okay?"

Not remotely, she answered. At least, she answered in her own mind.

"Daph?"

The first notes of concern entered the other woman's tone, and Daphanie felt like cheering.

"Daphanie, what's wrong? Why won't you look at me? Are you upset about something?"

She waited.

"Daphanie?" The last was louder, more urgent, and accompanied by Missy pushing out of her chair and bending over Daphanie's still form so that she stood directly in her friend's fixed line of sight.

Daphanie blinked in relief. She could see the worry that creased Missy's brow, and the concern in the blonde's soft gaze. Missy wasn't stupid. In another minute, two at the most, she would realize something was wrong. Then Daphanie could start to hope.

"Daph?" The luna tried one last time. When she got no response, she reached for a telephone on the bedside table and punched in a number. Daphanie couldn't see her, but she could hear it happening. She wanted to laugh with excitement.

When she heard more buttons being punched, Daphanie realized Missy was using a cell phone and tapping out a text message. Frustration tore at Daphanie's belly. She wanted to hear who the luna had contacted and listen to exactly what she said. Instead, the entire exchange took place in silence and Daphanie was robbed of even that small reassurance.

She heard the snick of the phone flipping shut and the clinking of glass. Water tumbled from one container into another, and a second later, Missy leaned over her again. The woman slipped an arm under Daphanie's shoulders and raised her slightly off the mattress. She felt the press of a tumbler against her mouth and a trickle of water across her parched lips.

She swallowed reflexively and with gratitude. She wanted to suck the water in like a thirsty camel, but even that small independence was denied her. All she could do was wait while Missy slowly tipped the contents of the glass into her mouth until it was empty. Daphanie longed to ask for more, but of course she couldn't.

She couldn't, she couldn't, she couldn't.

Couldn't was beginning to drive her a little bit crazy.

"Don't worry, honey," Daphanie heard, the words so quiet they barely qualified as a murmur. "Graham and Rafe and Asher will be back soon. You just rest. They'll be here in just a few minutes."

But Daphanie couldn't tell who Missy was trying to reassure—her unresponsive guest?

Or herself?

Months seemed to pass before Daphanie heard the crash of the front door banging into the wall behind it and the pounding of footsteps up the stairs. Unless she had seriously miscounted the last time she'd been on those stairs, whoever ran up them at that moment was taking at least two or three at a time.

When the bedroom door flew open and her nerves gave a shout of rejoicing, Daphanie knew it was Asher.

"Daphanie?" he demanded, his voice a low rasp. "Are you okay?"

She didn't answer.

Couldn't answer.

Goddammit.

She could hear his confusion, though, and pictured him looking at her still form on the bed, then at Missy's protective stance at her side.

"I thought you said she was awake?"

"She opened her eyes," Missy said, her tone apologetic and baffled. "I thought she was awake. I'm still not sure she isn't. She's just . . . not answering."

Daphanie wanted to; she *longed* to, but all she could do was blink. And not even a *meaningful* blink, for fuck's sake. If she could have managed even that, she would have felt better. If she could have rolled her eyes and fluttered her lashes and aimed meaningful stares at them, at herself, at the goddamned water pitcher, maybe she could have communicated something. Instead, she could just lie there like a lump.

Like a dead woman.

She heard Asher brush past Missy and take her limp hand in his.

"Daphanie?" he murmured, and the warmth of his touch felt like heaven on her chilled skin.

A flurry of footsteps marked new visitors. The smell of forest and sun and man identified them as Graham and Rafe. In other circumstances, her new olfactory perception might have given Daphanie a thrill, but at the moment she could have cared less. What she cared about was Asher and his gorgeous face sliding into her field of vision.

She noticed first that he looked tired. Lines of strain and fatigue bracketed his mouth and carved deep furrows between his brows. His expression held concern, frustration, and anger, the emotions swirling and competing behind his silver-gold eyes. But underlying it all was a deep well of tenderness that made Daphanie's heart leap into her throat and tears sting hotly behind her eyes.

The fact that she couldn't even cry nearly drove her over the edge. The sheer evil unfairness of being unable to experience the fullness of her *own goddamned emotions* made her want, for the first time in her life, to commit bloody murder. If Charles D'Abo had stood in front of her in that moment, Daphanie would have plunged a knife into his chest and ripped his heart out with her own bare hands.

She stared up at Asher and felt fear and love and rage well up in her chest until she thought her body couldn't contain them, but his expression didn't change. He couldn't see any of it.

Panic returned, hot and sharp and bitter.

"Daphanie," he repeated, more insistently. When she betrayed not the flicker of an eyelash, she saw him straighten and glare at Missy. "Why isn't she saying anything?"

"I don't know. She's been like this since she opened her eyes. She hasn't said a word, hasn't made a sound. She hasn't even twitched. It's like she's . . . not really there."

Daphanie wanted to scream a denial. Of course she was there! How could they think otherwise? How could they not tell that she was still herself? She just couldn't show them.

"Shit," she heard Graham curse from a few feet away. "You don't think the attack or the spell . . . damaged her . . . do you?"

Damaged her? Daphanie's mind gave a hysterical laugh. Was he talking about brain damage? Did he think she was a bloody frickin' vegetable?

"I don't know," Missy said quietly, but it was the uncertainty in her voice that made Daphanie want to scream.

How could any of them *think* that?

"Do you think we should . . . call someone?" her friend asked.

"Like the witch?"

"No." Rafe overruled Graham. "She's already seen her and told us what she knows. I think a doctor might be a wiser move. Medical tests might tell us . . . where she stands. I could contact a physician I know and ask him to visit."

"To hell with a physician," Missy swore, and the incongruity of it got everyone's attention, including Daphanie's. "I'm calling Annie. She has medical training, has a master's in neurobiology, and she's the smartest woman on the planet. Plus, if I can reach her, she'll be here in less than an hour. That should give you just enough to time to tell me where you're going to look for D'Abo next."

There was a grim silence, then Asher spoke.

"We don't need to look for D'Abo anymore. We found him."

"You *found* him?" Missy cried. "Then get him up here! Whatever is wrong with Daphanie, you know he did it to her. Drag his sorry ass up here and make him break the spell."

"We can't," Graham told her, firmly but gently.

"Why the hell not?"

The answer slapped Daphanie like a heavy hand.

"Because he's dead."

Nineteen

Humans have searched for the keys to immortality for as long as they've understood that, inevitably, they would die. From the mummification of corpses by the ancient Eqyptians to the Spanish conquistadors' questing for the fountain of youth, from the alchemists' search for the philosopher's stone to modern medicine's research into the genetic components of aging, humanity has always sought a way to live forever.

What the Others can teach us, however, is that nothing *lives forever. Vampires might exist indefinitely on a diet of the blood of other beings, and the sidhe might seem as eternal and ageless as time itself; but even they can die. All living things can be killed, somehow, in some way. So even for those creatures we humans jealously refer to as "immortal," the reality is that they, too, shall pass.*

—A Human Handbook to the Others, *Chapter Twenty-three*

The words fell on the company like a live mortar. Daphanie experienced a wave of nausea and a sick rush of vertigo.

Dead?

"Dead?" Missy parroted. "How can he be dead? If he were dead, wouldn't Daphanie be out of danger? Wouldn't the curse be lifted?"

"We assume it would," Rafe said. He sounded ruthlessly calm, as if every ounce of his will were trained on containing his fury.

Daphanie could definitely sympathize.

"The fact that nothing has changed lends credence to our theory that D'Abo was not the force behind this," the Felix continued. "Someone wanted us to believe he was responsible, most likely to shift blame away from himself."

"But how are we going to find out who that is? We have to find out," Missy insisted. "Daphanie is depending on us."

And she was.

"Oh, my God! Got here . . . fast as I could! She okay? Had . . . cell phone . . . turned off. They . . . make everyone turn . . . phone off. Please . . . tell me . . . she's okay!"

Daphanie could practically hear heads turning toward the sound of Corinne's voice. She could picture the woman framed in the bedroom door, clinging to it as if poised on the verge of collapse. In her mind's eye, Daphanie pictured her bent forward at the waist, her hands braced on her thighs as she gasped for air. The picture formed easily, colored by the fact that Corinne had barely gotten her words out because she was panting so hard. She sounded as if she'd just run a four-minute mile, and Daphanie could smell the slight dampness of perspiration on her skin.

"I could ask the same of you," Missy scolded, the shush of movement sketching her hurried path to the other woman's side. The sound of footsteps and rustling cloth painted the image of the reporter being herded into the chair beside Daphanie's bed. "What did you do to yourself?"

Corinne slumped audibly into the seat, and a soft thump made Daphanie envision the battered leather backpack she habitually carried in lieu of a purse sliding off the woman's shoulder to the floor at her feet.

Daphanie felt Corinne's gaze fix on her in concern. "Just ran. I'll be fine . . . soon as I catch my breath. Was on the other side of the park at the Historical Society when you called. Just grabbed everything and took off . . . faster than trying to get a cab."

Missy spoke with a frown. "I never intended for you to try to kill yourself. Daphanie's been unconscious almost since Asher brought her in."

Corinne gulped in a last deep breath. She blew it out in a long, controlled stream and then seemed to regain her focus. "Okay. Good. Well, not good, because I can see something's wrong, but good that she hasn't taken a turn for the worse, or anything."

Daphanie wondered silently how she thought it could get worse, but she could of course say nothing about it. She also was smart enough to realize she didn't actually want to contemplate an answer to that particular question.

"She's been just like you see," Missy told the other woman, her voice low and serious.

Corinne digested that information for a moment, then shifted her attention to the group gathered around

Daphanie's bed. Daphanie could have sworn she literally felt the change in direction of the other woman's energy.

"Tell me everything that just happened," Corinne ordered. "I need to make sure I have all the facts."

Rafe was the one who related the story of how Daphanie had wound up back in the guest room at the Winters' home.

"Daphanie and Asher went to her studio that morning so she could try to get some work done," the Felix explained briefly. "They were there for several hours and everything appeared normal. But just after noon, Daphanie experienced some sort of . . . attack."

Corinne swore, fluently enough that Daphanie wished she could laugh. She had teased the woman many times about having a mouth like a sailor. Corinne always responded that a reporter who couldn't curse was like a lifeguard who couldn't swim.

"Someone broke in there, too?" Corinne asked. "Why the hell didn't Logan and his boys stop them? What the hell did they think they were there for—"

Rafe cut her off. "Not that kind of attack. I'm referring to something more subtle. An attack of the spirit, as it were."

He offered a succinct outline of the events. It actually worked out well for Daphanie, filling in the parts of the story she'd missed by being either unaware or unconscious. Of course, hearing it now stirred up all the anger and fear and confusion she'd been working so hard to keep in check, but she couldn't afford to let those emotions overwhelm her, not when the information was so important. Almost as important as figuring out how the hell she could be in this predicament when the man she'd thought had placed her there was dead.

When the Felix finished, Corinne took a deep, shaky breath and spoke in a voice that did little to offer Daphanie reassurance. "In that case, I think you guys definitely need to hear about what I was able to dig up."

"Dig up?" Missy asked.

Corinne made a sound of confirmation. "Yesterday morning, I called Daphanie at your place."

Daphanie assumed she was referring to Asher's place.

"After hearing about the real break-in, at Danice's apartment, I thought Daph might be facing a rough morning dealing with everything. I was going to ask if she wanted to catch a movie or maybe hang out and watch a few DVDs."

Daphnie felt a surge of affection. Her friends really did love her just as much as she loved them. Given her current circumstances, it helped to remember that.

It helped a surprising amount.

"I never got around to asking, though," Corinne continued. "Before I could, Daph asked me to do her a favor instead."

"What kind of favor?"

"She told me she'd had another one of those dreams."

Since she already knew all about this part of the story, Daphanie had to struggle with her impatience. Not that she could do anything to hurry Corinne along, but she still had to struggle. Giving in to her emotions would feel too much like surrendering. When her emotions were the only things she could control, losing control of them would send her one step closer to madness.

"But she said that this time she was able to figure out what was going on," Corinne explained. "Or at least a significant element in them. So she asked me to find out what I could about a woman named Manon Henri."

Daphanie could feel the others frowning.

"Manon Henri?" Graham repeated. "Where did Daphanie pull that one from?"

"Trust me, I asked her the same question, but for an entirely different reason. I'd already come across the name when I was trying to get Daph some info on D'Abo. Forewarned is forearmed and all that."

Asher latched on to that tidbit. "Manon Henri and D'Abo are linked somehow?"

"*And* how," the reporter confirmed. "The thing was, I'd never mentioned the name to Daphanie, so I was surprised as hell to hear her spitting it back at me and asking me to find out more. When I asked her why, she explained that in the dreams she'd been having, she was convinced that she had taken on the persona of Henri. She made it sound almost like she felt she'd been possessed by the woman. It had really freaked her out, so I told her I'd found out what I could."

Everyone in the room leaned forward at the sound of the word "possessed." If she could have, Daphanie would have done the same. Corinne had definitely earned their undivided attention.

"At first I found a lot of mentions of her, but no real details. Like I told Daphanie, the basic sources say that Henri was a voodoo priestess who emigrated to New York from New Orleans sometime in the mid-1790s. She supposedly founded her own church here and then faded from the record. The part I found interesting was the church she founded is a little place called 'La Société de Bon Anges.' "

She didn't have to explain the significance of that to anyone. Daphanie felt the hair on the back of her neck stand up. Based on the tone of Corinne's voice, the story she'd uncovered didn't stop there, and Daphanie was impatient to hear it. She wished she could shout at the other woman to hurry.

"Go on," Rafe urged, and Daphanie would have kissed him if she could.

"Okay, so right away I could see there was a link to D'Abo, but I found it a little odd that all the histories of the city that I consulted gave that same spiel and nothing else. Since Daph asked me for more, I had to widen my search, so I spent the last twenty-four hours holed up at the New-York Historical Society over on West Seventy-seventh. Or at least every single one of those hours when I wasn't being escorted out by security and locked out after hours. The society has some very interesting information on Henri."

"Like what?" Asher bit out.

Corinne seemed to understand her audience's growing impatience. "Like, from what the stories say, Manon Henri was Marie Laveau before Marie Laveau was ever born. Meaning, she was the most recognized and feared voodoo priestess in Louisiana between about 1785 and 1795. The problem was that while Marie Laveau became famous for her charity work, philanthropy, and political activism during her lifetime, all Manon Henri was known for was having 'the blackest soul on the bayou.' And that, by the way, is a direct quote from one of the letters I read."

"How did she end up in New York?" Missy asked.

"Conflicting reports. When it comes to Manon Henri, I think just about everything is part of a conflicting report. Except for the part about her being 'snake mean and pure evil.' That's another quote, but I couldn't find a single source who disagreed with it," Corinne said. "Part of the problem is that no one could say for sure whether Henri was born a free woman of color or a slave. They did agree that she had mixed ancestry, and she seems to have been considered a quadroon. Certain rumors suggested her father was a white planter and her mother was his *placée*—his mistress; others that her father was a Creole politician and her mother a mulatto prostitute at a brothel in the Vieux Carré; and some that she was born to a slave of mixed Indian and African descent who had been raped by a French plantation owner. The first two could have left her a free woman, but the last one would have meant she was a slave herself.

"Personally, I can't say I'd choose any of those, but they could affect how she got up here. If she was a slave, she could have either been sold or brought up here by her owner. And all this talk about people 'owning' people really makes me want to take a shower."

She shuddered. "Anyway, if I were a betting woman—and, incidentally, I am—I'd place my money on her being free, because I also tend to believe the other story about how she got here, that she was run out of New Orleans by the terrified citizens after she was discovered practicing human sacrifice as part of her black magic rituals."

"Human sacrifice?" Missy repeated, sounding half a step from dumbstruck. "Is that really a part of voodoo?"

"No, and I learned an awful lot about that over the last day, too," Corinne said firmly. "I don't think what Manon Henri practiced was voodoo. Everything I've read about that religion confirms that the people who practice it are sane, ordinary men and women with a perfectly reasonable world view that includes honoring and invoking ancestor spirits called the *loa* to help them or offer them advice in times of need. It sounds like some do incorporate the occasional animal sacrifice of chickens or goats, but it's done as humanely as kosher butchering and the animals are then used to feed the congregation as well as the gods. What Henri brought with her to New York was something else entirely. It wore a pretty, colorful suit of voodoo, but it was a hell of a lot darker."

"I'm beginning to believe you are right about that," Rafe said, sounding grim and thoughtful. "What I would dearly like to know is whether Charles D'Abo practiced the traditional religion, or if he attempted to follow in Manon Henri's footsteps."

Daphanie heard the shift of cloth as Corinne shrugged. "If he performed the same rites as Henri, he sure as hell did it more discreetly. If there were human sacrifices being made at La Société, the police would have been all over them. I haven't heard so much as a whisper about that."

Asher caught the hesitation in her voice and pounced on it. "But?"

"But I found something else while I was digging through the Society's archives," she said. Daphanie heard her weight shift in her chair and the rattle of a metal buckle. She pictured the reporter reaching down and flipping open her backpack to pull something out. Then she heard the rustle of papers and imagined one of her friend's thick folders full of the fruits of her research. "I'd like to think I'm making too much of it . . ."

She trailed off, her voice troubled. Daphanie heard her riffle through the papers in the folder, stopping at one particular sheet. This she drew free and held for a long moment of silence.

"Look at this and tell me what you see," she said. Then she handed the paper to Asher.

Daphanie felt like a toddler in front of a candy story counter. She knew that somewhere above her, something very, very important was taking place, but she could do nothing about it. She couldn't hurry it along, couldn't stop it, couldn't do anything but feel her own impatience and strain for the audio clues to what her friends were doing and seeing and thinking.

She was going to lose her damned mind.

She heard the paper rustle as it changed hands, heard a quick, hissed intake of breath, heard Rafe mutter a curse in Spanish. Then she heard Asher murmur a single, strangled word.

"Daphanie."

Twenty

Ghost—*the noncorporeal specter of a deceased be-*
ing. While it can be confirmed that ghosts do exist,
they themselves do not qualify as Others, being a
rather more universal phenomenon. Ghosts may
spring from humans, from Others, or from any crea-
ture possessing a soul. With that being said, however,
many Others do seem to have the natural ability to
detect and to communicate with ghosts in a way that
can only be accomplished by humans with supernat-
ural gifts. Among certain groups of Others, to see a
ghost may be considered an omen of good luck.
  —A Human Handbook to the Others, *Glossary*

Asher felt as if he'd just seen a ghost.

The paper Corinne handed him was crumpled around
the edges as if someone had gripped it too tightly, and he
couldn't swear that someone hadn't been him. The single sheet was a slightly too dark photocopy of a photograph of a painting, and as such, the quality left something
to be desired. The background was blurred to an indis-
tinct blob of variegated charcoal, but the face in the fore-
ground was as familiar as his own.

The image in his hand was one he'd never seen before

and was obviously antique, and yet the face that stared out from the page possessed features he would have recognized in a crowd of thousands.

Daphanie.

"Where did you get this?"

"From the New-York Historical Society. It's a portrait of Manon Henri, dated 1796. Apparently, it's owned by the Frick, but has never been hung."

"Impossible."

"I said nearly the same thing, but the society has documents that back it up. Several letters about Henri refer to the portrait. More than one man acknowledged her beauty in one sentence and called her the daughter of Satan in the next."

Daphanie—the woman in the portrait, he corrected himself—had been painted from the torso up wearing an elegant-looking gown of the period that exposed the upper swell of her breasts above a rounded neckline. An elaborately folded and tied turban obscured most of her hair, allowing only a few, tiny pincurls to peek out near her temples. She wore a delicate string of beads around her neck and the same teasing smile he'd seen Daphanie wear at least a dozen times.

The resemblance left him stunned.

Behind him, Graham whistled through his teeth. "Holy shit."

"I am afraid I have to agree with that eloquent assessment," Rafe said, frowning down at the portrait. "I have never seen such a likeness. Daphanie could have posed for this just this morning."

Corinne nodded. "I stared at it for like half an hour before I found the tiniest little difference, but you have to look closely. See, the woman in the portrait has a mole at the end of one of her eyebrows. You can barely see it, but it's there."

"Oh, you're right," Missy exclaimed, crowding closer. "Good catch, Rinne."

Asher could only continue to stare, the uneasy feeling he'd had during the whole of Corinne's story intensifying until he felt as if thousands of stinging insects crawled over his skin.

"This is wrong," he murmured. "This means something very, very wrong."

Rafe nodded. "I think you are right. This feels . . . significant."

Asher looked back at Corinne. "What happened to Manon Henri after she came to New York?"

"That was the most difficult thing to discover," she told him. "The background I had by dinnertime yesterday. The end of the story took me until just before Missy called. I think that no one wanted to talk about it. None of the principal parties involved left so much as a mention of it, but there was one letter that dropped enough hints for me to put it together.

"In September of 1797, Manon Henri was interred in an undisclosed location in lower Manhattan. The undisclosed part is kind of a laugh. I mean, even if they *had* disclosed it, most of the cemeteries in Manhattan were closed and the bodies moved back in the mid-nineteenth century. No one wants to state flat-out how she died, but I think it's pretty clear that she was murdered."

"By whom?"

"Again, no one wants to admit to it, but I'm guessing it was murder by committee. That summer, just before she died, rumors had been flying around the city about her activities. Witnesses claimed to have seen her drinking human blood, consorting with the devil, sacrificing babies . . . the whole nine yards. A century before and she'd have been burned at the stake. That made a few people nervous but what really sealed her fate was when people heard her talking about a *nouveau régime* and had her followers referring to her as *la reine*."

"The queen of what?" Rafe asked.

"The world, according to her enemies. The last letter I read was written by the son of a man named Phineus Jay-Martin. The family were cousins a number of times removed of John Jay, the Supreme Court Justice. Anyway, in the letter, Phineus's kid, William, refers to his father's 'gentlemen comrades' and lets slip that Phineus and four of his closest friends—all prominent members of New York's elite—were responsible for putting an end to the 'evil harlot's quest for power.' They staked out the area that Manon was using for her ceremonies— pretty much where Eleventh Street and Avenue A meet today. At the time it was nearly on the water and completely outside the city. Her followers would set up a tent there and they'd perform the rituals at night when no one was around or likely to stumble across them."

"Except for the 'gentlemen comrades,' one assumes."

"Right. Though stumbling was the last thing they did. They kept watch on her for over a week, trying to decide what to do. Then on the night of September ninth, Manon Henri began to perform a ritual designed to call forth a particular entity called, among other things, Kalfou and invite it into her body. The goal doesn't appear to have been possession, but power-sharing. Henri was offering her body as a host to Kalfou in exchange for him giving her unchecked magical powers. For a woman already said to spread the pox with a look and to kill animals by pointing at them, God only knows what 'unchecked' might have looked like."

Asher flinched under a lash of memory. "Kalfou. D'Abo tried to call that name in the club when he wanted to curse Daphanie."

"It would have been appropriate," Corinne said, looking far from pleased. "Kalfou is the name of one of the Petro *loa*—the dark spirits of voodoo. Actually, he's their king, you might say. He's called the grand master of curses, charms, and black magic, and he's the guy who can open the door to the other world to let all the bad things in."

"Sounds like a real charmer," Graham growled.

"That's exactly what the 'gentlemen comrades' thought. They also seem to have suspected—as others have throughout history—that Kalfou was just another name for Satan himself, so William wrote that they felt they had no choice. They brought a small army of servants and slaves with them, and when the *Société* members were all inside and beginning the drumming to start the ritual, they collapsed the tent and set it on fire, killing all seventeen people inside. Reportedly, Manon was the only one to make it out, but as soon as they saw her emerge, they opened fire, shooting her twice in the stomach, four times in the head, and once in the heart."

Graham winced. "That seems excessive."

"Not if you believe Phineus's statement that the first six shots didn't kill her."

"Holy shit."

"William wrote that the men took her body with them and buried it in secret because they feared she had other followers who hadn't been at the ritual that night and who might attempt to raise her from the dead. Each man swore to take the location of the body to his grave. It sounds like they might have been traditionalists, though, and treated her like any other evil creature by burying her at a crossroads with a stake through her heart."

"Christ, I thought only vampires provoked those gruesome customs," Rafe said.

"I think they feared her more than a vampire. The irony, though, was that because these were all New Yorkers and none of them spoke Creole, they must not have realized that in Haitian Creole, 'Kalfou' means crossroads. They're apparently one of his major symbols."

Asher felt his blood chill. All at once, he feared he knew exactly what D'Abo had planned. "Has anyone ever attempted to raise Henri the way the men feared would happen?"

"There's no record of it, but I'd be surprised to hear about it. Like I said, none of them ever revealed where they'd put her body. Without that, a resurrection would be kind of a moot point, wouldn't it?"

"Not if they decided to raise her spirit into someone else's body instead."

There was a long, tense moment of silence.

In the end, it was Corinne who spelled it all out. "That's exactly what I was afraid of. I hoped I was overreacting, that it was just my writer's imagination spurred on by all those hours at the archive and the story of the attack coming so close on the heels of the shock of seeing that portrait. But now I don't think so. I think you're right. I think Charles D'Abo was trying to get to Daphanie so that Manon Henri can come back to life and take possession of her body."

Asher turned immediately to Graham.

"I need your best tracker," he bit out. "I don't care if the monster behind this has gone to ground on the moon. I don't care if he's the bloody ghost of Christmas past. You're going to find him, and we're going to stop him."

The alpha was already headed for the door. "That would be Logan. I'll call him right now. He'll bring at least two others, the best we have. We'll start trails from D'Abo's apartment, the *Société,* and the Callahans' apartment. One of them will lead us to something."

Rafe stepped into the doorway, blocking Graham and Asher from exiting. He must have caught the look in Asher's eyes, because he hurried to explain himself before the Guardian removed him bodily from the path.

"We might already have the most vital clue we could wish for." The Felix nodded at Asher. "Do you not still have the paper you discovered in D'Abo's grip?"

If Asher could have done so he would have lifted his boot and kicked his own hell-cursed ass. As it was, he had to content himself with calling himself nine kinds of fool while he fumbled in his pockets.

He couldn't have said what he'd been expecting to see. A neatly worded paragraph explaining everything and naming the villain in boldface type would likely have been too much to ask for. Apparently, even something as simple as a name was, too. Instead, Asher found himself frowning down at some kind of voodoo crossword puzzle and wishing he'd kicked D'Abo's corpse when he'd had the chance.

"What the fuck is this shit supposed to mean?"

It didn't even appear to be written in English, though if it had, it would have provided only marginal amounts of help. In the center of the small page an oddly arranged collection of letters formed what looked almost like a compass. He assumed the letters formed words, though he could make neither heads nor tails of them, couldn't even tell which way they were supposed to be read, whether to shift his gaze left to right or top to bottom or another direction entirely.

The two longest lines of letters ran straight across two planes of the sheet, intersecting roughly in the center. The right angles they formed, however, were each bisected with another word that did not follow a straight line but curved in an elongated S-shape from one end to the other. At the tip of each of the straight-line words, a triangle had been drawn almost like an arrowhead pointing toward the edges of the paper. D'Abo had also apparently indulged his artistic senses by adding small star shapes in each quadrant and inserting two others in place of missing letters in the S-shaped words. The whole mess was completed by a circle drawn around where the central words met with two small circles contained within at the top.

"What? Was he *high* when he did that?" Graham demanded, peering over Asher's shoulder to scrutinize the drawing. "That's a complete piece of horseshit. How the hell is that supposed to help us?"

Rafe reached for the paper, and Asher handed it over without hesitation. It wasn't as if the damned thing were going to provide them with any help.

The Felix examined the drawing for a moment in silence. He shook his head and cast Asher a look of apology. "I am sorry," he said simply. "I had hoped for more."

"Hadn't we all?" Graham grumbled.

"Still, we cannot discount that there may be a meaning here that we are at present unable to discern." Rafe gestured with the paper. "I will ask Erica to look at it. It may have a symbolic meaning, or the words may represent a spell. Magic often uses language of its own devising for such purposes."

"Fine," Asher bit out, "but I'm not going to sit around in the meantime and twiddle my damned thumbs. We need to get moving and find the mystery man. I'm not letting Daphanie stay like that."

The other men followed his glance to the motionless, wide-eyed form on the bed. He knew they sympathized with him, knew they cared for Daphanie themselves, in their own ways. Both men considered her a friend, a part of the extended family formed by the bonds between their wives and their brothers-in-arms.

But none of them could possibly understand how he felt, how seeing her helpless and vulnerable while he had been sworn to protect her cut like a killing blow to the abdomen. None of them could understand how the sight of her made him so weak he could barely summon the strength to stand and so enervated with rage that he could have lifted Atlas' globe with one hand.

Whatever he had to do to save Daphanie, Asher would do it. He didn't care if it cost him his own damned life. He was no good without her anyway. She had already ruined him for his solitary life.

"Of course not," Rafe agreed, clapping him on the

back. "We will waste no time. While Erica sees what she can discern from the message, we will gather the Silverback trackers and commence the hunt. One way or another, Asher, we *will* find him."

"Right. You and Asher come with me. We'll join Logan's group." Graham glanced at Missy and Corinne. "You two should stay with Daphanie."

Missy cast her husband a sharp look, and he shook his head. "No, don't argue. I'm not excluding you from the hunt for my own male-chauvinistic-pig reasons. Daphanie will need to be watched carefully and protected from both physical and magical attacks. I'm trusting you to see to that, Miss." His voice softened. "Plus, she is your friend. If she wakes up before we return, she'll feel better having you with her."

Missy nodded, her expression easing. "Of course. This building is warded so tight, it's a wonder light can get in, so I'm not worried about a magical attack reaching her while she's inside; but we'll make sure that no one can physically get to her. I'll ask Samantha and Annie to set up a guard outside, just in case."

Graham pressed a quick hard kiss on his wife's mouth. "Good idea. I'll catch Sam in the office on our way out and fill her in." He turned back to face Asher and his face wore an expression of fierce resolve. "Don't worry. I promise you, if the man responsible for this is still in Manhattan, the pack will find him. If he tries to leave, the pack will find him. There isn't anywhere he can hide from us. We won't stop tracking until he's found."

Asher nodded once, rage already clouding his vision. "And when he is, you can all stand back, because I'm going to kill him with my bare hands."

Twenty-one

A werewolf on the trail of an enemy is an amazing thing to witness, though not many humans get the opportunity. The Lupine's acute sense of smell allows him to track a person's or an animal's movements twenty times more easily than the best-trained bloodhound in the world.

Plus, since a Lupine can be fully aware of the source and behaviors of the creature he's tracking, he can make educated guesses to stay with a trail, while an animal, with its limited cognitive abilities, would likely be forced to give up the chase.

—A Human Handbook to the Others, *Chapter Five*

Daphanie screamed her frustration, then screamed again when no one took the slightest bit of notice. Admittedly, since not a single sound emerged from her throat, it must have been easy to ignore her, but that didn't make it any easier to deal with.

She wanted to talk to Asher. She wanted to tell him that she was all right, that she might be trapped inside her own body, but her mind was whole and healthy and missing him with a ferocity that was hard to bear. She wanted to speak his name and feel the heat of him as he leaned over her. She wanted to smooth her hands over the lines of worry on his face, the ones that only got deeper with the passing of every minute in this ridiculous nightmare.

And she wanted him to kiss her good-bye so badly it felt like a knife blade twisting in her heart.

Instead, she had to listen helplessly while he and Rafe and Graham marched out of the room on a maddening quest to save her from the forces of evil.

God, she felt like she was trapped not just in her body, but in the plot of a bad made-for-TV sci-fi movie. How the hell had this happened to her? How the hell had she gone from ten days before, when she'd thought *The Others* referred to a creepy Nicole Kidman movie, to this? How had it happened? And how could she make it unhappen?

"She hasn't said a word?" she heard Corinne ask softly, and Missy sighed as she made her way back to the bedside.

"She hasn't even twitched a muscle." Missy reached out to fuss with the blankets, tucking them more securely around her friend. "If her eyes weren't open and blinking every once in a while, I'd think she was in a coma."

"Would Annie know if that were the case?"

"I'm sure she would, if she were here. Unfortunately, she's been in Germany for the last week attending some kind of scientific symposium. She was supposed to be back sometime around now, but I haven't heard from her." Missy gave a short, unhappy laugh. "I'm almost afraid to call her in case she's not home yet. If she can't come, I don't know what to do."

"If she's not home, you'll call another doctor. We'll find out what's going on, Miss, and we'll find a way to help Daph. You know we always find a way."

"God, I hope you're right."

Daphanie heard the sound of Corinne rising and the soft glide of skin on skin as she took Missy's hand.

"I know I'm right," the reporter said, injecting her voice with the sort of confidence Daphanie associated with her. It was funny how she'd never considered before now that that kind of confidence could take effort to be achieved.

"Come on, though. I'm sure you've been up here with her since the moment Asher brought her through the door. You look ragged enough for that to be true. Come downstairs with me and get something to eat."

Missy shook her head, her fine blond hair shushing against the shoulders of her top. "I'll eat later. At dinner."

"It's past dinner, sweetie. When was the last time you looked at the clock? It's after seven."

"Seven? That's impossible!"

"No, just surprising. Our world might have stopped when Daphanie got into this mess, but the rest of world didn't. Come get some dinner. Even if you're not hungry, I am, and you know I suck as a cook. You'll have to fix us something to keep me from destroying your kitchen with my ineptitude."

"I shouldn't leave Daphanie alone. You heard Graham; someone needs to keep an eye on her."

"We're only going downstairs," Corinne pointed out, "and I think this place is the origin of the expression 'safe as houses.' You know it's like a fortress."

"But—"

"One hour, Miss," her friend insisted. "I'll let you come back up in a hour. But you need to eat and you need to rest. Don't make me threaten to sic Graham or Samantha on you."

Daphanie heard Missy sigh, and knew the woman had given in. "All right. One hour," she said, her voice now fading toward the hallway. "Then we'll both come up and sit with her. You can keep me company. We'll play gin, or something."

"Poker," Corinne corrected, her voice coming from outside the room as the pair headed for the stairs to the first floor. "I need to keep in practice for the next time I find myself in a strip tournament."

Missy's laugh floated back toward her, then Daphanie heard their voices disappear into the depths of the house.

She was alone.

It took a minute to push back the fresh surge of panic. Nothing had changed, she hurried to reassure herself. She had nothing to fear. Or at least, nothing new to fear. She remained in exactly the same situation she'd been in when she'd woken a couple of hours ago, and while that situation sucked and blew and scared her all the way to the soles of her feet, at least she could say it hadn't gotten any worse. That was something, wasn't it?

And something, as her mother would say, was always better than nothing.

The thought of her family conjured pictures of her sister's wrecked apartment, and Daphanie gave thanks yet again that Niecie hadn't been around to see that; it would have broken her heart. Daphanie's little sister

wasn't what she would call a homebody, by any means—
that was Missy's official title—but she was proud of
her things because she'd worked too damned hard to get
them. And she'd been so excited about the new apartment she and Mac had moved into just a month before
the wedding. Neither had been able to agree which of
their old places they'd rather be in—Danice had voted
for hers, Mac for his—so they'd compromised by
looking for something that would be *theirs*. Daphanie
intended to see that before they returned from the
honeymoon, the place looked exactly the way they had
left it.

She was also glad, Daphanie acknowledged to the
blank white surface of the ceiling, that Niecie wasn't
around to see her like this. Her sister would just have
worried, and Daphanie couldn't have stood that. Daphanie was the big sister; it was her job to ease worries,
not to cause them.

She didn't appear to be doing a great job of that at
the moment.

Exhaustion threatened to swamp her. She closed her
eyes, grateful to be able to at least do that much on her
own. Whether she was tired from the culmination of a
week's worth of worry or from the exertion of using
her senses in an entirely new way for the past few hours,
Daphanie wasn't sure, but in the grand scheme of things,
it didn't much matter.

The room was empty, so she had nothing to listen to.
The ceiling was unchanged, so she had nothing to look
at. And Asher was gone on the hunt, so she had everything to hope for.

When he returned, he would bring with him the answer to her prayers. She really believed that. She had to. Without that belief, she had nothing left but despair.

He would return as soon as he knew something, she reassured herself. In the meantime, she could do nothing except lie there and worry.

Sleep, she decided, would be a much more constructive use of her time.

Surprisingly enough, that resolve was all it took. Before the thought had finished forming in her mind, she slipped under, offering up one last prayer that the bad dream would stay away for one more night.

Daphanie woke again to utter darkness and to the stunning realization that she was sitting up in her bed.

Well, not *her* bed precisely, but the bed she'd been occupying in Missy and Graham's guest room. The details were insignificant. What *was* significant was that she was no longer trapped on her back and unable to move. She was *sitting. Up.*

Damn, it felt good.

Smiling, she reached out to flip the blankets off her legs and slide to her feet, but her hands refused to cooperate.

Goddamn it! Not again!

But either God wasn't listening to her, or he really had as much trouble with his name being taken in vain as her mother had always tried to tell her, because once again, she found she couldn't move of her own free will. Once again, her body had been removed from her own control.

This time, there were no lights burning in the small room at the top of the stairs, no sound of pages being quietly turned. She was entirely alone, but from the corner of her eye, she could see a small green light glowing from an object on the bedside table. It took her a second to figure out what it must be—a baby monitor.

True to her word to care for Daphanie while her husband took Asher and Rafe out to search for the big baddie, Missy had proved herself both resourceful and as big a mother hen as her friends always teased her about being. She had removed the baby monitor from her son's nursery and placed it next to Daphanie's head, just in case her friend called for help.

In other circumstances, the clever, protective gesture would have made Daphanie smile. In the present one, the smile fled quickly from her mind when she felt her body jerk into action without the slightest prompting from her.

Confused and more than a little freaked out, Daphanie felt her legs flex and swing themselves over the side of the bed. She felt her palms flatten against the mattress and press down to lever her onto her feet. She felt her center of gravity shift and her balance immediately compensate, and she felt another silent scream well up in the base of her throat.

Dear God, what was happening to her?

Daphanie's feet padded silently across the soft carpet, completely ignoring her frantic mental commands to stop! Halt! Desist! Cut it the fuck out! They moved her inexorably to the door, their betrayal soon joined by her hand, which reached out and wrapped around the cool glass doorknob, turning it with slow, deliberate care.

The latch barely made a click as it opened, and the door swung silently on well-piled hinges. The baby monitor would never register a sound, and Daphanie would be herded by her own out-of-control body onto the chilly wooden boards of the upstairs hall.

Daphanie choked back a sob. Why? Why the hell was this happening to her? Why the hell would someone do this? She had not asked to be born the spitting image of some evil witch from the eighteenth century, and she sure as hell had no desire to offer her body up as a sacrifice to allow the woman to rise from the dead.

Daphanie had plans of her own! She wanted to live her life, build a career. Marry the infuriating man with the huge white wings, and have a dozen fat, sassy babies with silver-gold eyes and the ability to jump off the roof without worrying about the fall.

The power guiding her didn't care about her plans. It forced her down the stairs, moving her along the edges of the treads to prevent the betrayal of noisy creaking.

Daphanie felt like a sleepwalker, only one without the comforting oblivion of sleep to shelter her. In her mind, she screamed and clawed and fought, wept and railed and struggled like a wildcat for her freedom. But in reality, she moved steadily forward on silent bare feet and glided out through the front door and into the night like a ghost.

Twenty-two

*It is impossible to call any one group or species of
Other in its entirety "evil." Throughout the pages
of this book, we have demonstrated that within the
society of the Others, an individual is no more likely
to act evilly than is a human, and the Others resent
any implication otherwise.*

*Of course, the Others also realize that their nat-
ural abilities give them the power to harm humans
more easily than they themselves might be harmed.
This is the reason for the existence of the Council
of Others, and that group takes its duties of govern-
ment and enforcement very seriously indeed.*

—A Human Handbook to the Others,
Chapter Twenty-one

Logan Hunter earned Asher's respect the minute he arrived at the doors of Vircolac clad in dark clothes and
bad temper. Graham had given him a brief overview of
the situation on the phone, and he had come to the club
with a small army of Lupine warriors led by himself
and two elite trackers.

"No one messes with a mate," he had growled in

Asher's direction after nodding respectfully to his alpha. "We'll find him."

The men had been quickly divided into three groups and sent to three locations to begin the search. Asher, Logan, Graham, and Rafe had all chosen to start at D'Abo's apartment. His killer had almost certainly been behind the attacks on Daphanie, and his scent there was more than a day fresher than it would be at the Callahans' place.

The police had been to the building on Eleventh Street by the time the men returned, but it was a simple matter to bypass the crime scene tape and the seal on the apartment door. It took Rafe barely more time to let them in than it had the first time.

Logan curled a lip at the smell of blood and decay in the empty living room, but he wasted no time getting to work. He moved all the way to the rear of the bedroom where D'Abo's scent was less likely to be mingled with others and worked his way forward until he hit on something different. Pausing near the doorway that led to a small galley kitchen, he turned his head from side to side, inhaling deeply as he went.

"I think I have it," he said. He snorted once to clear his nose and inhaled again, moving to stand directly above where D'Abo's body had lain.

"Yeah, this is it," he muttered, almost as if he'd forgotten the other three men in the room. The rest of the Lupines had waited outside the building. "Nasty little fucker. Smells like death and crazy."

He looked up at the others and grinned, a sharp, feral baring of teeth. "Let's go get him."

Asher had chuckled in grim satisfaction, and the sound had suited nothing so well as the Lupine beta's smile.

Logan led them briskly out of the apartment, his eyes narrowed and his head constantly moving as he followed the lingering scent of their quarry. They quickly turned onto First Avenue and headed south toward SoHo. Asher didn't care which direction they took, so long as it brought him closer to Daphanie's tormentor.

Logan didn't speak as he worked, but Graham and Rafe walked with Asher and attempted to be reassuring.

"I asked Samantha to call Erica and get D'Abo's weird little message to her right away," the alpha said, striding along at Asher's right shoulder. "You can count on Sam. She's my right-hand man."

Apparently, the fact that Logan wasn't talking didn't mean he wasn't listening, because he shot Graham a speaking look. The man just grinned and flipped him the bird. "Ignore my beta. He recognizes a figure of speech when he hears one."

"I only hope Erica recognizes the symbol," Rafe murmured from Asher's left. "I cannot help feeling that we'll be missing some vital piece of information until we discover what it was meant to convey."

"She'll call as soon as she knows."

"Soon cannot be too soon."

Listening to them debate back and forth around him made Asher feel like a man in one of those old images with an angel and a devil perched on his opposite shoulders. On another night it might have amused him.

On this night, he was focused on other things.

He followed Logan along First Avenue, watching

the Lupine move from shadow to light, shadow to light, as they walked past illuminated storefronts and darkened alleys. The sun had set before they even left Vircolac, and now the night deepened around them, pressing down on the oblivious city like a heavy cover.

Asher usually took no notice of the dark. He saw in it well enough that it inconvenienced him very little, and much of his work was done at night, as that tended to be the time of day when most humans found themselves stumbling into places they shouldn't have been or encountering Others they shouldn't have known. Tonight, however, the darkness left him feeling uneasy, as if it obscured things he needed to see and muffled sounds he needed to hear.

Still, he didn't miss it when Logan picked up his pace.

"Getting closer," the Lupine growled over his shoulder.

Asher broke into a trot and battled back his surprise. He hadn't expected results this quickly. Were they even out of the East Village yet?

Looking around him, Asher caught sight of a nearby street sign and cursed roundly. He knew exactly where they were, and suddenly he knew exactly where they were headed.

He increased his pace until he drew even with Logan. The Lupine glanced at him in surprise, then looked back when Graham shouted something about them being on the wrong damned trail, but Asher ignored them. He ran past the tracker, rounded the corner, and skidded to a halt exactly where he didn't want to be. In front of la Société de Bon Anges.

He hadn't expected, though, to see a familiar face peering through the window of the darkened storefront.

The woman turned at his approach and gasped. "What are you doing here?"

The rest of the search party caught up with Asher, and she gave a short laugh.

"*All* of you?"

Rafe shouldered his way forward. "Erica. I could ask the same of you. Didn't you get Samantha's message?"

The witch nodded, lifting her hand to show she gripped a crumpled piece of white paper in her fingers. "That's why I'm here. Though, really, if I'd known you were coming here yourself, I wouldn't have bothered. Why did you ask me to find out what the thing means if you already had it figured out?"

"Had *what* figured out?" Asher snapped.

Erica jerked back and gestured weakly toward the storefront. "That message on the paper is contained in a *vévé*."

"We didn't have it figured out," Rafe said, laying a calming hand on the woman's shoulder. "Running into you here was a complete coincidence. Explain what you have discovered."

"The message uses the letters of several words and phrases to form the pattern of a *vévé*," the woman explained, still eyeing Asher warily. "Even if I don't know voodoo, I know a *vévé* is a symbol that represents one of the major *loa*. Every *loa* has his or her own symbol that can be used to invoke the spirit during a ritual. That part I know in theory. In practice, I know some of them are pretty pictures that are often used in jewelry and decorations."

"So you recognized this as the symbol of whom?"

Erica grimaced. "I recognized it *was* a symbol, not which *loa* it represents. I hoped the words would give me a clue, but I don't speak French, let alone Creole, so I thought I'd come down here and ask. What are you all doing here?"

"The story would take too long to explain properly. Were you able to speak with someone who knew about this particular *vévé*?"

She shook her head. "The store was already closed when I got here, but if you look at the poster hanging on the near end of the counter, you can see the patterns listed and labeled. This appears to be the symbol of Carrefour, also known as Kalfou."

There was that name again, and with it, another connection to Manon Henri. Corinne had said that Kalfou was the demon with whom the priestess had once attempted to strike her bargain for unlimited power. Asher got a bad feeling at hearing Kalfou's name come up again during a search for the man they suspected of trying to raise Henri from the dead.

"From what I understand, he's not a very pleasant fellow, but the few words on this page that I can make out don't appear to be very nice, either."

Asher refocused on the witch, his gaze sharpening. "What words can you make out?"

She took a step backward and closer to Rafe, as if seeking protection. Asher didn't have time to reassure her.

"Only a couple," she said hurriedly. "I know that <u>bokor</u> is a word that means 'one who serves with both hands' and it refers to a voodoo practitioner who performs black magic. *Barriè* is a barrier, specifically the barrier between our world and the spiritual world where the *loa* live. And <u>*bizango*</u> . . ." She paused. "I thought that one was just a legend. The *bizango* were said to be a secret society of *bokor* dedicated to black magic, specifically various forms of necromancy. They were the ones who were said to raise people from the dead as zombies."

The silence on the street nearly deafened him. Asher heard the witch's story and found himself powerless to speak. No one else made a sound. He could have sworn no one even drew breath. This was what they had feared. This was the fate some nameless, faceless monster had planned for Daphanie. Asher would die before he let that happen.

"Really, though, I would think the names would be the important part," Erica continued. "I'm sure you must have recognized those. Have you done any research to try and identify them?"

Rafe's hand tightened visibly on the witch's shoulder until she squeaked in protest. The Felix immediately loosened his grip, but his expression remained hard and intent. "We couldn't make out anything," he informed her. "We thought it just a random collection of letters. What names did you find?"

"Only two that I could point to as definite names, but neither was complete enough to point to any particular individual," she said, sounding apologetic. "Maybe you'll have better luck."

"What. Names." Asher spat the words like bullets from a machine gun.

"Manon," she revealed. "And Sosa. But those could refer to almost anyone."

Not quite.

Everyone there—with the clear and unimportant exception of Erica—knew to whom the name Manon referred, but Rafe and Graham looked puzzled over Sosa. Asher suffered a jab of memory and a rush of adrenaline.

"Sosa is the name of one of D'Abo's followers," he said tightly, remembering how the angry man had roared his minion's name at the club, ordering him to attack Daphanie. That minion, in fact, had been the one to tear the small strip of fabric from her shirt. It made perfect, crystalline sense.

Except for one thing.

"I remember the man." Asher frowned. "He had all the personality and animation of a wet dishtowel. He just stared straight ahead of him unless he was given a direct order. I assumed he was one of the zombies D'Abo had bragged about creating."

"How did he move?"

He glanced at the witch. "What?"

"How did he *move*?" she repeated. "That is one of the characteristics that identifies a zombie. A so-called thousand-mile stare is common, but zombies always move slowly and carefully because they only do so when directed by the *bokor* who controls them."

Asher remembered seeing Sosa reach for Daphanie and recalled that he'd moved with remarkable quickness.

He told her and watched her shake her head very definitely.

"If he grabbed her that fast, he wasn't a zombie. They're not capable. He might have been brainwashed, or heavily influenced, but he was clearly just a follower."

Or had he been a subtle mastermind who had recognized the familiarity of Daphanie's features and seized an opportunity for action?

"So if he wasn't a zombie," Graham puzzled slowly, "then . . ."

"He is likely the very man we are looking for," Rafe acknowledged. "I thought Logan had led us to the wrong place, or that our quarry had laid a false trail, but it seems I should have had more faith."

"Thank you," Logan said wryly, emerging from the alley that ran alongside the building. "I could have told you that if you'd asked. Our guy was definitely here, recently. But he used the rear entrance. I would have gone in, but the place is full of people."

Erica pointed to a sign on the door. "Apparently, the Société is having a service tonight in honor of D'Abo. That's what the notice says, anyway. It called it a memorial service, but I figured that was impossible. If D'Abo were dead, your problems would be solved, wouldn't they?"

Rafe shook his head. "It turns out that Sosa, not D'Abo, was the man behind all of this. He killed D'Abo sometime last night, and now we're afraid he had further plans for Daphanie, as well."

The witch looked shocked. "Then you have to stop him. Is he at this memorial service, do you think?"

Asher thought that would be too much to ask. But he intended to ask anyway.

"We can only go and see for ourselves," Rafe said, taking the woman's elbow and ushering her toward the corner. "I thank you for your help, my dear, but we have reason to fear Sosa may be dangerous. You should take yourself home and out of harm's way."

The Felix murmured reassurances to the woman as he walked her toward the corner of Second Avenue and hailed a passing cab. While he bundled her inside, Asher turned to Logan and asked, "How many people did you see?"

"None," the beta admitted. "There are no windows back there, but the outside is lit up like a beacon, and I can hear people inside. Smell them, too."

"Sosa?"

"I don't know. I know he went in at some point, fairly recently, but his scent is all over the place. He comes here regularly, which makes it hard to pick out what's lingering and what's current."

Asher tamped down his frustration.

Graham jerked his chin toward the alley. "Let's go check it out."

He ordered the bulk of the Lupines to remain where they were, then led Asher, Rafe, and his packmate toward the darkened alley.

The alley turned out to be more of a narrow walkway, perhaps the remains of an old carriageway from the area's distant past. It led them around the side of the building to the actual alley shared by several of the buildings on the block and giving access to the rear exits. As Logan had indicated, the area immediately behind the storefront blazed with the illumination provided by a pair of floodlights mounted above a riveted steel door. Just to the left of the entry, an old and cracked wooden sign hung from a hook embedded in the brick. The sign read, *"Byenvini à la Société de Bon Anges. Antre kontanman."*

Below it, an old domed doorbell sat adjacent to the door's heavy handle. Farther down the alley, the pavement stretched into darkness, but in front of the Société there was light enough to read the look in another person's eye. There just weren't any unfamiliar eyes to be seen.

"Okay, we checked," Asher barked impatiently. "What do you suggest we do now? Because in about fifteen more seconds, I'm busting down the door and searching the place inch by fricking inch."

A faint sound had Graham turning his attention to the far end of the alley. He peered into the darkness for a couple of seconds and then grinned.

"I don't think that will be necessary," he murmured and gestured to the figure emerging from the shadows.

It was the shopgirl from that morning.

She had obviously gone home and changed clothes. Instead of the jeans and T-shirt from before, she now wore a loose white peasant blouse and full matching skirt tied with a multicolored sash dominated by bold swaths of red and gold. Her short dark hair had been curled and styled and pushed back from her forehead with a wide red bandeau. The heels of her tall black boots had alerted Graham to her approach, which halted abruptly when she spotted the men gathered at the Société's closed door.

"Hey, I know you," she announced with admirable powers of perception. "You two were at the store today looking for Papa D'Abo. Did you hear the news?"

Graham and Asher exchanged careful glances before Graham nodded. "We did." He gave the girl one of his fatally charming smiles. "I'm Graham. I'm sorry, but I don't remember your name."

"Daisy." The girl shrugged the strap of a large canvas purse higher onto her shoulder and sniffled.

"We were very sorry to hear about it, Daisy," Graham continued, injecting just the right tone of sympathy and friendship into his voice. "That's why my friends and I stopped by again. To pay our respects."

Daisy nodded, looking unsurprised. "A lot of people knew Papa D'Abo. Everybody misses him real bad." Her lips trembled, but she continued bravely. "Tonight's ritual is private, though. It's the *boule zen*. Mambo Amanda is in charge. There will be a public service in a few days, though. You're welcome at that. I'm sure we'll have the details in the store by tomorrow or the day after. You should check back."

Asher wanted to grab the girl by the throat and shake her until she told them where to find Sosa. He imagined using her as a human shield as he forced his way into the middle of the ritual and demanded Sosa as *his* human sacrifice.

Rafe's hand on his arm stopped him. The Felix nodded meaningfully toward Graham, who, Asher had to admit, was in the middle of one hell of a performance.

"Mambo Amanda?" Graham repeated with a small, perfectly gauged frown of confusion. "I'm surprised. I thought Sosa would be the one to perform D'Abo's ritual."

Daisy shook her head. "No, *houngan* Sosa was *la*

place for Papa D'Abo. His assistant," she explained. "So it was decided he should take all the highest-ranking *hounsi* with him and perform the *dessounin* in private."

Asher didn't understand half the words she spoke, but he didn't need to understand Creole to extract the gist of her message. Sosa was not at the Société tonight. He had specially selected a group of their most powerful initiates and taken them off to a secret location to perform an alternate, powerful ritual.

His spider sense began to tingle.

At the same moment, Rafe's phone beeped. He smiled at Daisy politely and stepped away to answer. Asher divided his attention between the Felix and the alpha, but frankly he was more concerned with getting as much information as they could from D'Abo's shopgirl. He could almost feel Sosa's slimy little throat beneath his hands.

"Of course." Graham nodded, looking wise and knowledgeable and completely convincing. "I should have figured. Are they performing the day-sue-nan at the traditional site?"

For the first time, the girl eyed him oddly. "At the crossroads? I assume, but no one other than the *hounsi* can attend. And three quarters of them weren't even invited. How did you say you knew Papa D'Abo again?"

Graham scrambled to cover his mistake. "Well, I just thought—"

Rafe leaped back toward the little group so fast, he nearly overshot and sent Asher bowling into a surprised Daisy. "Never mind. Thank you for your help. We will check back about the public memorial. Good night."

He grabbed Graham and Asher by the backs of their

shirts, jerked his chin at Logan as he propelled them all back toward the street.

"Hey, what the hell is this?" Graham complained, trying to free himself with a shrug. "I didn't screw up that bad. I could totally have salvag—"

"Not now," Rafe snarled, sounding in that moment every inch the jaguar. "We have to get back to your place."

"Why? What's going on?" Asher demanded, a frisson of dread snaking down his spine.

Rafe just pushed them faster until the small group was running toward the nearest avenue, the pack automatically falling in at their heels. The Felix's sense of urgency was contagious.

"Rafe!" Asher prompted, his stomach knotting. "What is *going on*?"

"Samantha has raised the alarm," he bit out. "One of the guards thought she saw someone exit the club about fifteen minutes ago."

"So?"

"So, she swears she thinks it was Daphanie."

Twenty-three

Evil is as evil does. The trouble being, of course, that from time to time, evil does some pretty nasty things.

—A Human Handbook to the Others, *Chapter Two*

Daphanie's body carried her unwillingly out of Missy's front door and down the street to the neighborhood's small, private park. She remembered glimpsing the black iron of the fence—hopelessly boring and of mediocre craftsmanship—and feeling the cool blades of grass under her feet; but that was the last thing she recalled before she opened her eyes to the sound of rhythmic drumming.

Frickin' *drums* again. Daphanie had grown to *loathe* the sound of drums. In fact, she was instituting a new rule that from now on, the bloody things were not allowed within seventy-five frickin' feet of her. On pain of death.

Daphanie wasn't quite sure how you went about killing a drum, of course, but she figured one would make perfectly nice kindling for her forge. She also imagined her hammer would make a beautiful music of its own as it blew right through layers of goathide and oak.

Gingerly, aware of an uncomfortable ache reminiscent of a wicked hangover, she turned her head to take in her surroundings. It took a few seconds for her to register that she could do so, that she'd done it of her own free will, and Daphanie had to bite back a whoop of glee. Finally, she was mistress of her own body again!

With a sense of gratitude and a vow never to take the action for granted ever again, Daphanie pushed herself into a sitting position and propped herself up against the nearest vertical surface. Judging by the feel of it, said surface was a rough brick wall, crumbling in places and coated here and there with moss. That, plus the cool damp of grass beneath her butt told Daphanie she was outside.

But where? The park down the street from Vircolac? She couldn't picture the sound of drumming going unnoticed in such a quiet, upscale neighborhood.

No, she must have wandered somewhere else.

She looked around, squinting against the glare of a bright light, and realized she was staring into a roaring bonfire. Averting her gaze, she blinked her eyes twice with slow deliberation until she could focus on the dimmer corners of her surroundings.

The bright glow of the fire cast most of the area into shadow, but she thought she could discern the outline of an enclosed area roughly forty feet square and bordered almost entirely by high brick walls. If she craned her neck, she could see that the wall against which she leaned belonged to some sort of building, as did the one directly opposite. On the left, the wall rose maybe a dozen feet in the air before ending in a cap of rough gray stone. The wall to her right reached about half that height with a gap of approximately six feet at the center spanned by a tall iron gate with a double door, currently shut fast. Matching iron rails surmounted the low walls on either side, bringing the fortifications on the street side of the courtyard into alignment with the others.

Within the small yard, Daphanie could make out one tree, a towering, stately old elm, as thick around as a child's wading pool. It stood just to the rear of the middle of the space, looking as if it had rooted there before the Revolution, its branches spreading out to canopy most of the yard.

The space beneath the branches remained largely empty, and open. The neat carpet of grass stretched from wall to wall, obviously thick and well tended, broken here or there by pale stones jutting up out of the sod.

Gravestones. And gravestones in Manhattan meant a churchyard, of which precious few remained. Daphanie knew the most famous, of course—the New York Marble Cemeteries, Trinity Churchyard, St. Paul's. She'd wandered into most of them during her teenaged morbid phase, but this one looked unfamiliar.

She thought she would remember it if she had seen it, if for no other reason than the appearance of the two distinctive graves in the back corner. One bore a stone sarcophagus with an effigy of a man—presumably the occupant—reclining along the marble lid. If she squinted, Daphanie could see writing carved into the side facing the yard, though she remained too far away to read it.

Next to the grand tomb, wedged into the corner, stood a plain, granite obelisk, about four feet tall and as thick around as a ten-year-old boy. It bore no writing, no carvings, no distinct marks of any kind, and yet around the square base, she could see a row of X-shaped marks drawn on the pale stone with something the color of charcoal.

Beneath the elm's leafy branches, near the wall behind the sarcophagus, Daphanie thought she saw the figures of five or six men gathered around a low table that all but groaned under the weight of food and flowers and all manner of decorations.

Her subconscious fit the pieces together in an instant.

Drums + fire + graves + me = Someplace I really *don't want to be.*

Keeping her eye on the figures on the far side of the small graveyard, Daphanie carefully braced her hands on the ground, steeled herself against the agony in her head, and eased slowly to her feet. She stood there for a moment, verifying that her legs would hold her and more importantly would obey her commands, before she began to sidle toward the gate. Her progress was slowed by her desire to keep to the shadows, but she had made it nearly as far as the corner between the church and the street wall when a deeper shadow blocked her path.

"Oh, no, Ms. Carter, you can't leave us," a man's voice said, slick and obviously amused. "After all, you're very nearly our guest of honor."

Daphanie didn't recognize the voice, but she recognized the presence. It felt as thick and black and oily as Manon Henri had felt in her dreams, and when she forced herself to look, she recognized the face.

Sosa.

Before her stood the man who had grabbed her at D'Abo's urging that night in the club. The man whose eyes had stared blankly into the middle distance while his "master" bellowed and blustered like a summer thunderstorm.

Tonight, Sosa's eyes looked anything but empty. Tonight they were filled with a kind of gleeful anticipation that had her stomach tightening and her instincts screaming in protest. Tonight they held a look of malice and an intent so evil she thought he must make Manon Henri a very suitable assistant.

Daphanie Carter had been a lot of things in her life, though, and a coward had never been one of them. She didn't care if her knees knocked, her teeth chattered, or her palms sweat. The only thing that mattered was that she would not cower before this monster. She hiked up her chin before she spoke to him.

"You're the one who placed a curse on me," she stated simply, and she felt a rush of satisfaction that the words emerged calmly and evenly.

She saw surprise flicker behind his cruel smile.

"Very good," he complimented her. "I had of course intended that you blame D'Abo for your predicament, but at this point, I suppose it hardly matters. Not that Charles will mind the confusion—"

"Because you killed him."

Anger tightened his features for an instant before he managed to soothe away the strain and resume his expression of amused condescension. "It is true that I never imagined his body would be found quite so soon—something I believe I owe to your friends. My plan had been to continue with the charade until tonight's work was complete, just to be safe. I do so like to wrap things up neatly, but he expressed the most distressing intention to attempt to stop the proceedings, and naturally I couldn't have that."

He corrected himself.

"We couldn't have that."

"You're planning to sacrifice me to Henri, to take away my soul and give her my body." That managed to surprise him, and she took a certain amount of satisfaction in knowing he had thought himself too clever for her. "I should tell you that I don't intend to let you do it. Did you think I would go along quietly? I happen to like being who I am. I have no intention of giving it up so you can be the bitch queen's chief flunky, the same way you were for D'Abo."

Sosa threw back his head and laughed. "Is that what you think? That I would do all this to be a servant? You foolish girl. When Manon rises, she will call down Kalfou Himself, *gran' maître* of all dark magics, and be granted all the powers of His world. She will become the new *loa*, Maman Manon, and in her gratitude to me, the one who raised her, she will make me the most powerful *bokor* who has ever lived." His eyes flashed with greed and madness. "I will serve *no* one, especially not a pretender the likes of Charles D'Abo. He was never more than the means to an end. And the end is near."

"Not my end."

Sosa leaned in close, so close that the smell of rum and tobacco on his breath made her stomach churn. His nose almost bumped hers, and she could count the red veins in his bloodshot eyes. "You will do as I command."

Daphanie shook her head. "No," she said quietly, her voice as resolute as her heart. "I won't."

"You have no choice," he hissed and jerked away. "You forget, *putain,* I brought you here, and if I have to, I can make you beg for the *coup poudre.*"

Stepping back, he raised his hand as if to strike her, and she could see for the first time that he gripped something tightly in his right fist. Her eyes fixed on the object and she frowned, an uneasy feeling clawing through her belly. It appeared to be a lump of clay or wax, crudely molded into an approximation of a human form.

The sorcerer followed her gaze and laughed, the high, evil cackle of a witch or a madman.

"Ah, yes, you see my *'tite Daph'nie, non?* She looks just like you, doesn't she? She should, since she is wearing your clothes and your hair."

Daphanie recognized the glittery fabric of her tank top instantly; she'd almost expected to see that. But it took a moment for his words about her hair to sink in.

An image flashed into her mind, absent of all context save a bowl of white porcelain. Her hairbrush in Danice's sink, balanced drunkenly in the shallow curve, *shed hairs clinging to the bristles.*

Her heart stuttered to a stop.

How stupid of them.

She and Asher had just assumed because they had noticed nothing missing after the break-in that nothing had been taken. A few fingers full of shed hair from a brush was only so much trash. Why would they even have checked?

It would be unlikely a doll could control you unless the bokor *had something of yours to bind the doll to you,* Erica had said. A warning, if she had only listened.

Something you've had for a long time and used or worn frequently is usually preferred, because the closer it is to you, the more of your energy it will have stored.

What could be considered closer to Daphanie than her own hair? It had literally been a part of her. And now it decorated the doll a madman intended to use to march her toward her own living death.

"Oh, yes," Sosa hissed, the firelight casting his features in sharp relief, making his eyes look as black as a well and his mouth as red as blood. "Maman Manon will be suitably grateful, especially when she looks upon her image and sees herself exactly as she remembers. In the beginning, I had thought any girl would do, provided she was not too old, not too fat or too ugly, but now I see that fate made me wait for you. The *loa* knew you were coming, and they made me bide my time until you came."

And here, Daphanie thought desperately, she had always believed fate was on her side. Had it deserted her now? Had it returned her to Manhattan, to her home and her family, and introduced Asher into her life only to end it now?

It hadn't, she assured herself. It couldn't. Men like Sosa might be crazy and cruel, but fate was impartial. Fate would always deliver what a person deserved.

Clinging to that thought, Daphanie hoped fate still believed she had been a good girl.

With her eyes on the madman and her heart with Asher, silently, earnestly, Daphanie began to pray for a miracle.

Twenty-four

The highly specialized variety of Other known as a Guardian is not to be confused with the human conception of the "guardian angel," something a Guardian would be the first to tell you. The Guardians of the Others are not sent by a benevolent deity, or any deity at all, but rather are assigned their duties of protecting humans from supernatural threats by the oldest and most respected member of their kind, an ancient and awe-inspiring figure known only as the Watcher. What he watches, no one is precisely certain, but given the success rate of his army in protecting and preserving the humans under their protection, one assumes it must be the human race in its entirety.

Not every human will fall under the protection of a Guardian during his or her life; in fact, very few of them will. But those who do find themselves under one of these creatures' sheltering wings can rest assured that while that Guardian lives, that human shall come to no harm.

—A Human Handbook to the Others, *Chapter Nineteen*

Asher had never known fear like what he faced when he returned to the Upper East Side and found the bed in Missy and Graham's guest room cold and empty. Unless it was the fear he felt when he stood with his back to the front wall of the Church of St. Mary the Consoler and heard Daphanie's voice calmly challenging the man who intended to end her life.

When he got his hands on her again, he was going to kill her. And then he was going to make love to her until she was permanently crippled and would never again be able to walk away from the safe place where he had left her. Just see if he didn't.

But first, he had to find a way to rescue her from the clutches of Emmanuel Sosa, something that he feared would be easier said than done, since the man would have made a hell of a military strategist. He had set himself up in a place that was both spiritually significant and easily defensible. Asher, Rafe, and the Lupines had discussed it as soon as they had gotten word of where Daphanie had been taken. Getting his woman out wouldn't be easy, but few of the important things in life were, and he knew nothing would ever be more important than this.

Thanks to the quick thinking of the female Silverbacks Samantha Carstairs had handpicked to guard the Winters' house while Daphanie was inside, her midnight stroll had not gone unnoticed. The Lupine who had been stationed across from the front door had been surprised to see it open just before eleven o'clock and even more surprised when Daphanie had emerged apparently under her own power. Surprise, though, hadn't kept her from doing her job.

Robin, the guard in question, had taken note of Daphanie's solo state and her awkward, shambling gait and gotten curious. Although Asher might have preferred that she had simply stopped his woman and marched her right back into the house, at least the Lupine had made sure to follow her, keeping Daphanie in sight as she entered the small fenced park a few short yards from the door of Vircolac.

The men there had taken Robin by surprise. She had seen three of them surround Daphanie and immediately leaped forward, only to feel a sharp blow to the base of her skull and then see nothing but the inside of her eyelids for approximately ten to fifteen minutes. When she'd regained consciousness, Daphanie had been gone, but her scent had been fresh. Angry and ashamed, Robin had followed the trail on foot all the way downtown to the Flatiron district and Mary the Consoler, tucked into a side street between Madison Square Park to the north and Union Square to the south. She had taken one look at the situation in the churchyard and run back uptown at top Lupine speed. By the time she'd collapsed in the front hall of Vircolac, Samantha's call had been made, Asher and the others had returned, and Robin—all of twenty years old and stupid with it—had been cowering on the floor at Graham's feet with her paws tucked to her chest and her belly exposed.

Asher had resented the five minutes it took to calm her down enough to tell her story, about the poor decisions she had made in allowing Daphanie to leave the building and then allowing herself to be taken by surprise when she should have been providing a rescue. Eventually, though, she had spilled her guts and Rafe had nodded, turning to Asher with purpose.

"I know the place. Not the church, but the area, and it makes sense. Broadway was one of the few major roads that existed in Manhattan during the eighteenth century, and I wouldn't be surprised to learn that an east-west road intersected with Broadway in that vicinity. It would have provided access from the farms to the populated area at the tip of the island. When Manon Henri was slain, that could very well have been a crossroads, and her killers would likely have considered it to be so far outside the city that a grave wouldn't be found or disturbed."

"They've taken Daphanie to Manon Henri's grave," Graham said, cursing and making Robin shake so badly her teeth rattled like castanets.

"What better place to raise her than at the site where she was buried?" Rafe asked.

Five minutes later, they had organized an army of Lupines and set off for the church.

At least Robin's description of the space had been accurate. Asher could almost have wished she had exaggerated the problems inherent to getting inside unseen.

The buildings on either side and the high brick walls in front of and behind the churchyard narrowed the possible means of access to strolling through the main gate—which was easily observed and even more easily defensible by one man with a sharp right hook—and scaling over the walls. The second option offered more secrecy, but it also left the invaders vulnerable to being picked off by bullets or spells fired by the voodoo priests inside.

The best way to go, he had finally acknowledged, would be to follow Rafe's risky plan, an idea he liked only marginally better than no plan at all.

Rafe's two-pronged assault relied on the combined forces of stealth and might to carry the day. The first ones into the yard would be he and Asher, but they wouldn't go over the walls; Sosa and his men would be expecting that. Instead, they would come down from the sky, relying on the cover of the elm tree to block them from view and on the fire to weaken the men's night vision. Asher would fly them up there and deposit himself and Rafe in the branches of the tree. Thankfully the thing was so huge and old, it would take their weight easily, and the breezy night air, the beat of the drums, and the crackle of the fire should combine to mask any sounds they would make.

Once inside the walls, Rafe would descend on the dark side of the tree, relying on his stealth, the uneven light, and the camouflage of his jaguar form to conceal him as he made his way to the rear wall of the church. Tucked into that rear corner was the small door that gave access directly from the sacristy to the graveyard. The Lupines would wait in the church and be ready to attack the minute Rafe reached the door and gave them the signal.

As Asher had grudgingly admitted, it was better than no plan at all, but only barely.

His own goal was Daphanie, pure and simple. Let Rafe worry about evening the odds against the angry witch doctors; all Asher wanted was to grab his woman and drag her to safety so he could beat the living hell out of her. Or kiss her bloody senseless. One or the other.

Taking a deep breath, Asher stepped away from the wall of the church, caught Rafe's eye, and nodded. The Felix returned the gesture and motioned silently for the small pack of restless werewolves to head into the church. Glancing quickly up and down the deserted street, the man nevertheless took the precaution of stepping back into the dubious privacy of the church's recessed entryway before he stretched, shifted, and blurred from the form of a tall, dark-haired man to that of a sleek, muscular jungle cat. By the time he padded back onto the sidewalk, Asher had done his own stretching and released his wings from their confinement along his spine.

Someone had asked him once how he folded his wings back into his skin so that it was almost impossible to detect them, even with his shirt off and his naked back exposed. Asher couldn't explain it. He just knew that when he folded them tightly behind him, they sank down into his flesh like the mattress of a convertible sofa bed—not the most glamorous of images, but a fairly accurate one. His body had been designed to hold his wings, and he could feel them inside him even when he wasn't using them.

Now, he would definitely be using them.

With a sharp jerk of his shoulders, Asher unfurled the full span of the feathered, white appendages and felt the thrill at the freedom of stretching muscles too seldom used. Wings were less of an exciting gift in the modern world than one might think; they tended to attract attention even when one was trying to be discreet, so Asher seldom used them for anything other than effect; and he'd found they had a perfectly satisfactory effect even when fully or three-quarters furled. But now he got to open them full and wide, and he saw a glint of envy in the Felix's eyes.

If the other man only knew what it felt like to truly fly, that envy would grow to more than a glint. Right now, though, Asher had a mission, and his mission was Daphanie.

He reached for the jaguar, pausing for permission before hefting the enormous cat in his arms and swaying a little under his weight. As a Guardian, Asher had been gifted with the strength necessary to bench-press a city bus, which he discovered in that instant was good, because Rafe felt like he weighed as much as one.

Grunting, Asher shifted the Felix in his grip, earning himself a pointed glare. Satisfied that he had balanced his load as well as possible, the Guardian bent his knees, flapped his wings, and launched himself toward the sky.

Daphanie stared at the doll in Sosa's hand, unable to look away. It was like staring at one of her own internal organs and seeing the blade of a madman's knife pressed against it. Only instead of a human heart, the voodoo doll looked like a deformed hand—Sosa might have a talent for magic, but he clearly lacked any talent for art—and the weapon the *bokor* pressed against it was his own index finger.

"I made you join us here." The man grinned, teeth flashing sharp and white in the firelight.

He ran the tip of his finger over the doll's legs and Daphanie felt the touch on her own skin. Bile rose in her throat and she fought the urge to shift her feet. She refused to give him the satisfaction.

"I made you lie still and I made you walk, *chère*. Shall we see if I can make you beg?"

His eyes glinted and his fingers bent the doll's legs in half. Daphanie fell to her knees with a sharp cry.

"Very nice." The *bokor* laughed. "If I had more time, I would make you dance, but the hour grows late and Maman Manon grows restless. Can't you feel her? I promise you, you soon will. She hungers, *chère*. It's time *pour le mangé loa!*"

Sosa shouted to the other men, who took up their drums and launched into a driving rhythm. There was no hesitation, no buildup. The only one not ready for tonight's ceremony was Daphanie, and about that, no one else would care.

The fire crackled, flames shifting in the night breeze. The same wind rustled the branches of the elm tree as Sosa grabbed her by her ponytail and dragged her toward the granite obelisk. Manipulating the doll, it seemed, was too much work. Sosa had grown impatient. He tucked the poppet into the pocket of his baggy trousers—the pocket on the side away from Daphanie, damn it—and relied on brute force rather than magic to compel her forward.

He began to chant even before he reached the pale monument. This, Daphanie now knew, was where Manon Henri's body had been hidden. Her killers might have taken the secret of the location to their graves two hundred and some odd years ago, but since then someone had discovered the truth and marked the spot with a statue. The Xs on the base, Daphanie could see, were drawn in groups of three, like those on Marie Laveau's tomb in New Orleans, in order to beg favors from the spirit of the priestess. Daphanie wondered hysterically how many of those requests had been in vain. She couldn't imagine that the woman who wanted her body for her own corrupt spirit felt particularly moved to help anyone but herself.

If Daphanie had hoped to make a break for it while Sosa was occupied with his ritual, she had hoped in vain. Instead of the way she remembered in her dreams, Sosa had the others dance. He occupied himself with chanting as he gripped her hair in one hand and grabbed a handful of powdered ash in the other.

"Madame Manon, fille de Kalfou," he called, his voice echoing in the small yard, *"Ouvrey baye. Ouvrey baye pou muem, Kalfou. Maît d'baye, gran Carrefour. Frè d'Legba. Modi Legba. Vo la gran maît tu! Kalfou, Manon gaye. Gaye asteur! Mange! Bwè! Gaye!"*

Sosa dragged her close to the fire and began to scatter the ashes on the ground where the grass had been burned away. At first Daphanie thought the motions were random, but as she watched she saw a pattern begin to emerge, then two. The first looked like a compass with arms that curled at the ordinal points instead of pointing straight. Stars decorated each of the ordinal arms as well as the corners of the drawing, and a circle enclosed the intersection of the arms with two smaller circles within so that it resembled a round, blank face staring out into the night.

The second pattern also sprang up around two crossed lines like the most basic of compasses, but instead of two ordinal lines, a single long snake slithered from west to east across the northern arm. Touching the belly of the snake, the point of an inverted heart seemed to pierce the animal, just as the blade of a knife pierced the heart.

Below the heart, a crescent moon hugged the southern arm. Again, stars twinkled in the corners.

The patterns should have looked pretty, or at least intriguing, but Daphanie could barely bring herself to look at them. Just the sight made her stomach heave, and when she looked at the second drawing, her head began to spin and her knees to weaken.

"Gaye, Maman Manon!" Sosa shouted, the excitement building in his voice. *"Gaye e pran ce ko po ou! Gaye, Maman! Gaye! Retournen a mwen! Gaye! Viv!"*

Daphanie could understand not a word of his hoarse, frantic shouts, but she didn't need to in order to understand the way the ground beneath the churchyard began to tremble. She didn't need to speak his language to feel the cold, thick blackness of that dreaded fog begin to seep into her consciousness; and she didn't need to understand to know that he had called on the spirit of Manon Henri to rise from her grave and take Daphanie as her sacrificial lamb.

Too bad the lamb had no intention of going quietly.

In her head and her heart, Daphanie fought. She fought harder than she'd ever fought in her life, drawing inspiration from the fresh breeze that shook the branches of the elm tree over their heads. She pictured the breeze stirring inside her mind, pictured it gathering strength until it became a steady wind and began to blow the insidious, heavy fog away. She concentrated until the wind became a gale, but still the fog crept forward until it threatened to pull her under the dark, oily blanket.

With the last of her strength, Daphanie gathered her will, gathered her breath, and screamed.

Twenty-five

For there is no greater magic in all the world than that of love.
   —A Human Handbook to the Others, *Frontspiece*

Asher crouched on a thick branch high in the canopy of the elm tree and watched the scene unfolding below him with fear, impatience, and barely suppressed rage.

He growled low in this throat when he saw Sosa bend the object in his right hand and heard Daphanie cry out in shock and pain, crashing to her knees at his feet. He wanted to launch himself straight onto the man's back and break his neck with a quick brutal twist. That wasn't the plan, though, and Asher knew that their best chance for retrieving Daphanie alive and unhurt rested with the plan.

Still, his resolve nearly deserted him when the *bokor* grabbed Daphanie by her long, high ponytail and dragged her across the small churchyard with brutal disregard. Hell, reason nearly deserted him. All he could think of was rage and revenge. He half rose from his crouch, his intention to swoop down, grab Daphanie, and fly away before Sosa even realized what had hit him. Only a supreme exercise of will stopped him.

He had been through this with the others. Of course,

his first instinct had always been to fly directly to Daphanie's rescue. What good did it do a man to have wings, after all, if he couldn't use them to save the woman he loved? As Rafe had pointed out, though, removing Daphanie bodily from Sosa's grasp wouldn't save her from him; not while he still possessed whatever charm he had bound to her energy. Asher needed both Daphanie and what he now suspected was the voodoo doll the *bokor* had concealed in his trouser pocket.

Asher waited anxiously for Rafe to pick his way along the yard's back wall to the sacristy door. The Felix used the shadows cast by the structure to his advantage, and the growth of moss and ivy in patches along the brick surface contributed to the camouflage of his roseate-spotted coat.

While Asher kept one eye on the man's progress, most of his attention remained fixed on Daphanie, ready to leap forward on a moment's notice, plan be damned. If he saw an imminent danger to his woman, he would act, and to hell with the consequences.

Fate allied itself with the good guys.

Everything came to a head in a single instant. After several tense minutes of scattering ash over the exposed dirt and shouting foreign words over the frantic beat of the drums, Sosa threw back his head and Asher could feel the change in the air. The ground seemed to tremble, the vibrations racing up the trunk of the mighty elm. Daphanie screamed, loud and shrill. And Asher's powerfully acute hearing picked up the soft scratch of feline claws on the antique wood of a darkened door.

Showtime.

Before Rafe even had his paw back on the ground,

Asher gave a deafening roar and beat his wings with one powerful motion. The action lifted him from his concealed spot, sending secondary and tertiary branches cracking and tumbling to the earth.

He dove into the yard at a breathtaking speed, letting his wings sweep him toward his target. A powerful backward beat halted him just before impact, allowing him to land on his feet before a startled *bokor*.

With one hand, he chopped the back of Sosa's wrist, deadening the nerves and loosening the man's grip on Daphanie's hair. With the other, he grabbed her around the waist and pulled her aside, shoving her away from Sosa and his minions.

He need not have worried about the *hounsi*. By the time Asher landed, the Lupines had burst through the church's rear door and fallen on the drummers and dancers like a pack of wolves. Which, at that moment, was exactly what they happened to be. Only Graham had remained in his human form, shouting orders as his packmates overwhelmed Sosa's men and pinned them to the grass.

Asher didn't even spare them a glance. All his attention was focused on Sosa and the fear and pain he had inflicted on Asher's woman.

"Asher," Daphanie shouted, pointing to the *bokor*. "The doll! He stole my hair!"

So that was what had sealed the spell; not the scrap of Daphanie's top, stolen that first night at Lurk, but strands of her hair probably gathered during the break-in at the Callahans' apartment. Not that the when and how mattered to Asher at this point. What mattered was confiscating the doll and watching Sosa die under his hands.

The priest turned out to be a smarter man than Asher would have guessed. Instead of instigating a physical fight he couldn't hope to win, Sosa pulled the voodoo doll from his pocket and placed his thumb over its mouth, cutting off Daphanie's urgent words.

"I can kill her, you know," the man snarled, his teeth bared and his eyes wild. "Just squeezing her like this is all it took to hold her paralyzed. I can stop her heart with my finger or break her neck with a flick of my thumb. But I don't want to do that. Maman Manon will not like it if I damage her new body before she even gets a chance to ride it."

The ground continued to tremble, a low quaking of the earth, and Sosa swayed from side to side, clearly unbalanced physically as well as mentally. Asher eyed the doll in his hand warily. What would happen if he dropped it? Would Daphanie's body be slammed to the earth as if from a great height? Would the impact snap her bones? Snap her neck?

Asher couldn't risk it. He searched his mind frantically for another way and glimpsed Rafe out of the corner of his eye slinking slowly around the perimeter of the light cast by the roaring bonfire. The Felix was slowly placing himself in a flanking position behind Sosa, pinning the man between himself and Asher. To the left, Daphanie stood frozen in the firelight, once again paralyzed by the *bokor*'s grip.

Silently, Asher urged the Felix to hurry.

"I wonder, though, if Manon would really mind so much. After two hundred years in the grave, she will likely be glad to feel anything, even if that includes a little pain." Sosa gave a maniacal giggle. "Shall we see?"

He jerked the doll's right arm behind its back, and Daphanie screamed. Asher's glance flew to her, and he could see by the way her limb now hung at an unnatural angle that the priest's little game had dislocated the shoulder. Her face had gone the color of kindergarten paste and a cold sweat beaded along her brow. She breathed in soft, agonized whimpers, and Asher felt hatred like he'd never known.

"Touch her again, and I will rip your heart from your chest and make you taste it," he promised, his voice low and tight and murderous.

"But I didn't touch her," Sosa giggled. "She's all the way over there, see?" He pointed to her and grinned. "I never touched Daphanie. Only *'tite Daph'nie, non*?"

He reached for the doll's left leg, and Rafe sprang.

Asher moved almost simultaneously, and the two men—one Guardian, one jaguar—caught the *bokor* between them in a living vise.

Sosa screamed.

Rafe the cat clamped his powerful jaws around the man's left arm and dragged him to the ground, glowing, golden eyes fixed on the doll in his hand.

Asher pinned the man's legs beneath his own body and wrapped his hands around Sosa's throat the way he'd fantasized about doing a thousand times. Without his meaning them to, his fingers began to tighten, choking off the man's windpipe.

The priest fought fiercely, using his right hand to claw at Asher's compressing fingers. His eyes widened and began to bulge as Asher continued to press, and he renewed his desperate struggles to free himself, twisting and thrashing against the fingers pressing on his throat and the jaws clamped around his arm. The harder he struggled, the deeper Rafe sank in his teeth, until blood began to flow into the dirt.

The trembling of the earth intensified.

"Asher, no!" Daphanie shouted, her voice barely audible over the fury and hate roaring in his ears. "You're giving Manon what she wants! You're making Sosa her sacrifice!"

He heard the words, but the meaning hardly registered. Nothing mattered but taking revenge on the man who had hurt his woman.

Dimly, he was aware of Rafe releasing the priest's arm and snarling at him, but he was too far gone to care. The Felix grabbed him by the ankle and tried to pull him off Sosa, but he struck out blindly with one leg, kicking as hard as he could and knocking the big cat halfway across the yard.

As if from a great distance, he heard Daphanie shouting his name and begging him to stop. He saw her turn and stumble toward the obelisk that marked Manon's grave. The earth heaved and knocked her down, but she dragged herself right back up again, cradling her injured arm to her belly.

He felt Sosa's struggles begin to weaken, and a thick, oily, black fog began to creep into his mind, obscuring his consciousness. He watched impassively as Daphanie dragged her feet across the ground, obliterating the *vévé* the *bokor* had drawn there, but a gleeful, unfamiliar voice in his head whispered that it was too late, that the girl was pretty, but Asher was strong and he would do just fine for a new chance at life . . .

Daphanie screamed again and ran toward him, but

the earth buckled beneath her and drove her to her belly in the dirt.

"Asher! No!"

Using her one good hand to brace herself, Daphanie levered herself to her knees and began to crawl.

Sosa was almost still now, and Asher's awareness was shrinking until all that remained was a tiny pinprick of light through which Daphanie's face was barely visible.

She reached out to him, sobbing in pain and fear, and the voice in his head told him to ignore her, but her hand brushed his cheek and she whispered, "Don't," and the pinprick of light got a little bigger.

"Asher, don't," she begged, her palm cupping his face. "I love you. Please don't."

And suddenly, the earth went still.

Light flashed in Asher's mind. The fog disappeared and took the strange voice with it. His fingers flexed and fell away from Sosa's throat. The *bokor* drew in a desperate, choking gulp of air, and Asher focused on his woman's tearstained face.

He reached out and brushed away the moisture with fingers that trembled. "I love you, too."

Daphanie smiled, her mouth curving and her whole face lighting up in an expression of such pure joy that his heart could barely contain the pleasure of it.

She grabbed his hand and brought it to her lips, kissing the fingers that had very nearly taken a man's life. For her.

"I love you," he repeated, his voice stronger, more certain.

Daphanie laughed. "And that," she told him with quiet certainty, "is magic."

Epilogue

And they all lived happily ever after.
—This Book, *Right Here, Right Now*

Daphanie set the last book back on the shelf beside the entertainment center and grinned with weary satisfaction. It was done. Finally, the apartment was put back together and ready for Danice and Mac's return.

"Not a moment too soon." Asher's arms closed around her waist and gathered her to him, careful of her still-sore shoulder. She leaned back against his chest and savored the magic of his presence. "Their flight should be landing any minute. A few minutes in a cab, and they'll be walking through that door."

"Good," she sighed. "I can't wait to see Niecie again. Three weeks might have seemed like a tiny little interlude to her, but it felt like forever to me."

"That's probably because she was on her honeymoon and you weren't," Asher pointed out.

"Oh, right. She was soaking up the sun on a tropical beach—and breaking up the monotony of it with hot bouts of newlywed sex—while I was being possessed by the spirit of an evil voodoo queen. I have no reason to be jealous, and absolutely no reason to resent the fact that she wasn't here to help me out through the most difficult nine days of my life."

He raised an eyebrow at that and she smiled sheepishly.

"All right, that last bit might have been a little irrational, but I can't help it. When you think about it, she's the reason I got into that whole mess to begin with. If it hadn't been for her and her wedding, I wouldn't have moved back to New York, learned about the Others, and met that obnoxious imp who deserted me after placing me in the path of the man who turned out to be a psycho black magic voodoo priest."

"Tru-ue," Asher acknowledged, "but without all those things you also wouldn't have met me."

"I know." Daphanie grinned. "That's why I haven't asked you to hunt down the imp and strangle him for me, because without him, I wouldn't have been at Lurk that night. It's also why I cleaned up Niecie's apartment instead of letting her find it like it was. Because she led me to Quigley and Quigley led me to you. I don't know whether to hit her or hug her."

"Wow, you've got a mean streak."

"A potential mean streak," she corrected. "After all, I didn't use it just now, and I almost never do."

"Hm, then maybe I shouldn't leave that extra wedding present I got for your sister in the guest room. After all, we wouldn't want her to think we were being mean . . ."

Daphanie pulled back and eyed him curiously. "What extra present? You didn't tell me anything about an extra present."

Asher just gestured to the door down the hall.

Daphanie looked at him suspiciously for a moment before turning and hurrying down the hall. He followed, grinning.

When she opened the guest room door and gasped, he was standing behind her looking quite pleased with himself.

"What do you think?" he asked.

Daphanie burst out laughing and had to slap her hand over her own mouth to muffle the sound. After all, she didn't want to wake Niecie's "present."

The guest bed was the only piece of furniture still visible among the stack of boxes and bags piled up around the spare room. Daphanie herself had made it up last night, smoothing the pale blue coverlet into place and plumping the pillows to downy perfection. And that was how she had left it, empty and pristine. Asher had laid his present right in the middle.

Passed out and snoring, a bright silver bow pinned to his chest, Quigley the imp lay amid the wreckage of a sixpack of empty root beer cans.

"I think it's perfect," Daphanie whispered, stepping back out into the hall and closing the door firmly behind her. "Now let's get the hell out of here before she comes home and finds it."

"Do you think she'll like it?" he asked as he locked the apartment door behind them and led her to the elevator.

"I think she deserves it, and that's even better."

Asher gathered her to him once more and leaned down for a kiss. "I don't think I deserved to meet you," he murmured, his lips curving in a tender smile, "but I'm going to try deserve you in the future."

"It doesn't matter if you deserved me or if I deserved you," Daphanie told him. "We had to find each other."

"We did?"

She nodded firmly and rested her head against his chest, knowing she would be content in his arms for the rest of her life.

"We absolutely did. It was fate."

Coming soon...

NOT YOUR ORDINARY FAERIE TALE
ISBN: 978-0-312-35722-1

Available in November 2011 from St. Martin's Paperbacks

Don't miss these other novels in The Others series from
New York Times bestselling author
Christine Warren

PRINCE CHARMING DOESN'T LIVE HERE
ISBN: 978-0-312-94794-1

BORN TO BE WILD
ISBN: 978-0-312-35719-1

BIG BAD WOLF
ISBN: 978-0-312-94795-8

YOU'RE SO VEIN
ISBN: 978-0-312-94792-7

ONE BITE WITH A STRANGER
ISBN: 978-0-312-94793-4

WALK ON THE WILD SIDE
ISBN: 978-0-312-94791-0

HOWL AT THE MOON
ISBN: 978-0-312-94790-3

THE DEMON YOU KNOW
ISBN: 978-0-312-34777-2

SHE'S NO FAERIE PRINCESS
ISBN: 978-0-312-34776-5

WOLF AT THE DOOR
ISBN: 978-0-312-94553-4

And look for Warren's story, "Devil's Bargain," in the sensational anthology

HUNTRESS
ISBN: 978-0-312-94382-0

AVAILABLE FROM ST. MARTIN'S PAPERBACKS